Playing a Player

USA TODAY BESTSELLING AUTHOR

IVY SMOAK

This book is an original publication of Loft Troll Ink.

ISBN: 9781519739766

2024 Edition

To my permanent roommate.
I will win our next Nerf gun battle.

PART 1

CHAPTER 1

I sat down on a stool in my half empty apartment and sighed. Callie had been the last of my single friends. Now she was married and I was roommate-less. I looked down at my bridesmaid dress. It was poofy and hideous, and it made me look like a troll. I glanced at the clock on the wall. My first interviewee for a new roommate would be stopping by early in the morning. I had never lived with someone I didn't know before, and the thought made my stomach churn. I slid off the stool and stumbled slightly. Being single at a wedding always seemed to make me drink too much. All these weddings I had been attending were just a horrible reminder that I currently wasn't even dating anyone. I kicked off my high heels, went straight to my bedroom, and collapsed on top of my bed in the ugly, poofy dress.

***

A knock sounded on my door.

I groggily opened my eyes. "Huh?" I put my hand on my forehead. "Ow." My head throbbed. I looked at the alarm clock on my night stand. *Who would bother someone at 8 a.m. on a Sunday?* "Go away!" I mumbled into my pillow.

The knock sounded again.

"Oh, crap!" I had completely forgotten about the interviews. I pushed myself off the bed, ran to the front door, and pulled it open.

"I'm so sorry, I..." I stopped talking when I saw who was standing there. He was nearly six feet tall, lean, yet strong at the same time. He had a chiseled jaw that made my own jaw drop. He had hazel eyes, dark hair, and tan skin. I didn't know who he was, but he definitely wasn't here answering my ad for a new roommate.

"Hi," he said. His voice was deep. He smiled down at me. "It's nice to meet you." He stuck out his hand. I could feel my face flushing. *Oh God, I'm still in the horrid bridesmaid dress!*

"Hi." I shook his hand awkwardly. His strong fingers sent a shiver down my spine. I felt like I was still drunk. I quickly pulled my hand away. "I'm sorry, I think you have the wrong apartment."

He looked down. "32 C?"

"What?" Was he guessing my bra size? I crossed my arms over my chest.

He took a step forward and knocked on the front of the door with the knuckle of his index finger. "It says 32 C."

"Oh, right." *Of course he's referring to the room number.* "I'm sorry, what did you say your name was?"

"Rory."

"You're Rory?" I had done some light stalking earlier in the week, and Rory was one of the only people on my list that didn't have a Facebook. Maybe that was because I had been looking for a girl.

"Yes, can I come in?"

"Um...okay?" I stepped to the side to let him pass. He must realize that I would never share an apartment with a male stranger.

"It's Keira, right?"

"Yes." I tucked a strand of hair behind my ear. I was having trouble not staring at him. He was so handsome.

He nodded and looked around the room. "How big is the bedroom?"

"That's rather forward." *Shit, did I just say that out loud?*

"What?" Rory laughed. I wasn't sure if it was because of the expression on my face or because of what I had said.

"I mean it's right forward. I mean, it's over there." I pointed to the door next to my bedroom. My heart was beating out of my chest. I needed a cup of coffee. And some Advil. And for this sexy stranger to not be staring at me in this hideous dress.

"Can you give me a tour?"

"Of course. This is the living room," I gestured with my hand to the open area in front of us. There was a small couch and a T.V. "And here's the kitchen." It was open to the living room. "And the two bedrooms and the bathroom are over there." There was a small hallway that was open to the kitchen, and both bedrooms were connected to it. I walked toward the bedrooms. I could hear him following me. "This is my room," I opened up the door and immediately slammed it shut. There were clothes scattered all over the floor, including every bra I owned because I didn't know which would work best with this dress. "But you won't be going in there, so of course that doesn't matter."

Rory laughed. His laugh was deep and alluring. Everything about him was charming. I looked down at my feet and opened up the bedroom door next to mine. "This would be your room. I mean, this is the second room." *What is wrong with me?* I stepped to the side to let him go in.

"It's bigger than I pictured." He put his hands in his pockets and walked over to the window. "Nice view."

"Mhm." I was looking at him. I glanced away when he turned around. "And the bathroom is right next to this room." I walked out and opened up the bathroom door. I had left a box of tampons sitting on the vanity. I swatted them off the counter and into the bathtub just before Rory walked in. "Just normal bathroom stuff in here. Toilet, shower."

He walked by me and pulled the shower curtain to the side.

Shit.

"Oh, there's something in here," he reached down and picked up the box of tampons. It felt like my whole body was melting.

"That's nothing." I grabbed them out of his hand and threw them behind the door. "Just trash."

His body was close to mine. He smelled like cinnamon. He was smiling at me. I wanted to laugh it off, but I was too mortified.

I took a step back. "Okay, that's everything." I walked out of the room and back toward the front door.

"Don't you have any questions for me, Keira?" he asked.

"Oh, right. Yes." I turned to the counter in the kitchen and opened up my laptop. I slid onto the bar stool. A moment later he slid into the one right next to me. I gulped.

I laughed awkwardly as I waited for my computer to load. As soon as the screen lit up, I clicked on my roommate questionnaire. "Okay, how old are you?"

"26."

Same age as me. I typed out his answer on the document. "What do you do for a living?"

"I'm the executive chef of La Patisserie, right down the street from here. It's only open for lunch. You should come check it out sometime."

Is he asking me out? No. No, he'd be working. He's just being polite.

"Do you prefer to shower in the morning or at night? Oh, I'm sorry. You don't have to answer that. It's just, I wanted to see if our schedules would conflict."

"At night."

"Okay. That's actually nice, because I shower in the morning, and that way we wouldn't run into each other. But I don't take long showers or anything. I won't be in your way at all." I looked back at my computer screen. "Do you keep odd hours? Like, do you stay up late or wake up late? Anything like that?"

"That depends on what I'm doing. But normally, no."

"That's good. Are you single? I don't mean that in a weird way. It's just that my past three roommates all got married after just living here for several months. I'm looking for something more long term. Someone. Someone more long term. In a roommate kind of way."

"I'm not getting married anytime soon." He shifted slightly in his chair and his knee bumped into my thigh. "So you don't have to worry about that."

I crossed my legs away from him and continued to stare at my questionnaire. "Do you have commitment issues or something?"

"Is that really on your questionnaire?"

I turned my computer away from him. "It's number five, yes," I lied.

"I don't have issue committing to my living situation."

"So why are you leaving your current apartment?"

"I don't get along well with my roommate. And it's far away from work."

"Why don't you get along with him? Or her?"

"He's always trying to shower at night."

"I see."

Rory laughed.

Geez, he was laughing at me. I looked back at my list of questions. "Do you mind sharing clothes? Oh. No. Never mind. I'm sorry, this is kind of embarrassing. I thought you were going to be a girl."

Rory laughed. "I get that a lot."

"Right. Because of Gilmore Girls?"

"Mhm." He looked at me and raised his left eyebrow. "Is that going to be a problem?"

"Um, I don't know. You're the first person I'm interviewing. I definitely won't be discriminating based on sex." *Oh my God!* "I mean, if you're male or female. I mean, you're male, obviously. Just in general. I won't be breaking any laws."

Rory laughed again. "Well I don't mind sharing my clothes with you, if that helps."

"Oh." I could feel myself blushing. "I think that's all my questions."

"When are you looking for someone to move in?"

"Right away."

"Okay. Well I'm in if you want me."

I do want you. But not as a roommate! "I'll get back to you soon, Rory. There are several other people stopping by today, so I can't make any promises."

"Keep me in mind." He stood up and walked over to the door.

"I will." *How could I forget meeting you?*

"Nice dress by the way."

I laughed awkwardly. "I was up late at my friend's wedding. Actually, she was my last roommate. And I was a bridesmaid. I didn't pick this out. I don't normally wear things like this."

He smiled. "It looks good on you. Oh, and here's my card." He pulled a business card out of his wallet and handed it to me. "Make sure to stop by the restaurant. I hope to hear from you soon."

"Yeah, okay. Bye, Rory."

"Bye, Keira." He gave me one last smile and left.

What the hell was that? I ran to my room to change before the next interviewee arrived.

CHAPTER 2

I opened up my laptop and scrolled through the list of remaining applicants. Any one of these girls could be a serial killer. Or a man. A knock on the door brought me out of my trance.

I slid off the stool and headed to the door. I took a deep breath before opening it. *Please just be a normal girl.* I opened the door and smiled. "Hi, you must be Piper." I extended my hand to her.

She shifted uneasily before shaking my hand. As soon as her hand fell from mine, she grabbed hand sanitizer from her purse and squirted a large glob in her hand.

"I just washed my hands," I said.

"I'm sure you did." Her tone was accusatory.

"Did you want to come in?" I asked as politely as I could muster.

The girl nodded and walked past me. "This doesn't really look like the pictures."

"Lots of the furniture belonged to my previous roommate. I was hoping to split the cost of some new stuff with whoever takes her place."

"The price is a little high then, don't you think?"

"It's just half of what the rent is. It's the same that I pay."

"Does it at least include utilities?"

"No." This girl wasn't very nice.

"How often do you clean?"

"Whenever anything needs to be cleaned."

"My last roommate was really sloppy. I don't want to live with someone like that again."

"I really do clean a lot. I just vacuumed the living room and cleaned the bathroom. And I never leave dishes in the sink. That's actually a pet peeve of mine too."

"It doesn't look clean."

"Excuse me?"

Piper looked around the room. "Can I see your bedroom?"

"Why?" My answer was a little snappy, but I couldn't help it. Who was she to come into my apartment and criticize me? Besides, I was supposed to be conducting the interview, not her.

"To see if you're sloppy or not."

"Why don't you just believe me?" I thought about the clothes strewn around my room, which now included the hideous bridesmaid dress. I was sloppy. It was like this stranger could see right through me.

"Because you have shoes in the middle of your kitchen floor. That's a cooking hazard, surely."

"What?" I tilted my head and looked over her shoulder. Sure enough, my high heels from the wedding were still on the floor. "Oh, I got home late last night from a wedding. I must have just overlooked them. I promise that I don't usually leave shoes laying around. I keep all my personal stuff in my room."

"And why can't I see your room?" she countered.

"Well...um...like I said, I just got back from a wedding. And I didn't really have time to tidy up my room..."

"Thanks, but no thanks." Piper walked past me and out the door.

What the hell?

***

Seven interviews and seven duds. And Piper hadn't even been the worst. I put my face in my hands. There were only two days until the end of the month. If I didn't choose someone soon, I'd have to pay next month's rent solo. I could afford it, but I'd have to take the money out of my savings.

I bit my lip. In the back of my mind, I was thinking about Rory. Actually, I couldn't seem to stop thinking about him. He had been the nicest one. But I couldn't live with someone I was attracted to. That would be uncomfortable. And I had only asked him half of my questions because I had been too embarrassed. I barely knew anything about him.

He really was the best option, though. I picked up Rory's business card from the counter. His restaurant was open until three. I glanced at my computer screen. It was only 2 o'clock. Maybe if I went down there, I could get to know him better before rashly asking him to be my roommate.

Before I could chicken out, I grabbed my purse and hurried out of my apartment. I made my way down the street, searching for the restaurant. It was nestled between a Starbucks and a pizza place. I had never noticed it before. I pushed the door open and a bell rang to announce my arrival. The small restaurant was deserted. It was past lunchtime, though, so maybe their usual crowd had already left. I looked around. I wasn't sure if I was supposed to sit down or wait for a hostess. There was a man at a counter in the back staring at me.

"Can I help you, miss?"

Oh, I'm supposed to order back there. I wound my way between the small bistro tables to the back of the restaurant. There was a chalkboard behind the counter. All the menu items were in French, but the descriptions were in English.

"I'm sorry, I don't really know how to pronounce anything. Can I just have a turkey sandwich on a croissant?"

"Sure thing. Did you get that, Rory?" The man looked over his shoulder.

"Got it!" Rory said from somewhere I couldn't see.

"That will be $7.50, miss."

"Okay." I grabbed my wallet out of my purse. Just as I pulled out a ten dollar bill, Rory walked up to the counter. An apron was tied around his waist and his hair was mussed up. He looked even sexier than he had earlier. There was a dot of flour on his cheek. And he was smiling at me.

"This one's on me, Jerry."

Jerry looked at Rory and then back at me. "I actually need to use the restroom. I'll be back." He winked at Rory and walked away.

Rory put his elbows on the counter and leaned forward slightly. "I hope you're bringing me good news, Keira. You saw how short of a walk it is from your apartment to here."

"I actually haven't made up my mind yet." I put the money on the counter and slid it toward him.

"Lots of good contenders, huh?" He slid the bill back toward me and put the plate with the sandwich on it down on top of the money.

"There were a few." I laughed, remembering Piper storming out of the apartment. "Actually most of them were horrible. There was this one girl who thought I was too sloppy to live with. She was super rude."

Rory leaned forward on the counter. "I don't mind if you're a little dirty."

The way he said it made my heart race. I could feel my face blushing. "I don't mind paying, Rory. I didn't come here to get free food. You just mentioned it, and I've never been here..." I shrugged my shoulders. I couldn't seem to control my rambling around him.

"It's on me. I insist."

"Are you trying to bribe me?"

"I'm just being nice. But if you're accepting bribes, then yes, it is a bribe."

"Well, thank you." I grabbed the sandwich and my money and made my way over to one of the tables. *Geez, could I be any more awkward?*

CHAPTER 3

A chair squeaked. I looked up and Rory was sitting down on the other side of my table, regarding me curiously.

"Are you done working?" I asked.

"No, not yet. I didn't want to miss talking to you, though. Look, I know you don't want a guy roommate."

"It's not that." I laughed uncomfortably. "Actually, yeah. It is that. It's just kind of awkward."

"Well, I'm not planning on walking around naked, if that's what you're worried about."

"Oh, God no. No. I mean yes, don't do that."

Rory laughed. "I mean, as long as we're not attracted to each other, it really shouldn't be a problem."

He's not attracted to me? That's kind of a rude thing to say. I shifted uncomfortably in my chair. "Right, of course. I mean, I'm definitely not attracted to you. I like...glasses. I mean, guys with glasses. And the whole tall, dark, and handsome thing is really overrated. I should say tall, dark, and not handsome, am I right? Gross. Ugh." I laughed awkwardly and shoved the rest of my sandwich in my mouth. *What the fuck?!*

He lowered his eyebrows slightly. I hadn't meant to offend him. And it was a lie. He was dreamy.

"Okay. And we can just make a pact," he said.

"Hmm?" I had a mouth full of food.

"To just be friends. To not start liking each other."

I choked on my bite of sandwich. It took me an agonizingly long time to swallow. "I don't like you," I lied.

"So what's the problem then?"

"I guess there isn't one." *Because there's a million!*

His eyes grew bright. "So the room is mine?"

"Um...yes." *What the hell am I doing?*

"Thanks, Keira, I really appreciate it." He got up, walked around the table, and wrapped his arms around me.

I could feel his muscles pressed against me. "You're welcome." My whole body felt tingly. I had a strong urge to kiss him, but instead I patted his back awkwardly. He released me from his hug. He was all smiles.

"Does tomorrow evening work for you?"

He does like me! "Yeah, I'm free tomorrow."

"Great, me and a couple friends will move my stuff in then."

Of course. Geez, I'm already acting like an idiot. "Sounds good."

Rory picked up my plate. "Thanks again, Keira." He headed back behind the counter. I quickly grabbed my purse and fled the restaurant.

CHAPTER 4

"You're not serious?" Emily stared at me in disbelief. She was my oldest friend. Ever since we had been randomly assigned as roommates in college, she had been my biggest confidant. And I needed her advice now more than ever.

"I didn't mean to agree to him moving in. It kind of just happened."

"You were doing that thing, weren't you?"

"What thing?"

"Where you just keep rambling because you're nervous."

Oh, that thing. When did I ever *not* do that? "He does make me really nervous. Emily, I've never been so instantaneously attracted to someone before. He's so handsome."

"Which is why you shouldn't live with him."

"Well, we agreed to just remain friends. So..." I shrugged. "There isn't really anything to worry about."

Emily stared at me skeptically.

"I was kind of hoping you'd tell me that it was a good idea."

"Why on earth did you think I'd tell you it was a good idea? It's actually a really terrible idea, Keira."

"How is it that bad of an idea? All the other candidates were awful. He was the only one who I could actually see myself living with."

"So put out another ad."

"I need a new roommate before the end of the month. He's moving in just in time. Anyone else would take too long."

"Well then, it seems like you already made up your mind." She smiled at me.

"So you think it *is* a good idea? I mean, you live with a guy. And you're so happy."

"You mean my husband?" Emily laughed.

I couldn't help but start laughing too. If that was the only argument I could come up with, then maybe letting Rory live with me really was a bad idea.

"Are you sure you don't want to just call him and tell him you made a mistake?"

"Geez, I can't do that."

"Of course you can. It's not like you have to ever see him again."

"But I don't want to not see him. I'm actually kind of excited about getting to see him every day."

Emily smiled at me. "I don't know what you want me to say. I feel like it's a bad idea. But you were my only roommate before I got married. So what do I know?"

I laughed. "I can't believe I'm actually going to do this."

"I know. What if he's a serial killer?"

"Emily! Why would you even say that?!" I tossed one of the pillows off the couch at her. She knew that was my biggest fear of living with a stranger.

"I'm just kidding. You're going to be fine."

"Yeah. I'll definitely be fine." I bit my lip. "What's it like living with a guy, by the way? It's pretty much the same as living with a girl, right?"

Emily started laughing again. "No, not at all."

CHAPTER 5

I just finished moving the rest of my bathroom stuff to my bedroom when I heard a knock on the door. My heart was beating fast. I glanced in the mirror. I was wearing my nicest pushup bra with a low cut tank top and a pair of jean shorts. Maybe I could change Rory's opinion of me. I didn't really want that stupid pact.

A few seconds later I opened the door. Rory was holding a large box and his two friends were hidden behind boxes of their own.

"Hey," Rory said as he made his way into the apartment. He put the box down in the middle of the living room floor. "Keira, this is Connor and Jackson." He gestured to his two friends.

"Hey," Connor said. "Rory, you didn't tell me that your new roommate was smoking hot."

I could feel myself blushing. "Do you guys need help with anything? I cleared space for you in the kitchen and bathroom cabinets."

"We have a lot to bring up. Maybe you could help me unpack?" Rory asked.

"Sure, of course."

I walked over to the boxes and sat down. I pulled the tape off the first one and opened it up. It was full of boxers. I lifted up a pair. A box of condoms was underneath of it. A huge box. *Does he buy them in bulk? Who needs this many condoms?*

Rory cleared his throat.

Shit. I threw the boxers down on top of the box of condoms.

"Maybe the one marked kitchen?" Rory suggested before heading back out of the apartment.

I quickly closed the box and pulled the tape back over it. *Why did I touch his boxers? What is wrong with me?* I found the box labeled kitchen and started to unpack the glasses.

***

By the time they moved the rest of Rory's stuff in, my apartment had been transformed into a bachelor pad. My small couch had been pushed to the side and dark leather furniture had replaced it. There were beer mugs lining the counter and a dartboard hung up on the wall.

I turned my head when I heard the door creak back open. The three guys were carrying a case of beer and a few pizzas.

"Did you want to join us, mademoiselle?" Jackson asked. He had a kind smile. The three of them sat down in the living room.

"No, that's okay, guys. I'm just going to hang out in my room."

"Don't be ridiculous," Connor said. "We're going to be over a lot. We need to get to know you better." He tapped the seat between him and Rory on the couch.

"Um..." I looked over at Rory. He was smiling at me. He had such a sexy smile. "If you're sure I'm not imposing."

Connor popped the top off a beer and held it up for me. I walked over to the couch, sat down, and took the beer bottle. Jackson was sitting in a chair across from us.

I could feel Connor's eyes on me as I leaned over to grab a slice of pizza. "So you guys are going to be over a lot, huh?"

"Well, Rory always hosts poker night on Tuesdays," Jackson said.

I looked over at Rory. He shrugged his shoulders.

"And he throws a hell of a party," Connor added.

"He forgot to mention that." *What had I gotten myself into?*

"Actually, we were thinking about doing a kind of housewarming party. If that's okay with you, Keira?" Connor asked.

"Sure. When were you thinking?"

"Friday?"

"Do you need me to do anything?"

"No, we've got it covered. Just wear something sexy." Connor's hand brushed the side of my arm.

I gulped. I didn't want Rory's friend to like me. I wanted Rory to like me. I shifted slightly closer to Rory on the couch. But Rory responded by scooting away from me. Jackson smiled at me. I could tell he wanted to laugh. He had seen me move away from Connor and then Rory move away from me. *Geez, why is this so awkward?*

"So, Keira, tell us about yourself," Jackson said.

I finished chewing a bite of pizza. "I'm a freelance writer for The Post."

"That's a stimulating job. Do you enjoy it?" Jackson asked.

That was a strange way to describe my work. *Stimulating.* "It's actually a lot of fun. I basically write about whatever I like and sometimes they'll pick up the story."

"That's considerably better than pushing paper all day." Jackson smiled. He seemed like a genuinely nice guy.

"And what does your boyfriend do?" Connor asked.

"Really smooth," Jackson laughed and leaned back in his chair.

"Um...well...he isn't, I mean, I don't..." I tucked a loose strand of hair behind my ear. "I'm not seeing anyone right now."

"Single and sexy? Rory, you were really holding out on us," Connor said.

I looked at Rory out of the corner of my eye and saw him shrug. *He didn't mention it because he doesn't think I'm sexy.* I was suddenly very aware of the fact that I was alone in my apartment with three men I barely knew. I stood up. "I've never played darts before."

"I can show you how," Connor said quickly, and got up off the couch. He walked over to the dartboard and picked up the darts off the table.

I sighed and walked over to him. He handed me a dart. I threw it toward the board and the dart sunk into the wall. "Oh, shit."

Connor laughed. "Here, let me show you." He placed a dart in my hand and got behind me. He put one hand on my hip and the other around my hand that was holding the dart. I glanced over my shoulder at Rory, but he was talking to Jackson. If anything could come out of this, I was hoping to make him jealous. But he wasn't even looking at me.

"I'm going to put the rest of the beers in the fridge." I shimmied out of Connor's grip, grabbed the case, and walked into the kitchen. I opened up the fridge and let the cool air hit my face. I took a deep breath. I needed to get a grip.

"Ahem." I looked up and Rory was leaning against the side of the fridge.

"Oh. Hi." I put the carton of beers down in the fridge. "Your friends seem...nice."

He leaned in close. I could feel his warm breath in my ear. It made chills shoot through the rest of my body. "Connor only does one night stands, Keira. Just a heads up. One friend to another." He leaned back against the side of the fridge and regarded me. I wanted his warm breath against me again.

"And what do you do? I mean, just one friend curiously asking another."

He laughed, grabbed a beer out of the carton, and headed back over to his seat.

He really doesn't like me. He was looking out for me, one friend to another. Or was he trying to make me avoid Connor? I closed the refrigerator door. I was now even more uncomfortable. And I suddenly remembered Emily joking around about Rory being a serial killer. A chill ran down my spine.

"You know what, I'm pretty tired," I called to them from the kitchen. "I'm going to go to bed."

CHAPTER 6

I sat down at the kitchen counter with my bowl of cereal. The pizza boxes were still on the coffee table and beer bottles were scattered around the living room. I wasn't used to living with a guy. And Rory's friends would be back tonight for their weekly poker night. Emily had been right. Living with a guy was very different than living with a girl. I was a little sloppy, but at least I didn't leave trash all over the apartment.

The bathroom door creaked and Rory walked out. He was wearing boxer briefs. *And nothing else.* I spit out my bite of cereal.

Rory looked over at me. "You okay?"

"Yeah, this milk has gone bad. It's rancid. Don't drink it. I'll throw it out." I had just bought it yesterday afternoon. I grabbed a paper towel and wiped off the counter. Then sat back down and took another bite of cereal.

"I thought you said it was bad?"

I hadn't realized that Rory was still standing there. *God his abs are amazing.*

He walked over to the fridge and brought out the half gallon of milk. He opened up the top and sniffed it. "It doesn't smell bad, Keira."

"Yeah, I know. I lied. I don't know. I was just surprised to see you. I've gotten used to living alone, I guess." I looked down at the bulge in his boxer briefs and then back at my cereal. My cereal didn't look nearly as appealing.

"Did you want me to wear more to breakfast?" He was smiling at me. He was clearly enjoying my reaction to his half naked body.

"What? Psh. No. Rory, I mean, wear whatever makes you comfortable. That wasn't it at all. You're not bothering me. I'm cool. Totally cool. Heck, maybe I'll start walking around in my underwear. It's just so comfortable in here. Between us, you know?"

"I'm going to go put on a shirt." He walked back into his room and reemerged as he pulled a t-shirt down over his head.

He made himself a bowl of cereal, walked over to me, and sat down beside me at the kitchen counter. I quickly took another bite of cereal. I hadn't realized that I'd been staring at him.

"So, I take it you don't do one night stands?" he asked, without looking at me.

"Oh no, I do them. I do them all the time."

Rory laughed and looked over at me. "Oh, you're serious?"

"Why is that thought so funny?"

Rory shrugged. "I don't know, you just don't seem like the type."

"Yeah." I pushed my cereal around with my spoon. "I'm not."

"You lie a lot, you know. I have no idea what to believe and what not to believe."

"I don't lie. I just sometimes don't know what to say when I'm nervous. Not that I'm nervous around you. You know what, I'm going to finish my breakfast in my room. I have a lot of work to do today." I grabbed my bowl of cereal and slid off the stool.

"So you work from home?"

"Yeah." I opened up my bedroom door and quickly closed it behind me. *Why am I so awkward?*

***

I finished up the article I was working on. I was holding my bladder, hoping that Rory wouldn't be in the kitchen anymore. I opened up my door a crack and looked out. The coast was clear. I tiptoed past Rory's door and quietly opened up the bathroom door.

"Um, excuse me," Rory said calmly.

"Oh my God!" I shrieked. Rory was standing there peeing. "Oh my God!" *Stop staring at his penis!*

I turned around and ran out of the bathroom. I started pacing the hallway. This was not going well at all. This wasn't working. *How am I going to get the image of that out of my mind? Geez, do I even want to?*

When Rory emerged I started yelling, even though I knew he was the one that should be upset with me. "You said you wouldn't walk around naked! You can't go walking around with your huge penis everywhere! I mean penis. Normal, average penis." My face was turning scarlet.

He looked amused. "Keira, I wasn't walking around. I was taking a piss...in the bathroom."

"With the door unlocked!"

"You should have knocked."

"But..."

"Let's finish this discussion later. I'm going to be late for work." Rory walked past me and out the front door. Before he closed it he put his head back in. "Huge, huh?"

"I said average!" I ran back into my room.

CHAPTER 7

I watched Rory as he flirted with a girl on the couch. I hadn't realized that poker night wasn't just for his guy friends.

"Hey, Keira."

I looked up and saw Jackson standing next to me. "Hey, Jackson. So, I was wondering. Is that Rory's girlfriend?"

Jackson started laughing. "No."

"Why is that so funny?"

"Rory doesn't do the whole girlfriend thing."

"Oh."

"You like him, huh?"

"What? No." So Rory didn't date and neither did Connor. I looked away from Rory and turned my attention back to Jackson. "Do you do the whole girlfriend thing?"

Jackson rubbed the back of his neck with his hand. "I actually just got out of a relationship. I only just started hanging out with Rory and Connor again recently. My ex hated them."

I laughed. "So what are you guys? Like the wolf pack or something?"

"You mean like from the Hangover?" Jackson started to laugh.

"You're all a bunch of sluts," I hissed.

Jackson laughed again. "Is that what you think? Well, I heard that you're kind of a peeping Tom."

"What?"

"Rory told me about the bathroom incident this morning."

"Oh God." I was completely mortified. "Who doesn't lock the door? If I had any idea that he was in there, I wouldn't have gone in. It's not like I was being discreet about it."

"He said you tiptoed in."

"It was an accident!"

"Mhm."

I looked over at Rory. He was smiling at me. He knew exactly what Jackson and I were talking about. I needed to change the subject. "I thought poker night was like a guys thing?"

"Rory didn't tell you?"

"Tell me what?"

Jackson smiled down at me. "This is going to be more interesting than I thought. Come on. It's time to get started."

My brow furrowed as Jackson walked over to the table that they had set up earlier. It was nice of them to ask me to join, but was I missing something? *What had Rory not told me?* I followed Jackson over to the table and sat down in the last seat, which was between him and Connor. There were two other girls at the table that I didn't know. And no one bothered to introduce us. Which was fine, because they both had huge breasts, way too much make up, and I instinctively didn't like either of them. Especially the one that Rory was staring at.

"Okay, winner chooses the person and the article of clothing for each round," Connor said and winked at me.

I swallowed my sip of beer. "What?" I looked over at Rory, but he was too busy staring down another girl's shirt.

Jackson put his elbows on the table and leaned over to me. "I told you it was going to be interesting," he whispered. "We're playing strip poker, Keira."

I could feel my jaw drop. *What the fuck?* "Rory, can I talk to you?"

"Yeah." He reluctantly pulled his eyes away from the girl to his left. He stood up and walked over to the kitchen. I followed him, fuming.

"You're turning my apartment into a brothel?!"

Rory laughed. "Well, it was going to be a normal poker night, but then you saw me naked this morning. So I figured this wouldn't be a big deal."

"Well it is a big deal."

"You don't have to play. I can call someone else to be our sixth."

Jealousy seared through me. *Do I want to do this? Can I even change his opinion about me?*

Rory was no longer even looking at me. His eyes were back on the girl that he had been flirting with.

"Fine. Game on." I turned on my heel and went back to the table. Maybe I could make him jealous too. Connor had his arm on the back of my chair. I sat down without flinching and smiled at him. Besides, I knew how to play poker. It wasn't like I was going to lose.

Connor dealt out the first hand.

I knew how to play, but it didn't mean I was lucky. I exchanged one card, but my hand still sucked. I had a variety of suits and no pairs or anything in a row. "I fold." I put my cards face down on the table. Connor was smiling at me.

"Okay, full house," Connor said and placed his cards on the table, fanning them out to the side.

Everyone else at the table was silent.

Connor drummed his hands on the table. "Take it off, Keira!"

I felt my face already blushing. "What do you want me to take off?"

"Hmm." Connor studied me for a minute, before reaching over and lightly touching the bottom hem of my tank top. "How about this?"

Luckily I was wearing a nice bra. I reached down to lift off my shirt, but before I could, Connor pushed the fabric up the sides of my torso. My body tensed. His fingers pressed against my flesh as he pushed my tank top up over my bra. I gulped. No one had ever undressed me before. I locked eyes with him as I put my hands above my head. He lifted my tank top off over my head and pulled it slowly down my arms. Connor whistled approvingly as he tossed my shirt on the floor. But Rory didn't even look at me. I bit my lip. *This isn't working.*

Connor dealt out the next hand. The girl to the left of Rory won. She straddled Rory and pulled his shirt over his head. *What a slut.* I watched as his hand slipped down her back and grabbed her ass. I rolled my eyes at them as Jackson laughed. I looked over at Jackson. *He was laughing at me!* I lightly pushed his arm. The girl next to him gave me a look to kill. *Geez.* I put my hands back on my lap.

A few rounds later, I was a little more than tipsy. Everyone except Connor had lost their shirts. And the girl next to Jackson had lost her skirt. I was pretty sure she was losing on purpose. I exchanged one card and smiled. I laid my hand down on the table. "Four of a kind."

Connor tossed his cards down in disgust.

"Hmm." I looked around the table. Rory leaned back in his chair and crossed his arms. He looked me up and down. I loved the feeling of his eyes on me. He smiled at me. He thought I was going to choose him. *Not today, Rory.* I looked over at Connor. He was pouting, but I could tell he wasn't really upset. "Your turn, Connor."

Connor gave me a seductive smile. I wanted to make Rory jealous. I was glad I was wearing low rise jean shorts. I stood up, walked behind Connor's chair, and slid my hands over his shoulders and down his chest. I leaned in, pressing my breasts against his shoulder, as I grabbed the bottom of his shirt and pulled it up. I moved my fingers up his chiseled abs and slowly lifted his shirt over his head. He caught my wrist in his hand.

"I need another drink. Come with me," he said.

I gulped, but followed Connor into the kitchen. I didn't have much of a choice, since his hand was still wrapped firmly around my wrist.

When we reached the fridge he touched the middle of my chest, pushing my back against the cold stainless steel.

"I know what you're doing."

"What?" My face flushed.

"You're trying to make Rory jealous."

"I don't know what you're talking about. I don't like Rory. Besides, we have this like roommate pact thing or something. So even if I did, I wouldn't pursue it. But I don't anyway, so it doesn't matter."

"Do you want my help or not?" Connor put his hands on either side of me.

I looked over at Rory and watched as he pushed the girl's hair behind her shoulder.

"Okay," I sighed.

"You'll owe me a favor, though."

"What kind of favor?"

"I'm sure I'll think of something."

I bit my lip and peered around Connor's shoulder. Rory was still completely enthralled by the woman sitting next to him. Maybe I could use Connor's help. "Okay, deal."

Connor opened up the fridge, grabbed two beers, and popped the caps off. "Cheers." He held up his bottle.

I felt like I was making a deal with the devil. I hit my bottle against his and followed him back to the table. He dealt out the next hand. After I picked up my cards, Connor immediately scooted his chair out, grabbed my waist, and pulled me onto his lap. I laughed as he lightly nipped my shoulder blade.

"Stop trying to see my cards, Connor!" I pressed my cards against my chest.

"Fold," Connor whispered into my ear. I wiggled out of his grip and sat back down in my chair. I looked at my hand. I was dealt a flush. It was likely that I would win. I stole a glance at Rory. He was definitely looking at me now. And he didn't seem happy. Maybe this was working. I put my hand face down on the table, refusing to even exchange any of my cards. "I fold." *What is Connor planning?*

Rory laid out his hand. He had a straight.

"Not so fast," Connor said. "Four of a kind. Read 'em and weep, Rory."

Rory scowled.

"Stand up," Connor said to me.

My heart was racing. *Please don't take my bra.* I stood up and faced him. He moved his hands to my waist and then slowly unbuttoned and unzipped my jean shorts. He hooked his fingers in my belt loops and pulled me toward him. I could feel his warm breath against my belly button. I held my breath as he pulled my shorts down my hips. The rough fabric fell down my thighs, and his fingers lightly pressed against my skin. He let go of my belt loops and placed a kiss just above my panty line. *Oh my God.* I felt everything below my waistline clench with desire. I took a step back and tripped over my chair and onto Jackson's lap.

"Hey there," Jackson said, and smiled at me.

"Oh God, I'm sorry." I quickly got back up and kicked my shorts off my ankles.

Everyone seemed to be staring at me. I was completely mortified. At least my thong matched my bra. I usually didn't care about things like that, but I had wanted to feel sexy tonight. Because I wanted Rory to think that I was sexy.

"I think I'm done for the night," Rory said and stood up.

"Oh, good," the girl sighed next to him. "I'm not wearing any panties anyway."

Slut!

Rory grinned, leaned down, and lifted the girl over his shoulder. She screamed in protest. He slapped her ass and disappeared with her into his bedroom.

"We're going to go too," the girl said that was sitting next to Jackson. She gave me a nasty look.

"Sorry, Keira," Jackson said. He stood up and grabbed his shirt off the floor. The girl next to him was staring longingly at his abs. I turned back to Rory's door. I suddenly remembered I was just wearing my underwear. I put my arms across my chest.

Jackson and the girl walked out of the apartment arm in arm. *Poor girl.* She probably had no idea what she was getting herself into. *Or does she?*

CHAPTER 8

Connor cleared his throat.

Oh God, we're alone.

"So about that favor..." He touched my knee and began to trail his fingers up my thigh.

I took a step back. My ass pressed against the poker table. "You didn't help me at all."

"I tried my best." His fingers continued to trail up my thigh. "You like playing hard to get." He pressed his palm against my underwear.

I couldn't help the moan that escaped from my lips. *Oh my God, what am I doing?* I stepped to the side, away from his hands. "No. No, I like playing poker." I picked up the deck of cards from the table.

"Forget about the favor for now. Do you like to gamble, Keira?"

"Not really."

I heard distant moaning. I turned toward Rory's bedroom. "Yes!" the girl shouted from inside.

My stomach churned. "What do you have in mind?" I asked, trying to ignore the girl's screams of pleasure.

"Well how about this. If you get me naked first, you can do whatever you want to me. And if I get you naked first, I can do whatever I want to you."

I gulped. "You're wearing more clothes than me."

"I have shorts and boxers, and you have a bra and a thong. Two versus two."

I sat down. "Deal."

Connor smiled and shuffled the cards. He passed out five cards to each of us. I picked mine up and tried to hide my smile. They were all hearts. And I was only one card away from a straight.

I looked up at Connor. "Are you going to exchange any of your cards?"

"I'll pass," he replied.

He must have a good hand. I looked back down at my hand. A flush probably wasn't going to cut it. I picked up the card that was out of order and placed it face down on the table. "Hit me."

"Oh, I'm planning on it."

What did he just say?

He gave me the card off the top of the deck. This time I couldn't suppress my smile. I already had a 3, 4, 5, and 6. And the card I just got was a 7 of hearts. "You first."

Connor smiled as he placed his hand down. "A straight."

I pretended to pout. "Oh, me too." I spread my cards on the table. "Except it's also a flush. Boom." I made an exploding noise and spread my fingers in the air.

"Did you just *boom* me?"

"You're just jealous of my awesome game. Take off your shorts, Connor."

"You have a good poker face." Connor stood up, unbuttoned and unzipped his shorts, and unceremoniously pushed them to the floor.

My eyes gravitated to the bulge beneath his boxers. *Oh my God.* He must be huge. *Or is he already starting to get an erection? Is that the tip of his penis hanging out from the hem of his boxers?* I looked down at my hands that were knotted in my lap.

"Do you like what you see?"

"Are you talking to me?"

"There's no one else here, Keira."

"Well, I wasn't looking at anything. I mean, you just took your pants off in my apartment and I barely know you. I didn't mean to look. Not that it's not worth looking at. I'm sure it's very nice." I could feel my face turning red.

"Nice, huh? You're not going to think it's nice when it's spreading your tight pussy wider than it's ever been."

Did he seriously just say that to me? I gulped. His dirty words seemed to have a direct line to my groin. I could feel my panties getting damp. I crossed my legs. I had only been with three men. And they had all been my boyfriends. Why was I so turned on by this sexy stranger? He was supposed to be helping me out with Rory, not trying to seduce me.

"Now let's get that bra off." Connor rubbed his hands together before dealing out the next hand.

I could feel my heart racing. I glanced down at my cards. Three of a kind. I could work with this. I put one card face down and waited for Connor to hand me a new one off the top of the deck. He was staring intently at his cards. He exchanged one of his cards and then handed me a new one.

Four of a kind!

"Sorry, Connor, but I think I've got you again. Four jacks." I fanned my cards out for him.

"I feel like you're cheating."

"Right, because I desperately want to see you naked."

"Well, go ahead." Connor stood up. His erection was definitely visible now.

"Look, we barely know each other. And I'm kind of tired. And we've both had too much to drink. Let's just call it a night."

"We're about to know each other real well." He grabbed my hand and placed it on his erection. I couldn't help but wrap my hand around his cock. I had never felt one so massive before.

"Let me help you out," he said, and pulled his boxers down. I moved my hand away and watched his cock stand to attention. When I didn't move, Connor took a step toward me, grabbed my ass and lifted me onto the poker table. His cock was pressed firmly against my stomach.

Holy shit.

He grabbed a fistful of my hair, tilted my head back, and kissed me. He shoved his tongue in my mouth, possessing me. *How many millions of times had he done this before?*

"Connor," I pushed on his chest. *This isn't me. I don't do one night stands.*

He ran his index finger along the top of my panty line. I felt my hips rise off the table.

What am I doing?

His other hand spread my thighs apart. He pressed his palm against my clit again and another moan escaped from my lips. I couldn't help it. I hadn't had sex in months.

"Fuck, you're so wet. You're dripping through your thong."

"We shouldn't be doing this."

"Is there something that you want?" he asked, ignoring me. Somehow, even though he was the one that was naked in my apartment, he seemed to have all the power. "Do you want me to fuck you with my fingers?"

I whimpered at his dirty words.

He leaned on top of me, pressing his erection against my stomach again. "Trust me, this will definitely make Rory jealous," he whispered in my ear. "He's going to be so pissed that he didn't get you first."

"Get me first?" I slid away from Connor's hands, knocking a few beer bottles off the table.

Connor shrugged. "Yeah. Isn't that what you want? For him to be jealous?"

"Who are you guys? What, do you just pass women around like objects?" *Are these guys prostitutes?! Does that make me a prostitute? Shit!* I ungracefully climbed off the table.

"You're not seriously going to leave me like this?" He gestured to his massive erection.

I stared at it for a second and then tried to focus my eyes on the poker table. "Thank you, for, er...well, an interesting night. But I'm not interested in being whatever it is you think I am."

"Keira, a deal's a deal. I'm cashing in on that favor. How about you put those lips to good use." Connor began to stroke his cock as he looked at me.

I put my hand out in front of me to block his erection from view. Part of him was still visible past my fingertips.

"Okay, night." I turned around and ran to my room, locking the door behind me.

CHAPTER 9

I heard Rory moaning. Every now and then his bed frame would tap against the wall. I turned sideways, grabbed my pillow, and covered my ears. I was already so turned on. Hearing him moaning was making it even worse. *Who has sex for this long?*

This was ridiculous. I never realized how thin the walls were in this apartment. I rolled out of bed, grabbed my pillow and comforter, and stormed out into the living room.

Holy hell! Connor was sprawled on the couch. On his stomach. *Naked.* I quickly turned around and ran into Rory. I yelped and dropped my pillow and comforter on the floor.

"Looks like you had fun." Rory peered over my shoulder.

"What? No."

"You seem to have worn Connor out."

"Oh." I laughed awkwardly. "No. He wore himself out."

Rory looked at me skeptically.

"That sounded weird. That's not really what I meant. I don't think he was masturbating or anything."

Rory laughed.

"I didn't sleep with him, if that's what you were referring to."

"Then why is he passed out naked on our couch?"

"Actually...I think he might have a drinking problem." I leaned down and picked up my comforter and pillow. "Excuse me."

Rory stayed where he was standing, blocking my path through the hallway.

"You know what? I think it was really rude of you to have a strip poker night in my living room without asking me first," I said. Why wasn't he moving out of my way? *What an asshole.*

"It's *our* living room."

"Right. Well, try to be a little more considerate next time."

"I warned you about Connor."

"I'm not talking about Connor, I'm talking about you." I took a deep breath. I wanted to slap his beautiful face.

"It won't happen again. Sorry." Rory ran his hand through his hair. *His sex hair.*

"And can you please keep it down in there? I can't sleep with all that ruckus." *Geez, I sound like an old maid.*

Rory smiled at me. "Sure thing. I'm actually going to bed now. I just came out to get some water." He stepped out of my way. "But I'll try to keep it down," he whispered.

I walked past him and back into my room. *What is his problem?* I tossed my comforter and pillow back on the bed. I heard faint murmurs from outside my room. I walked over and pressed my ear against the door. It sounded like Rory and Connor were arguing. I stepped back from the door. I just wanted this night to end. I flopped down on my bed and put my pillow back over my head.

***

My alarm clock buzzed and I slammed my hand down on the off switch. I wanted to get out of the apartment before Rory and that girl woke up. I didn't want to have to see her. I quickly got dressed and grabbed my notebook.

I closed the bathroom door and brushed my teeth. I sighed as I heard Rory's door squeak open. *Crap.* I finished getting ready and walked out into the hallway and toward the front door.

The refrigerator door was open. The girl Rory had been with was bent over rummaging through my food. She was only wearing a men's t-shirt. I turned away from her and walked past the kitchen. I noticed that Connor was no longer in the living room.

"Oh, hey!" the girl said.

"Hi." I felt a little rude for not knowing her name. This whole situation was extremely awkward. "I'm heading out. See you."

"Where are you going?" she asked.

"To the coffee shop down the street." I held up my notebook. "To work," I added.

"Oh, great. Will you bring me back a latte? Extra whipped cream?"

"I'm not coming back for a long time. Great meeting you though!" I left the apartment before I could hear her response.

CHAPTER 10

I waited until Rory's restaurant was open before heading back to the apartment. I just needed some time to myself. Letting Rory move in was proving to be a big mistake. I should have trusted my gut. But maybe if I set some ground rules it wouldn't be so bad. I definitely needed to talk to him about his friends being over all the time.

I sighed when my apartment door was unlocked. I'd add "locking the door" to my list of rules. I opened it and froze. Rory and Jackson were in the living room, hiding behind furniture with Nerf guns in their hands.

"Oh my God! What are you doing?!"

"Hey, Keira," Jackson said and stood up from his hiding spot. Rory immediately shot him in the chest.

"Shit." Jackson turned to Rory. "Obviously that doesn't count." He turned back to me. "We're having a Nerf war. Do you want to play?"

"No." *Am I living with children?* "Try not to break any..."

"Lighten up," Rory said and aimed his gun at me. He pressed the trigger and a Nerf dart hit my left breast."

"Fuck that hurts!" I put my hands over my mouth. I hadn't meant to curse. But I also didn't realize how much those foam darts could hurt. "What the hell, Rory?!"

Rory kept his gun aimed at me.

"Don't you have work?"

"I took the day off."

"You're on my team," Jackson said. He grabbed a smaller gun out of his back pocket, threw it over at me, and then crouched down behind the couch.

Rory fired another shot at me, but I dove behind the kitchen counter. My heart was racing. I used to play this with my brother when we were little. The guns were more sophisticated now, and they shot farther and harder. I cocked the gun and put my finger on the trigger. I peeked my head above the counter. Rory shot another dart and I ducked just in time as a dart flew past me.

I had an idea. I crawled around the other side of the counter, stood up, and pressed my back against the hallway wall. I peered around the corner. Rory grabbed my wrist, pulled me down on the floor, and held down my hand with the gun in it. He straddled me to keep me in place and pulled both my hands above my head, holding them down with one of his hands.

This is so hot.

Then he shot me twice in the stomach.

"Ow!" It hurt even worse at close range.

"Keira's dead!" he shouted over to Jackson.

I laughed as I tried to squirm out of his grip. He leaned down and whispered in my ear. "When you're dead you can't speak. So stay quiet."

I heard Jackson curse under his breath. Rory was still pressing me to the floor. I liked the feeling of his hands on me, holding me down. It was embarrassing how much this turned me on.

Rory looked down and smiled at me.

Does he like this as much as I do?

He released me far too soon and peered over the back of the chair. "I have an idea." He picked me up and held me against his chest as he ran toward Jackson. "Meat shield!" Rory yelled.

I screamed as Jackson's darts hit my back. I wrapped my arms around Rory's neck and my legs around his waist, and I felt his hand slide to my ass. *Oh God. Is he grabbing my ass because he wants to, or because he has to in order to hold me in place?* I heard several shots, but only a few more hit me.

"Shit, you got me," Jackson said and tossed his gun onto the couch.

Rory set me down and pumped his fist in the air. "Victory!" He tossed his gun next to Jackson's. "And now I need to take a piss. Don't follow me," he said and winked at me.

"That was an accident!" I called after him.

Jackson sat down on the couch with a sigh.

"Where's Connor?" I asked and sat down in the chair across from him.

Jackson shrugged. "I don't know. I talked to him this morning, though. I know you like Rory, but I was actually a little surprised that you and Connor didn't hit it off better."

I felt my face blushing. "We kind of did. I mean, he's nice, but I don't really do one night stands."

Jackson turned to face me. He looked surprised. "Why do you assume that's what Connor wants?"

Because Rory told me that's all Connor wanted? "I mean, isn't he like Rory? Doesn't he like...sleep around?"

"Connor? I mean, maybe now. I'm sure he isn't looking for anything serious, but he's not an asshole."

"What do you mean maybe now?"

"Well, he got divorced last year. When I met him in college, he was already dating Cindy. So maybe he's only into one night stands when he's single. I just can't really picture that." Jackson shrugged.

"Oh." *Why had Rory lied to me?*

Rory came back out of the bathroom. He looked back and forth between me and Jackson.

"Jackson, do you mind giving Rory and I a minute alone?" I said. "I wanted to discuss some roommate stuff with him."

"Sure. I actually need to get going anyway. I have a fitting for this divine new Armani suit."

"Very fancy."

"I have one every Wednesday. Just the usual."

"Are you serious?"

"No." Jackson laughed. "See you guys later."

After he closed the door I looked over at Rory. He was staring at me. He walked over and sat down on the couch.

"Your friends are interesting," I said.

Rory laughed. "Yeah." He leaned back and put his feet up on the coffee table. It wasn't my table, but I still cringed. "So, you wanted to talk?"

"Mhm. I was thinking maybe we should set up a few ground rules. So that this works out."

"Okay. Have I done something wrong?" He looked genuinely concerned. But for some reason it seemed like an act.

"No, not really. It's just that your friends are over a lot. I didn't realize that all three of you would be moving in." I laughed awkwardly.

"I know what this is about, and you have nothing to worry about. I already asked Connor to stop bothering you. It won't be a problem again."

"He wasn't bothering me."

"Oh, my misunderstanding then." He scowled slightly.

"Anyway, that's not what this is about. I just mean in general, are they really going to be here all the time? Is it never just going to be us? Or, just me I mean. Because it would be weird if it was just us. Not that I want to be alone with you. I didn't mean that in a sexual way at all. Like, not at all, Rory. Obviously." *What the hell?*

"Obviously." He took his feet off the table and put his elbows on his knees. "They won't be here all the time. They helped me move in. And I told you about poker Tuesdays. And today I had off, so I asked Jackson to come over. Besides, you weren't even here."

"Yeah, about that. I felt like I had to sneak out of here this morning because of your sexual escapades."

"Is that what you classify as a sexual escapade?" Rory laughed. "You need to get out more."

I could feel myself blushing.

"Oh, and by the way, you were kind of rude to Kelly this morning." He hesitated for a moment. "Or was her name Kim?"

"Come on." I didn't know her name either, but I also hadn't slept with her. I had been rude though. "Okay, fair point. I'm sorry, I just felt really uncomfortable because I had to listen to you two banging all night. I'll apologize the next time I see her, if that makes you feel better."

"You probably won't be seeing her again."

I rolled my eyes. When I said he could move in, I thought he was a nice guy.

"And I probably won't see Jackson or Connor again until the party on Friday."

"Okay." This conversation wasn't going well. "I just want to get a heads up when you're having people over."

"No problem."

"And about last night. It was really inconsiderate of you to invite me to a game of poker and then change it to strip poker without even telling me. It was really uncomfortable."

"I told you that you didn't have to play."

"That's not the point. If it's happening in my home, I'd just appreciate a heads up."

"Okay, I will let you know in advance whenever I'm going to be having fun."

"You're being a little dramatic."

"Am I? You're attacking me."

"I'm not attacking you, I'm just trying to make it so that we can live comfortably together." *Crap, I am attacking him.*

"Look, if you're just going to make up a bunch of rules for no reason..."

"I've told you all the reasons."

"Right. Well maybe I want to set some rules too. Is that okay? Or is one of the rules that I'm not allowed to make up any rules?"

"Yeah. Of course."

"Great." He stood up. "I'd prefer if you didn't hook up with my friends."

CHAPTER 11

I lay awake in my room, staring at the ceiling. *Why doesn't he want me to hook up with Connor?* He had stormed off before I had gotten to ask him about it. First he had lied about Connor being a player, and then he had asked me not to hook up with his friends.

Does he like me?

This was stupid. We were both adults. I looked at my alarm clock. It was only twelve thirty. He was probably still up. I climbed out of bed and pulled on my silk robe. Before I lost my nerve, I knocked on his door.

A moment later he opened it. He was only wearing boxers. And glasses. I hadn't really been serious when I told him I liked guys in glasses. But they were so sexy on him.

"So, you wear glasses?" I asked. *Obviously.*

"Sorry," he said. "I should have told you. But it's only when I'm not wearing my contacts."

"Oh, no, that's fine. I was just rambling the other day anyway. I mean, who doesn't like tall, dark, and handsome? Glasses are nice though. They look good on you."

He lowered his eyebrows slightly.

"I like what you've done with your room." *Are those handcuffs on his bedpost?*

He lifted his arm and put his hand on the doorframe to block my view. "Thanks."

"Why did you lie to me about Connor? Jackson told me that Connor doesn't really sleep around."

"I guess I was just rambling."

"It doesn't seem like you ever ramble."

He shrugged.

"Why don't you want me to date Connor?" I didn't really want to hook up with Connor, but I wanted to know Rory's reasoning. I needed to know if he liked me, because this tension was driving me crazy.

"Well, if you two dated and then broke up, things would be awkward here."

"Right." I tried to keep my eyes on his face, but I found his abs really distracting. "No other reason?"

"Look, Keira, you're a cool girl. Hell, I don't know any other girls that would have joined in on our Nerf battle."

"Thanks."

"And I don't want to fuck this up. I'll follow your rules. And I know that I can't stop you from hooking up with my friends. I'll revoke the rule if that's what you want."

"That's not what I want."

I saw his Adam's apple rise and fall. "So what do you want?"

You! I could feel myself gaping at him. I bit my lip. I wanted to tell him to forget about our pact. I wanted so badly to kiss him.

He smiled at me. "Look, it's late. I'm going to get some sleep."

"Right. Of course. Goodnight."

I stepped back and he closed his door in my face. *That was weird.* I walked back to my room and climbed into my bed. It definitely seemed like he liked me.

***

I heard movement in the kitchen. I glanced at my alarm clock. It was 7 a.m. I was still tired, but I had an idea. And I didn't want to miss this opportunity. I got out of bed and put on a lacy push-up bra and a pair of matching panties. I walked out of my room and into the kitchen before I could chicken out.

Rory had his back to me. He was wearing just his boxers and cooking something on the stove. It smelled amazing.

"Good morning," I said and walked toward the fridge.

"Hey, Keira." He didn't turn around to look at me. "Do you want some pancakes?"

"Absolutely. Thanks." I sat down at the kitchen counter and admired the muscles on his back. Every time he flipped a pancake his muscles would awaken. I could watch him cook all day.

When he finally turned around, he didn't even seem to notice that I was just in my sexiest underwear. *Notice me!* He put down a stack of pancakes in front of me and sat down on the stool next to me.

"These are really good," I said.

"Well, I am a chef," he said and smiled at me.

We continued to eat in silence. Now I just felt awkward. I thought he'd find this sexy and alluring. But he didn't even notice. Or maybe he thought it was awkward.

"Where are your clothes?" he finally asked as he took another bite.

You're supposed to kiss me, not quiz me! "Since we're just friends, I figured you wouldn't mind if I walked around like this. Besides, you walk around in just your boxers."

"That's fine. I don't mind at all."

"Good."

"Good." It looked like he wanted to laugh. He was so infuriating. And now I was growing increasingly more embarrassed.

"What are you doing today?" Maybe I could somehow salvage this conversation.

"I have work and then I need to get some stuff for the party tomorrow night."

"What kind of stuff?"

"Just the usual stuff."

"Of course." I literally had no idea what he was talking about. But I didn't want him to think I was a loser.

Rory finished his pancakes and picked up his plate. "Oh, you have some syrup on your face."

"Crap, where?"

He tapped the side of his lips.

I reached up and wiped the corner of my mouth.

"No, other side," he reached over and brushed his thumb along my bottom lip.

He's going to kiss me! A dull ache was spreading through my stomach. *My lingerie to breakfast trick had worked!*

But instead, he removed his hand from my face and licked his finger. *Fuck that was hot.* Somehow that was even sexier than him kissing me.

"What's it like to have a one night stand?" I blurted out.

Rory lowered his eyebrows. "Why do you want to know exactly?" He put his plate back down and rested his elbow on the counter.

"Well, I was thinking about having one."

"Really? I thought you didn't do one night stands, Keira."

"I don't. But maybe I should. You certainly seem to have a lot of fun."

"Mhm."

"So, I was thinking, maybe you could teach me how."

"You want me to teach you how to have a one night stand?"

"Yes." *With you.*

"Why the sudden change of...ethics?"

"Well, there's this guy that I work with that I really like. But he isn't looking for anything serious. And I can't seem to get him off my mind. So I thought maybe I should try him out. It out. It, as in a one night stand."

"Aren't you a freelance writer? I thought you just worked from here?"

"Well there's an office. For meetings and stuff. It definitely exists."

Rory was smiling at me. "Okay. I can help you out. If that's what you really want."

"Yeah, that would be great."

"Okay. Do you mind doing the dishes? I need to get going." He walked away and went into his room.

CHAPTER 12

"And then he just walked away?" Emily asked.

"Yeah."

"You're right. He's madly in love with you."

"Don't make fun of me."

Emily laughed. "I'm sorry. But this is what you do. You always read too much into everything." I had met Emily for lunch at a restaurant near her office. I needed advice, and she was always ready to give it.

"He asked me not to date any of his friends. I'm not crazy to assume that it's because he likes me."

"But you said yourself that he isn't looking for anything serious. Is that really what you want?"

"Of course not. But I can't get him out of my head. Maybe this will make me get over him."

Emily stared at me skeptically.

"Or maybe he could fall madly in love with me."

"I knew it! So, your plan is to get him to give you advice about how to have a one night stand. And then realize that you mean with him. And then he'll fall madly in love with you? Is that the gist?"

"Maybe."

"Keira, you don't have realistic expectations at all!"

"I do." I didn't. I really wanted more. All my friends were married. I felt like I was falling behind.

"And what the heck happened to your agreement? I thought you made a pact to not start liking each other?"

"Well, yeah, but clearly we both like each other already. So the pact is void."

"Clearly." She scrunched her face to the side.

"Stop looking at me like that! I never wanted the pact to begin with."

"I know, I know. Look, I have to go. If I'm late my boss will kill me. But think about what you're doing, Keira. That's not you. And odds are, he really isn't looking for anything serious. Because he's told you that. This is an awful, awful plan."

Why did she always think all my plans were so bad? "But..."

"Just think about it, okay? I have to run. But Jim is going to be out of town tomorrow night, so I can make it to your party after all. Maybe I can be your wingman." Emily winked at me and walked out of the restaurant.

***

I sat down on the couch and stared at the blank notebook page on my lap. I hadn't been able to write a good article since Rory had moved in. And now I was playing with the idea of writing a piece about his lifestyle. About how dating was devolving into meaningless hookups.

I heard the creak of the front door and looked over as Rory walked in. He tossed his keys onto the kitchen counter.

"Hey! So I was wondering if you wanted to start those lessons?" I asked.

"Right now?"

"Yeah."

"Okay, just let me go change." He came back out of his room while he was still pulling a white t-shirt over his head. His jeans sat low on his waist and hugged him in all the right places. He sat down next to me on the couch. "What exactly do you want me to teach you?"

"All of it." He smelled like cinnamon. It must be from something he made at work. I found myself wanting to lick his skin. *Calm down!*

"You seemed to be doing pretty well with Connor the other night. I didn't even believe you when you said you two hadn't hooked up."

"That was just fooling around. It was all him."

"Well that's how it works. I'm usually the one being forward. And then if the girl responds, I know she's interested."

He hasn't been forward with me at all. "So, what if the guy isn't being forward? Is there something I could do in order to let a guy know that I'm interested in hooking up?"

"Yeah, just be flirtatious and slutty."

I have been! "I've tried that. It doesn't seem to work."

"So maybe he's gay."

"No he's definitely not gay. I've heard him having sex."

"In your office?"

"No. No, that's not what I meant. I've heard about him having sex. From other people. He has sex with women and people talk, you know? Normal office stuff."

"No, not really."

"Okay, well he's not gay. He's straight. Just take my word for it."

"I'm sorry, Keira, but maybe he's just not that into you."

I bit my lip. "Oh." *Of course. Of course you're not into me.*

Rory was staring at me.

"Well maybe I just don't know how to be forward enough. Maybe you could show me exactly what a girl would do if she was interested in you. I mean, have you ever slept with a girl who you didn't find super attractive?"

"No."

"Well, just show me what to do." This wasn't working. *He's not attracted to me.*

Rory sighed. "Okay. So obviously if I'm sitting at the bar or something, she'd come and sit right next to me."

I can do that. I'm doing it right now! "Good to know." I scribbled that down in my notebook.

"You're taking notes?"

"I don't want to forget anything. Keep going."

"Lots of flirtatious touching. So when you laugh, touch his shoulder. Or put your hand on his thigh."

"Hand on thigh, got it." I bit my lip. "Wait, like right above the knee?"

Rory put his hand on the middle of my thigh. "Higher is better."

Yes it is. I gulped.

"And if you really want him to know you mean business, slowly move your hand up his thigh. He'll get the picture, unless he's an idiot." He moved his hand off my leg.

I scribbled that down. *I've got you just where I want you now, Rory.*

"Also, laugh at all his jokes. You don't want to wound his confidence if you're trying to take advantage of it."

"Done."

"And wear something that makes you seem easy."

"Like what?"

"Doesn't really matter as long as it's tight and barely covers anything."

"So like, legs and boobs?"

"Yeah." He ran his hand through his hair. "And it's gotta accentuate your ass."

Great, he likes big butts. Maybe that's the problem. "Anything else?"

"You should definitely invite him to the party tomorrow night."

"Who?"

"The guy you're crushing on."

Shit, I can't do that, you're already coming! "He's usually pretty busy. He probably can't make it."

"Even just asking him will let him know that you're interested. Besides, doing something together outside of work might make him put his guard down."

"Okay, he'll be there." *What the hell is wrong with me?!*

"Great."

"Oh, one more thing. A little while ago I told him that I wasn't attracted to him. Because we were talking and I got nervous. So I think that maybe that has something to do with him not thinking I'm interested."

"Yeah, that'll do it. But really, guys like the chase. If he was into you, he'd probably be even more forward than before."

Fuck.

"But that doesn't mean that you can't try being more flirtatious yourself. Okay, I gotta go take a shower. I hope that helped."

"Yeah, it definitely did. Thank you."

CHAPTER 13

I had to listen to Rory's bed springs squeak and a strange woman moaning with pleasure again all night. When I finally woke from my fitful sleep, I went straight to the mall. I needed to find the perfect outfit for tonight's party. But my efforts were proving fruitless.

"Thank God you're here, Emily. I need your help." I opened up the dressing room door for her. She was using her lunch break to help me find something to wear.

She came in and sat down on the bench. I turned around and she started laughing.

"You're not helping!" I yelled.

"I'm not laughing at you, I'm laughing at the dress."

I turned toward the mirror. "Okay, fine, it's horrible. I need something sexier." I was short and it seemed like it was impossible to find a dress short enough for Rory's standards. Maybe the girls that he usually hooked up with all shopped online.

"How about this one?" Emily pulled out one of the dozens of dresses I had on the rack and handed it to me. It was black with some sheer material on the front. It actually looked pretty short.

I slipped out of the dress I was wearing and started to put on the one she handed me.

"Why are you trying on such sleazy dresses anyway?"

"Can you just zip me up?" I held my hair up out of the way. I turned around after she had zipped up my dress. "How do I look?"

"Hot."

"Really?" I looked in the mirror. *Finally!* The dress hugged my ass and the hem ended just a few inches below it. The neckline plunged insanely low, but there was some mesh that helped make it a little less inappropriate. It was tight at my waist and somehow made my ass and breasts look even bigger. I pulled out my list from my purse. *Barely covers my breasts and legs, and definitely accentuates my ass. Check, check, and check.*

"What is that?" Emily grabbed the paper out of my hands and started reading it.

"It's nothing." I tried to snatch it back from her but she sidestepped me.

"Seriously, Keira, what the hell is this?"

I sighed. "It's a list of tips that Rory gave me on how to let a guy know that you're interested in a one night stand."

Emily started laughing. "This is his advice? He sounds like such a tool."

"He's not." This time when I reached out I was able to grab the paper back. I shoved it into my bag. "He thinks I like some guy at work. He wasn't giving me advice on how to get with himself. At least, he doesn't realize it."

"From work? You work from home."

"Ugh! I know. I get flustered around him and say stupid stuff. That's why I needed his advice."

Emily smiled at me. "So, does this dress fit all the criteria?"

"Yes, it does." I knew it was slutty, but I felt so sexy in it. Maybe this dress would give me the confidence I needed around Rory.

Emily turned the tag over and whistled. "Eighty bucks for a dress?"

"It's fifty percent off."

"Still."

"It's the only one that works. I'm going to get it." I quickly took it off and put my clothes back on. If I didn't check out soon, I'd change my mind. I hated spending money. If I didn't, I wouldn't have needed a new roommate in the first place.

"Do you have shoes that'll work?" Emily asked.

"Yes." I had bought a pair of six inch heels for my one year anniversary with my most recent ex. They were still in the box because he had broken up with me before we went out to dinner to celebrate. *I'm so bad at dating.*

"Okay, you better check out before you change your mind then." Emily knew me so well. We had been roommates all four years in college and had also lived together when we first moved to the city. She met her future husband the first day she started her new job, and they got married a year later. Maybe that was my problem. I needed a job where I had to go into the office every day. Just the thought of doing that made me shudder. I couldn't write in an office. It was too stifling.

I brought the dress to the checkout counter and looked it over. I was already having reservations. It was too short. And too slutty. I turned to Emily. "Maybe I should try on..."

"You're getting it." She looked around for a salesgirl and waved her arm in the air. "We're ready to checkout!"

The woman walked over and took the dress out of my hands. "That will be forty dollars."

I reluctantly handed her my credit card. "When are you coming over tonight?" I asked Emily.

"When does the party start? I'm so excited to finally get to meet Rory."

Hmmm. "I actually don't know. When do parties usually start?"

"Just ask Rory. Stop being weird."

I grabbed the bag from the salesgirl, and Emily and I walked toward the exit. "I feel like if I was cooler I'd just know."

"Give me your cell phone."

I pulled it out of my purse and handed it to her. She quickly typed out a message and pressed send.

"Oh my God, what did you just do?!" I grabbed the phone out of her hands and stared down in horror. She had texted Rory:

"Hey roomie, when does the party start? I need to tell my date. Can't wait to put all that advice you gave me into action. Looking forward to a sexy evening." There was even a winky face emoticon at the end.

Before I could figure out something to type so that I could somehow rectify the situation, his response came.

"9."

"It starts at nine. What is wrong with you?" I asked and put my cell phone in my purse. Maybe he would just think I was drunk or something.

"What did he say back?"

"He said it starts at nine. Actually, he just typed the number nine."

"Really? Hmmm."

"Why? What does that mean?"

"I think maybe you're right. It kind of seems like he's jealous that you're bringing someone. No one just types a number unless they're pissed. He does speak in full sentences, right?"

"Yes. And I'm not bringing anyone, so he won't be jealous for long. This is working out really well. Actually, way better than I thought."

"I think you should bring a date. Making him jealous is a pretty good tactic."

"I already tried that with his friend."

"Yeah, but that was his friend. If it's a stranger, he might be more territorial."

"But where do I find a date?"

"I don't know, just bump into a stranger on the street and ask him. I have to go. I'll see you at nine."

***

I clutched my shopping bag and walked around downtown. I wasn't sure if Emily literally meant I should bump into someone or not. She hadn't answered my text. But I wasn't sure what else to do. So I wandered around looking for someone to run into.

And then I saw the perfect guy. He was handsome, but not as handsome as Rory. It looked like he tried hard to make himself look good. Perfectly styled hair, really white teeth, and super tan. I quickly moved to the center of the sidewalk so that I'd be in his path. When he stepped to the left to avoid me, I made a sharp turn left and half ran into, half shoved him. His briefcase fell open and documents scattered all over the sidewalk.

"What the hell?" he said under his breath.

"Oh my God, I'm so sorry. Let me help you with those." I quickly grabbed some of the papers before they blew away.

"It's okay," he smiled. "You need to pay more attention to where you're going."

"I know, I was just thinking about what I needed to pick up for this party I'm going to. Oh! Let me make this up to you. I'm throwing this really big party tonight. Do you want to come?"

"Oh. Um. What kind of party is it?"

"It's a party for my new roommate. Like a housewarming party, but a lot crazier. There's going to be tons of people and it's going to be a blast."

"Where is it?"

"Let me write down the address." I pulled a piece of paper out of the small notebook in my purse, wrote down my address, and handed it to him.

"You're not asking me to be your date, are you?" The man suddenly looked uncomfortable.

Why do all strangers think I'm un-dateable? "No, I actually have a date," I lied. "I just thought you'd have fun."

"Oh good, because I'm..."

"It's fine. Just come if you can. I'm really sorry about running into you." I quickly walked away.

CHAPTER 14

"Hey, Rory?" I knocked on his bedroom door. I had just put on my new dress and I couldn't pass up the opportunity to ask him to zip it up for me. If I moved my arms just so, I could probably do it myself, but I was trying to be as flirtatious as possible. That's what he had instructed. And I was going to follow all of his advice.

"Hey, Keira," he said as he opened the door. He lowered his eyebrows slightly when he saw my outfit.

I walked into his bedroom without asking permission. The feel of his eyes on me was making me blush. "Could you zip up my dress for me? I can't quite reach the zipper."

"Um, yeah, sure." He put one hand on my waist and slowly pulled the zipper up my back, letting his fingers trace my skin before the zipper did. He moved my hair to one side and then fastened the clip at the top of the dress. His hands lingered for a moment and then he pulled back.

I turned around to look at him. He was looking at my breasts. *Yes!*

He shook his head and looked up at my face. "I see that you took my advice."

"Yeah, what do you think?"

I spun around once to let him see all the angles. This dress didn't leave much to the imagination, but I hoped that he'd want to see what was underneath.

"It looks good on you."

"Is it sexy enough?"

"Um, yeah it looks good on you," he repeated. He rubbed the back of his neck with his hand and looked back toward his door.

He wanted me to go. But all I wanted was for him to think I was sexy. I sat down on the edge of his bed, leaned back slightly, and crossed my legs. "So who's coming tonight?"

He put his hands in his pockets and looked down at the floor. "Just a few of my friends." A knock sounded on the door. "I'm going to go get that. Close the door behind you, okay?"

I sighed and got off the bed. I was trying to be sexy but all I had succeeded at was making him uncomfortable. I walked out of his bedroom and closed the door.

"Damn, Keira, you look amazing."

I almost jumped. I turned around and looked up at Connor. "Oh, hey, Connor."

"So I'm pretty sure it worked," said Connor.

"What worked?"

"Making Rory jealous." He handed me a bottle of beer.

"Wait, really?"

"Well he basically threw me out the other night."

"You really think he was jealous?"

"It sure seemed like it. But maybe we should continue where we left off, just to make sure."

"You know, Jackson gave you up. He told me that you're actually a nice guy."

"Do you want me to be a nice guy?"

I rolled my eyes at him. "Everyone likes a nice guy, Connor." I looked over at Rory. More people were coming in and he was already talking to some girl.

"Then why are you staring at Rory?"

"I've only ever dated nice guys. Maybe I need a change."

"Here's to being something that we aren't." Connor lifted up his beer bottle and tapped it against mine. "Good luck with Rory." Connor smiled at me and walked away.

"Was that him?" Emily grabbed my elbow and led me over to the kitchen.

"No that's Connor, Rory's friend that helped me try to make him jealous."

"He seems into you. And he's really good looking."

"I know. But I like Rory."

"Okay, which one is he?"

"He's the unbelievably gorgeous one over there." I pointed to where Rory was standing. He had ditched the girl and was now talking to a few guys near the couch. He smiled over at me.

"I can see the appeal," Emily said. "He's kind of dreamy."

"Dreamy and a total slut."

Emily laughed. "So, what did he tell you that you need to do?"

"Flirt with him by touching him a lot."

"Of course he did. How about you go try that out."

"Okay, come with me. I'll introduce you." The two of us walked over to Rory. "Hey, Rory."

Rory turned away from his guy friends.

"This is my friend, Emily." I gestured to Emily. "And Emily, this is my new roommate." I touched Rory on the arm. *Geez, he's so muscular.*

"Nice to meet you," Emily said and shook Rory's hand.

"Likewise. I was beginning to think that Keira was a weird loner."

I laughed and lightly pushed on his shoulder. "Oh, stop it."

Rory laughed and gave me a strange look. "So, where is that guy you're crushing on?"

"He is..." I looked around the room. "Not here yet apparently. Maybe he stood me up." I laughed and lightly pushed Rory's shoulder again. *Shit. I'm only supposed to do that when he makes a joke.*

"Okay. Nice meeting you, Emily," Rory said and turned back to his friends.

Emily grabbed my arm and guided me over to the couch. "That was probably the worst flirting I've ever seen," she said and started laughing. "What is wrong with you?"

"He makes me nervous!"

"That was so awkward." She laughed again.

"Help me, please."

"What else did he tell you to do?"

"To rub his leg. Upwards."

"Quite the innuendo. Okay, so we just need to wait until he sits down somewhere."

I glanced over at Rory. He was still standing in the same spot, but a few girls had gravitated toward him. *Not good.*

"Hey."

I looked up and saw the man I had purposely bumped into on the street earlier. "Oh, great, you came!" I stood up. "I forgot to get your name."

"Patrick," he said. "And you?"

"I'm Keira. And this is my friend, Emily."

Patrick nodded his head and looked around the room. "Nice place."

"Thanks. Help yourself to a drink." I pointed over to the kitchen counter that was acting as our bar. "And I'm sorry again about bumping into you."

Patrick laughed. "No problem at all, Keira." He smiled and walked over to the kitchen.

"You bumped into him?"

"That's what you told me to do."

Emily laughed. "That's not exactly what I meant. Oh, look!" She pointed over to Rory. He had just sat down at the poker table. There was one seat open next to his.

"I'll be right back," I said and walked as quickly as I could in my heels over to Rory. I touched his shoulder and said as seductively as possible, "Is this seat taken?"

Rory looked up at me and eyed me suspiciously. "It's all yours."

I sat down.

"Hey, Keira," Jackson said. "I heard you invited someone to the party. That must have broken Connor's heart."

I laughed. "Connor is fine. I'm not exactly what he's looking for. What are you guys up to?"

"Scoping out our options." Jackson laughed. I wasn't sure if he was just joking, but I needed to make my move.

"Oh, is that so?" I put my hand on Rory's knee and slowly moved it up his thigh. I could feel his body tense. "Have you found anyone enticing?"

"Keira."

Me?! "You find me enticing?"

Rory put his hand on top of mine, stopping it from going any higher. "Where's that guy from your work?"

"You know what, I'm not sure where he went. Maybe I should go find him." I leaned in close and whispered in Rory's ear. "Thanks for the advice, I think it's working." I winked at Rory, stood up, and walked back over to Emily.

"How did it go?" she asked.

"Pretty well I think." I sat down next to her. "He seemed flustered."

"Did he give you any other advice?"

"No, that was pretty much it."

"I guess we'll have to just wait and see then," Emily said.

***

A few hours later I didn't seem to be getting any closer to winning Rory over. He was flirting with some girl. "I'm going to go talk to him again," I said to Emily. I had made a point to go over to him about every half hour to flirt with him. I walked over and tapped on his shoulder.

"Keira."

"Rory. Can I talk to you?"

"I'm listening."

I grabbed his arm and pulled him to a corner. "Your advice sucks. It's not working at all. Is there anything else I can do?"

He smiled at me. "Hmm. That's quite the predicament. Are you sure you've tried everything? I haven't seen you talk to anyone all night except for Emily."

"That's not true." *He's been watching me?!*

"Keira, did you even invite him?"

"Of course I did." I pointed over to Patrick.

"You mean Patrick?" Rory laughed. "You guys don't exactly seem to be hitting it off."

"Yeah, well, I just met him on the street. I don't think he's interested in me."

"I thought he worked at your office?"

"Yes! Isn't that what I said?"

"No."

"Oh, right, of course you wouldn't know. The street is what we call our office. Like office nicknames. Working on the street? It's just an inside joke at my office. You wouldn't understand."

"Okay."

"And I have tried everything. None of your advice worked."

"That's because he's gay."

Seriously? Damn it, Patrick! "He's not gay."

"Well, he hit on me about an hour ago."

"Oh, please, Rory. I don't think you really know how to tell if someone is hitting on you. I could hit you with a bat and you wouldn't know I was hitting on you."

"That's rather violent of you. But I am curious, why would you think that I don't know if a girl is hitting on me?" He raised his left eyebrow.

If he knows I'm hitting on him, why is he acting like this? It's so frustrating! "Just tell me what else I can do."

"You could just pull him to the side and yell at him. Guys really like that kind of thing."

"I've already tried that."

Rory laughed.

Shit, he's just messing with me. "Wait, what? That's terrible advice."

"And if you've tried that and he's still not getting the hint, you should probably just make the first move."

"I can't do that."

"Because he's gay?"

"No! Because I don't know if he likes me."

Rory looked over at Patrick. "It looks like he might like the guy he's talking to right now."

"Damn it, this isn't even about Patrick. I don't even know him."

"Wait. Are you serious? I'm shocked and appalled that you would lie to me. You've absolutely never done that before."

"Ugh." I stormed off to go find Emily. I had never been more embarrassed in my life.

CHAPTER 15

"Clearly he knows that you were talking about him," Emily said.

"Yeah, he's just been messing with me this whole time." The party was winding down and there were only a few people left. Surprisingly, Rory was just talking to a few of his guy friends.

"Well, he did tell you to make the first move. Maybe he wants you to come on to him."

"I've been flirting with him all night. I think I'm done embarrassing myself."

"I'm sorry that your master plan didn't work. It's probably better that it didn't, though. If he doesn't want a relationship, it's going to be so awkward living with him once you've had sex. Like...really awkward, Keira."

"I know."

"It's getting late. I'm going to head out, okay?"

"Okay." Emily gave me a hug and left me alone on the couch. A few minutes later, Rory sat down next to me.

"I'm surprised that you're alone," I said.

"Yeah, well, someone kept interrupting me all night long."

"Well I'm sure that person wasn't trying to be annoying."

"She wasn't. She was more cute than annoying."

Cute? I didn't want him to think I was cute. "I think she was probably going for sexy."

"I kind of got that vibe. She's definitely sexy. But she's also cute and innocent, and doesn't exactly know what she's getting herself into."

"I think she realizes what she's getting herself into."

"Well, it doesn't matter because she's also completely off limits."

"Which makes it sexier, doesn't it?" I put my hand on his thigh. *Maybe it's not too late.*

Rory looked into my eyes. "Damn it, Keira, what are you doing?"

"I'm following your advice." I thought about the girl he had liked during strip poker. She had been really forward. She had even straddled him at one point. I took a deep breath and straddled Rory on the couch.

His Adam's apple rose and fell. "I've noticed."

"Please don't make me beg."

His hands slowly slid up my thighs and grabbed my waist. "This isn't what you want, Keira."

"Yes it is." I could feel his erection growing beneath me. I had never wanted something so badly in my life.

"You have no idea how to have a one night stand."

"Maybe you can show me."

"Keira..."

I leaned forward with my hands on the back of the couch and gyrated my hips against his erection.

"Fuck it." He grabbed the back of my head, pulled my mouth to his, and kissed me hard. The way his tongue collided with mine sent chills down my spine. He wanted this just as badly as I did.

I moved my hips again and he moaned into my mouth. I felt his hands drift to my back. He quickly unzipped my dress. I sat back on his lap and let the straps fall off my shoulders. The way he was looking at me made my heart race. He pulled my waist up toward him so that my stomach was just a few inches from his face. I loved the feeling of his hands on me. He grabbed the hem of my dress and pushed it up my thighs and over my ass. I could feel his warm breath against my skin. He kissed the inside of my thigh. My body trembled under his mouth. *Oh God.* I wanted him so badly. It felt like I had waited forever for him to touch me. He kissed the inside of my other thigh.

"Rory."

He kissed my stomach in response. My whole body began to quiver as he kissed down the front of my thong and between my thighs. "Keira, you're so wet for me."

"I know," I moaned. *Why is he torturing me?* "I've wanted you this whole time."

He pushed my dress up the sides of my torso. I grabbed it and pulled it the rest of the way off. I had been in front of him in just my underwear before. But this time was different. This time he was looking. He ran his hands down the sides of my torso as he stared at the top of my breasts. His touch made my skin tingle. I could feel my nipples getting hard just from his gaze.

"I've wanted you too." He grabbed my ass and stood up. I wrapped my arms around his neck as he carried me through the hallway. He slammed my back against the door to his bedroom and kissed me again. I wanted him to do me right here, pressed up against his door.

"Are you sure this is what you want?" he whispered in my ear.

"Yes. I want you."

He opened up the door, carried me into his room, and threw me down onto his bed. He stared down at me as he grabbed his t-shirt from the nape of his neck and pulled it over his head. I had never seen anyone sexier in my entire life. His six pack and muscular arms made him look like he was straight out of a magazine, posing for something other than shirts. He started to unbutton his pants. I moved off the bed, knelt down in front of him, and pushed his hands away.

I locked eyes with him as I slowly unzipped his pants. I wanted to taste him. If this was just one night, I wanted to enjoy every second of it. I wrapped my fingers in his belt loops and pulled his jeans off his hips. The bulge in his boxers made me gulp. I slowly pulled his boxers down and his erection sprung free. *It's huge.* I had never seen a cock so big before. And tonight it was all mine.

I let my fingers slide down his happy trail as I put my lips around the tip of his cock. I swirled my tongue around his tip, tasting his salty pre cum. Just the taste of him was making me even wetter. I wrapped my fingers around the base of his dick. He was so big that it barely fit in my hand. He was staring down at me, daring me to go further. I slid my lips down his shaft.

Rory groaned.

He was so big that I couldn't take him all. *He's going to feel so amazing inside of me.*

Rory grabbed a fistful of my hair and shoved the rest of his thick cock into my mouth. I felt it enter the back of my throat but I didn't choke. I wanted him in my mouth. I grabbed his ass and used it as leverage as I went up and down his shaft. I tightened my lips around him.

He groaned again.

I liked hearing him react. I swirled my tongue around his base. I wrapped my lips tighter around his shaft and took him all the way to the back of my throat. When I pulled back, he grabbed my hair again and slammed his cock back into my mouth. I was so turned on it was getting hard to concentrate. He continued to guide his cock in and out of my mouth. *Oh God, he's fucking my mouth.* He thrust his hips faster and faster. I could barely focus. *Fuck this is hot.*

He pushed his dick even deeper, making my nose rub against his happy trail. I sniffed, trying to stifle my sneeze. But I couldn't. I sneezed.

Rory laughed. "That actually felt really good." He was smiling down at me.

I didn't want him to laugh at me. I wanted him to think I was good at this. I was going to make him cum in my mouth. I swirled my tongue around his shaft and bobbed my head faster. He slid his cock in and out of my mouth faster and faster.

"Keira." His cum shot into the back of my throat. I reached up to feel his abs tighten as he found his release. He continued to pump his cock in and out of my mouth, shooting more hot cum into my throat. I drank him down hungrily. He released his grip on my hair and I pulled back and licked my lips.

"You're not as innocent as you made me think." He pulled me to my feet and pushed me back down on his bed. I looked up at his face. He looked hungry, hungry for me. He kicked off his pants and boxers and knelt down in front of me. He kissed the inside of my thigh again. I wanted his huge cock inside of me.

He kissed my hip and then right above my panty line. I leaned up on my elbows to watch him as he took my thong between his teeth. *Holy shit.* I lifted my ass so he could pull it down my hips. The feeling of the lace and his warm breath made every inch of me feel aroused. He pulled my thong down my legs and let it fall to the floor. I watched him as he slowly took off one of my stilettos and then the other. My heart was beating so fast. He kissed the inside of my ankle and slowly up my leg as he traced his palm up my other leg. *This is torture.* He stopped when his head was right between my thighs.

"Rory, please," I begged.

"Don't worry. I'm going to claim every inch of you."

I didn't have time to react to his naughty words because he put his lips around my clit and sucked hard. *Oh God.* I arched my back. He thrust his tongue deep inside of me. I moaned as he began to swirl his tongue against my walls.

He grabbed my hips, pulled me to the edge of his bed, and spread my thighs wide. He thrust his tongue even deeper inside of me, completely possessing me. His lips moved back to my clit as he placed a finger against my wetness. He put the tip of his finger inside of me and then pulled it back out, teasing me. I tilted my head back and moaned.

He sunk his finger deep inside of me.

Yes!

"You're so tight." He sounded as eager as my body felt. He slowly moved his finger in and out of me.

"Faster," I groaned.

Rory pumped his hand faster and placed his lips back around my clit.

"Rory," I gasped. I could feel him smile against my skin. He swirled his tongue around my clit as his fingers slid in and out of me faster and faster. I lifted my hips up, but he pushed them back down with his free hand. He held me down as his experienced fingers explored deep inside of me. He pumped his hand faster, matching the rhythm with his strokes against my clit. He hitched his finger up, hitting a spot I didn't even know existed. I felt myself clench around him. My orgasm washed through me as he continued to thrust his fingers and suck on my clit.

When my body relaxed, he kissed my clit gently. He looked up at me and slid his fingers into his mouth. *Oh my God.*

"Fuck you taste good, Keira."

Did he seriously just lick his fingers?

He leaned down and placed one last stroke against my wetness, making my whole body shiver with pleasure. "You're very responsive."

"To you."

Rory frowned at me. "Close your eyes."

I followed his instructions, even though it was hard to look away from him. He pulled me to my feet and left me standing in the middle of his room. I heard him open a drawer. He came up behind me. "You need to remain unattached. This is purely sexual." I felt something silky fall on my face.

"What is that?"

"A tie." He tightened it and knotted it behind my head.

"But I want to see you." The silky fabric blocked out his bedroom.

"This will make you focus on the pleasure, not me."

"But..."

"Just focus on my hands." His voice was firm and demanding. It made me wet all over again. His hands slid up my waist. He unhooked my bra and slid it down my shoulders and arms. I heard it drop to the floor. I was completely naked in the middle of Rory's bedroom. He grabbed my breasts and pulled me back against his torso. I felt his cock against the small of my back. It was already erect again, ready to fill my aching pussy.

I pushed my ass out toward him and arched my back.

"You're so sexy, Keira." He kissed the side of my neck as he moved one hand to my stomach and slowly let it dip between my thighs. He lightly stroked my wetness. I pushed my ass against his cock again. He quickly spun me around so that I was facing him. I wanted to see him, but instead I let my hand brush against his chiseled abs. Somehow not being able to see made this even sexier. He grabbed my ass, lifted me up, and collapsed on top of me on his bed.

He buried his face in my neck, kissing my skin softly, as his hand wandered to one of my nipples. He squeezed the tender skin. I could feel both my nipples getting hard in response.

"Rory," I moaned. I wanted to see him. I wanted to watch what he was doing to me.

He moved his mouth down to my other nipple and sucked on it hard.

I couldn't take it anymore. "Rory. I need you inside of me."

I could feel him smile against my breast. The springs squeaked as he got off the bed. I gulped as I heard the rip of foil.

"Rory?" The waiting was agonizing. *What is he doing?*

His fingers lightly touched my clavicle and wandered down between my breasts and down my stomach. I knew he was staring at my body, watching me respond to his touch. I so badly wanted to see him. "I want to see you."

He grabbed my hips and flipped me so that my stomach was on his bed. My heart was beating so fast. He pulled my hips to the end of the bed so that my feet were on the ground. "Spread your legs," he said. His voice sounded tight.

I moved my legs apart and jutted my ass in the air. He ran his fingers down my spine and over my ass.

"What do you want, Keira?"

"You," I panted. The waiting was driving me insane.

"You want my cock deep inside your tight pussy? Is that what you want?"

I whimpered at his words.

"I can tell you like it rough." He rubbed his hand over my ass. "You're dripping from just my words. Now tell me what you want."

I had never been so aroused in my life. I couldn't take it anymore. "Fuck me, Rory. Please fuck me."

"Keira, I'm going to fuck you." He grabbed my hips. "Hard." He thrust himself deep inside of me, deeper than anyone had ever been.

I gasped. He moved slowly, stretching me wide. His cock was so big that it hurt. But he was being gentle as I adjusted to the thickness of his massive erection. And soon all I could feel was the pleasure. My whole body felt alive. I arched my back and he thrust himself even deeper, filling me with every inch of him.

I moaned. *Fuck this feels good.* He grabbed my hips and pumped his length in and out of me. I pushed against his mattress to match his thrusts. He dug his fingers into my hips as he moved faster. He tilted his cock up against my g-spot and my whole body shuddered.

"Yes!" I pushed against the edge of the mattress and forced him even deeper.

He grabbed my hair and tilted my head back. I arched my back as he slammed his hard cock inside me. I could feel myself clench around him. But before I could come he pulled out of me and flipped my body over again. I felt the bed sag as he leaned over top of me. But he wasn't touching me. I wanted him back inside of me.

"Rory, please," I begged. "I'm so close."

Finally I felt his fingers on the sides of my face. He slowly lowered my blindfold.

"You wanted to see me?"

"Yes." He was even sexier than I had remembered. His hair was mussed up and his body glistened with sweat. I wrapped my arms around the back of his neck and kissed him. He seemed surprised, but immediately kissed me back. While he kissed me, he guided his cock back inside of me.

I let my hands wander down his strong back. I grabbed his firm ass and gyrated my hips.

He bit my lip softly and pulled away. He looked down at me. His hands were on either side of my face. With every thrust his biceps flexed, making me tremble. He was so sexy. He slammed his massive cock deep inside of me and groaned. I reached up to grab the back of his neck so that he'd kiss me again. But he grabbed my hands and held them firmly over my head.

He moved his hips faster and faster. "Come for me, Keira."

His words were my undoing. I tilted my head back and let myself surrender to him. I felt myself clench around his massive erection. My whole body shuddered as my orgasm crashed down on me. I could feel his cock pulse inside of me as he came, making me shudder again. He groaned as he found his own release. He pulled out and collapsed on the bed beside me.

I turned and stared into Rory's piercing hazel eyes. A one night stand seemed a lot like the best sex I had ever had. *Crap.*

PART 2

CHAPTER 16

I watched Rory's chest rise and fall with each breath. I bit my lip. This wasn't how I was supposed to be feeling. *It was supposed to just be a one night stand!* I had been so focused on getting him to want me that I never really thought about how I'd feel if it actually happened.

Emily had warned me that I couldn't handle this. And she was right. She was always right. Why did I never listen to her advice? Sex had never just been sex to me. It was sensual and intimate and romantic. It was all those things with Rory too. *No.* It was better. He knew my body better than I did myself. He had made me feel things I had never felt before.

Rory moaned in his sleep and turned toward me in the bed. The smell of cinnamon mixed with his sweat was the most intoxicating aroma I had ever smelled in my life. A part of me wanted to flee his room so I wouldn't have to look at him anymore. But something was holding me back. If this really was the only time I'd ever be with him, I wanted to revel in it. I wanted to remember the curve of his biceps and how soft his skin was and how his muscles felt pressed against me. Just the thought made me shudder.

I reached out and lightly touched the scruff along his jaw line. How long would one night stands be all he wanted? He'd eventually want more. Marriage, children, the big picture? He had to. I definitely wouldn't mind waking up to his beautiful face every morning.

I shook my head. *What am I doing?* Staying here in this moment was just going to make living with him harder. All he wanted was sex. He couldn't have made that any more clear. It didn't matter how I felt. I forced myself to quietly climb out of his bed.

I was able to find my shoes in the dark, but I had no idea where my thong and bra were. It didn't matter. I just needed to get out of there. I quickly went into the hallway and closed the door behind me.

***

The sounds of pots and pans banging woke me up. I slowly sat up and hugged my knees into my chest. I couldn't go out there and see him. It didn't matter what I tried to tell myself. I liked him and I wanted it to be more. But he was a player. There was nothing I could do to change that.

I slowly got out of bed and pulled on my silk robe. Now I had to act like everything was back to normal, even though it wasn't. I took a deep breath and walked out to the kitchen.

Rory had his back turned to me. He was wearing a pair of boxer briefs and cooking something at the stove. I wanted to go up behind him and wrap my arms around him. Instead I sat down at the counter.

"Hey!" I said. My voice sounded weird and high pitched.

Rory turned his head. "Good morning," he said with a smile and went back to cooking. He started whistling.

I put my elbow on the counter and rested my chin in my hand. "You seem awfully cheery this morning."

He ignored my comment and placed some eggs and toast on two plates and walked over to me. He placed one plate in front of me and sat down beside me. "Yeah, well." He shrugged. "Does great sex not put you in a good mood?"

I could feel my face blushing. "Great sex?"

He leaned toward me slightly. "Yeah, great sex."

"You're awfully cocky."

"Well you should have heard yourself screaming my name." He raised his eyebrow. His hazel eyes seemed to bore into mine.

I gulped and looked down at my plate. "I doubt you really thought it was great." I pushed the eggs around with my fork.

"What do you mean?"

For some reason I wanted to cry. I didn't want to flirt with him at breakfast like last night meant nothing. I couldn't joke around about sex like he could. It meant more to me than that. "Thanks for breakfast, Rory. I'm going to eat in my room. I have a lot of work to do." The stool squeaked against the floor as I stood up.

"Keira." He grabbed my wrist. "I meant what I said. I had a lot of fun last night."

"Okay."

"Tell me what you meant." He rubbed his thumb against the inside of my wrist.

I wanted him to hold me like this forever. I looked up at him. "I thought you didn't sleep with girls you weren't attracted to."

"I never said I wasn't attracted to you, Keira."

"Yes you did. At your restaurant."

Rory dropped my hand and rubbed the back of his neck. "Oh. Right. I actually just said that so that you'd let me live here."

My wrist tingled where he had touched me. "You lied to me?"

Rory laughed. "Like you haven't lied to me."

"I've never lied to you."

"Seriously?"

I sat back down in my stool. Maybe honesty was the best approach here. "Fine. I never wanted that pact, Rory. I only agreed because I was nervous. And I ramble when I'm nervous. You're so handsome." I held my breath. It was all out there now.

He laughed. "It's okay. I knew."

"Was it really that obvious?"

"When you started using all my advice on me, yeah. You made it pretty obvious. And before that, I had my suspicions. Like when you walked in on me in the bathroom."

I laughed. "That was an accident!"

He gave me his panty dropping smile.

"Rory, it was."

"Well, anyway," he said as he stood up. "It's good we got that out of our systems. Now we really can just be friends." He lightly slapped me on the back as he put his slice of toast in his mouth and walked back to his bedroom.

What?!

***

I wiped under my eyes with the back of my hand and pressed the number for Emily's apartment. The door buzzed open. I grabbed it and slowly made my way up the stairs.

As soon as Emily opened her door, her face fell. "Keira?" She stepped to the side so I could walk in.

"Is that the food?" Emily's husband, Jim, said as he walked into the room. "Oh, hey, Keira. Um, I'm just going to..." he pointed to something and left the room. He must have seen my face.

"What the hell did he do to you?" Emily sat down on the couch.

"He didn't do anything," I said as I took a seat next to her. "Last night was perfect. He's so perfect."

"No one's perfect, Keira."

"He is. He's everything I've been looking for."

"You always do this."

"Do what?"

"Build people up. He's not perfect. He's a player. He's probably slept with a hundred women. That's disgusting. You don't want to be with a guy like that."

I felt sick to my stomach. "I do." I dropped my voice so Jim wouldn't be able to hear me. "It was the best sex I've ever had."

"Well it should have been. He's had enough practice."

"Emily."

"Keira! You knew you could never do a one night stand. Why the hell did you sleep with him?"

"I couldn't help it. He's just so..."

"Womanizing?"

"No. Sexy."

"Okay, so you had a great night. Maybe you should just talk to him about it."

I started to cry again. *What the hell is wrong with me?* "I did. I told him I never wanted that stupid roommate pact. I even told him I thought he was really handsome."

"And?"

"He said he was glad we got it out of our systems. And that now we could really just be friends."

"Ouch."

"Yeah." I wiped away my tears again. "How am I supposed to live with him now? I'm going to have to listen to him having sex with other women every night. I can't do this!"

"I realize that this is not the right time to do this, but..."

"Don't you dare say it, Emily." I tried to pout but her facial expression made me laugh. She always did this.

"I can't resist." She smiled. "I told you so."

I laughed and tossed a pillow at her. "I really hate you sometimes."

There was a loud buzz, signaling that someone was downstairs waiting to be let in. Jim walked back into the room and pressed the button to let them into the building.

"Stay for lunch," Emily said and stood up. She grabbed three plates and began to set the table. "I'll be right back." She disappeared into the bathroom.

As soon as Emily closed the door, Jim walked over to me. "Why don't you just make him want *you* again?" he said in a low voice.

"Oh, geez, you were listening to us?" I asked. Jim had witnessed me being a complete mess more times than I wanted to remember. But he had never offered me advice before.

"Super thin walls." He shrugged.

I looked at the bathroom door. "Emily would surely tell me that is terrible advice."

"Yeah, well Emily's not a guy."

True. "So you mean, like, try to seduce him?"

"Try to turn the tables. Make him want you instead of the other way around."

"But that involves pretending like I don't like him."

"Guys like the chase. I don't know what else to tell you."

Emily came out of the bathroom and grabbed some glasses out of the cupboard. "What do you want to drink, Keira?

"Do you even have to ask?"

She laughed. "I'll open a bottle of wine."

CHAPTER 17

"Hey, guys!" I called as I walked into my apartment.

Rory turned his head toward me, but I didn't look at him. Jackson and Connor were sitting in the living room with him, watching a baseball game. I stumbled slightly as I kicked off my flip flops and walked over to them. One bottle of wine had quickly turned into two. The more I had to drink, the better and better Jim's advice seemed to be. I had hatched a plan in my head that I thought was pretty good. And it started with me ignoring Rory.

"Are the Phillies playing?" I asked.

"Do you follow baseball, Keira?" Jackson asked.

"A little. Mostly I like watching the sexy players." I sat down Indian style between Rory and Connor on the couch. My knee was pressed against Rory's thigh, but I pretended like I didn't notice. "Cole Hamels is a total dreamboat."

"Typical," Connor said.

"Don't be so quick to judge me, Connor. I'm just not that into baseball."

"So what sports do you follow?"

"Football. I'm a huge Eagles fan. And it's not just cause of the tight pants."

"Really?"

"Why are guys so surprised when I tell them that?"

"Sexism at its finest," Jackson said.

"Thank you, Jackson!"

"Well I don't believe you. Girls always pretend to be fans of the local teams. And then you actually sit down and watch a game and they don't even know what a field goal is. I bet you can't even name any of the Eagles' past quarterbacks," said Connor.

"Psh. McNabb, Vick, Kolb, and Foles. Boom." I made an exploding noise and spread my fingers in the air.

"You are full of surprises, Keira." He lifted up his beer bottle to me. "But I really wish you would stop *booming* me. That is so 2009, right Jackson?"

"So 2009," Jackson agreed.

"You guys are weird," I said.

"What were you up to tonight, Keira?" Rory asked. It was the first time he had spoken since I arrived.

"Actually, I had an amazing evening. I went out with some friends." He didn't need to know that going out meant hanging out talking about him. And that my friends were Emily and her husband. I looked over at him. "What were you up to tonight?"

Rory put his hand out, gesturing to his friends, somehow flipping the switch so that it looked like I was the one that was curious about his life.

"Oh, come on!" Connor yelled at the T.V. "Well, that's the end of that game. Why do they suck so much this year?" He switched the channel to ESPN.

"You know, I never understood why guys love this channel so much. You literally just watched everything that happened. Why do you need to hear about it again?"

"Apparently you wouldn't understand because you're a woman," Jackson offered.

"Mhm. Does anyone want anything?" I asked and stood up. They were all silent. I took a step and tripped over Rory's foot. Before I could fall, he grabbed my waist with both his hands. His fingers slid up slightly underneath my shirt.

"You okay?" he asked.

"Yeah, I'm fine." It felt like my heart was beating out of my chest. I loved his hands on me.

He slowly let go of me. I smoothed my tank top back down as I walked into the kitchen. I looked over my shoulder and saw Connor whispering something to Rory. *Weird.* I took a deep breath and leaned against the counter. Rory had to have felt that too. There was just something between us that I couldn't put into words. I grabbed a bottle of water out of the fridge, walked back over to them, and sat down between Rory and Connor again.

"I think we're actually gonna get going," Connor said and stood up.

"Right," Jackson agreed.

"Geez, I won't complain about ESPN anymore. You guys can watch whatever you want. I was just curious."

Jackson laughed. "I'm actually just really tired from the party last night. See you later, guys."

"Later," Connor said and followed Jackson out.

I looked over at Rory and instantly snapped my head back to the T.V. He was staring at me so intensely. Had he asked them to leave? Whatever I was doing was clearly working. My knee was still pressed against his thigh, and now it was hard to ignore it. Maybe he was going to suggest a repeat of last night. I stared at the T.V. screen without actually seeing it.

"Are you drunk or something?" Rory finally asked.

"What?"

"I don't know, you're acting weird."

"Trust me, you'd know if I was drunk. I get like ridiculously horny when I'm drunk." *What the fuck?!* "I mean corny. Ridiculously corny. I just can't stop making stupid jokes." I could feel my face turning red. *Calm down.* I had been doing so well. I took a deep breath.

"Good to know."

"Why did you ask your friends to leave?" I wanted to be bold. I wanted to follow up with, "Did you want to be alone with me again?" Instead I pressed my lips together, hoping I wouldn't say anything else stupid.

"I didn't ask them to leave."

"Um...I'm pretty sure you did."

He put his arm behind me on the couch, making sure not to touch me. "Actually, I was hoping to talk to you."

"About what?"

"I just want to make sure we're okay."

"We're fine."

"When you disappeared all day, I thought...well, I just wanted to make sure you're okay with me still living here." He scratched the back of his neck with his hand.

"Trust me, Rory, we're fine. Geez, you're acting like I'm in love with you or something. It wasn't even the best sex I've ever had."

He lowered his eyebrows slightly. "Okay then."

"Let's just pretend it never happened, buddy," I patted him on the shoulder.

His eyebrows lowered even more.

I'm so good at this. "Do you want to watch a movie or something?" I grabbed the remote and turned on the T.V. guide channel.

"Sure."

"Actually, you know what? Watching all those hot baseball players really got me hot and bothered." I stood up and looked down at him. "I just started this great new book called *Made of Steel.* I think I'm just going to spend the rest of the night in my room, if you know what I mean. Night, Rory!" I turned around before I could see his reaction.

I hoped I hadn't taken it too far. Confessing that I was reading an erotic novel and was super turned on by it probably just freaked him out. Or maybe it made him think I preferred a book over him. I closed the door behind me and sighed. This was going to be so hard.

I sat down at the desk in my room. I looked down at the notes that I had taken the other day, about how dating had recently turned into meaningless hookups.

The front door opened and closed. Rory was probably going out to find some girl to hook up with. Just the thought made me feel jealous. And angry. And depressed. Somehow I needed to stay on track with my plan. I sighed and looked back down at my notes. I lifted up my pen. Maybe writing about my experiences would make it less personal and more like work. It was time to take Jim's advice and completely turn the tables on Rory.

CHAPTER 18

I peeped out my bedroom door. The girl that had been screaming Rory's name all night was standing in the kitchen. *I can do this.* I walked out of my room and into the kitchen.

"Hey," I said as cheerily as possible.

She turned around. "Oh my God." She put her hands over her mouth. "You have to believe me. I had no idea Rory had a girlfriend."

"What?" I laughed. *I wish.* "Oh, geez, I'm not Rory's girlfriend. I'm just his roommate."

"Holy shit, thank God. I almost had a heart attack."

"Wow, that would have been super awkward. But no, no, we're definitely not dating. I'm Keira, by the way." I stuck out my hand.

"Izzy," she said and shook my hand.

"Do you want some cereal? I was just about to eat."

Izzy looked at the cabinet she had opened. "Yeah, that would be great. I'm sorry, I didn't mean to go through your stuff."

"Don't worry about it." I grabbed the milk out of the fridge. "The bowls are in the next cabinet over."

"Great." She grabbed two bowls while I got the cereal and spoons.

"Is cinnamon toast crunch okay?" I asked.

"Um, yeah." She sat down next to me at the kitchen counter. "Wow, I can't even remember the last time I had this. I've gotten so used to eating bland cereal with high fiber and less sugar that I tricked my mind into thinking it was good."

I laughed. "Ew. I can't even swallow that stuff."

Izzy laughed and took a bite. "So, is it weird living with a guy? I feel like that would drive me crazy. Especially Rory. I mean, have you not seen him or something? I'd be drooling every day."

I shrugged. "We're just friends, so it's not really awkward at all. And he's not even my type. How did you two meet?"

Izzy's face turned a little red. "Um, we ran into each other at the bar down the street from here."

The way she had worded it made it seem like they already knew each other. But the way she said it made it seem like they had only just met last night. I figured it was better not to ask any more questions about that. "Oh, the last time I was there they were having a karaoke night. It was so much fun."

"They were doing it last night too! It really was a lot of fun. Mostly because Rory is a terrible singer."

"Is he?" I started laughing. For some reason I couldn't picture him singing at all. I just pictured him standing in the corner being unbelievably sexy. It made me like him even more knowing he was willing to put himself out there and embarrass himself in public. Especially since I seemed to embarrass myself several times a day. *Stop thinking about how much you like him. Focus.*

"Good morning."

We both looked up at Rory. He was giving me a strange look.

"Izzy was just telling me that you're a fantastic singer, Rory." I took a bite of my cereal.

Izzy started laughing.

Rory continued to stare at me. "Keira, can I talk to you for a second?"

"After I'm done my cereal. So, Izzy, what do you do?"

"I'm trying to be an actress. And when I'm not at auditions, I work as a waitress."

"That's awesome! Have you been in anything I may have seen?"

"Yeah, there was this local used car commercial I was in a few months back."

Rory slammed one of the cupboards.

I smiled to myself. *Befriend the women he sleeps with...check.*

***

"Yes, definitely call me. We'll have to go to that bar together next time and show Rory up."

Izzy laughed. "See you later, Keira!"

I closed the door behind her. Rory was staring at me as I made my way over to the couch. I sat down and pretended I didn't notice him.

"What the hell, Keira?"

I looked up at him. "What?" I said as innocently as possible.

He sat down next to me. "She was here for like two hours. The rule is breakfast and that's it. No chatting. Couldn't you tell how awkward that was for me?"

"Oh, come on. That seems awfully rude. I promised you that I'd be nicer to the girls you bring over. I was just doing what you wanted me to do. And Izzy is really nice. You should definitely go out with her again."

"I'm not going to go out with her again."

"Why?"

"You know why."

As his words hung in the air, my heart skipped a beat. For a second I let myself believe it was because he liked me. I shook away the thought. He just meant because he didn't date. One night stands. That was it.

"Well, I thought she was really great."

"If you like her so much, you can date her."

I laughed. "You wish."

He laughed too. "Yeah, I wouldn't protest against that."

I rolled my eyes. "You're such a slut, Rory."

"A slut?" He raised his eyebrow at me.

"Oh, don't look at me that way. Guys can be sluts too."

"How does wanting to see two girls make sweet, sweet love make me a slut?"

"Sweet, sweet love?" I scrunched up my nose. "And what would you know about that? You've never made love to anyone in your life."

"You don't really know that much about me, Keira." He leaned back and put his hands behind his head.

"What, you're telling me that you've been in love? I don't even believe you." I so badly wanted to know this information. I was quickly losing my grip on the situation.

Especially when he was this close to me on the couch. I swallowed hard. I wanted to know everything about him.

He shrugged. "I don't know. I went out with this girl my first two years of college."

If I had been in a cartoon, my jaw would have dropped to the floor. "So you do date?"

"No, I *did* date. Huge difference."

"What happened?" I tried not to sound too eager.

"It was a long time ago."

Shit. I needed to know. "It couldn't have been worse than how any of my relationships ended. Seriously, what happened? Maybe a female perspective on the situation is what you need."

"I don't really need another perspective. She cheated on me. End of story."

So that's it. He doesn't trust women. He keeps his distance because he doesn't want to get hurt again. I suddenly felt awkward, sitting there analyzing him. "Sorry, that sucks. It's definitely her loss, though. Because you're awesome to live with," I quickly added.

Rory smiled at me. "Thanks."

"So, be nice to the girls you bring home, but don't talk to them for a long time?" I needed to get out of there. He was sexy, and funny, and broken. I loved dating guys that needed help. It was my weakness.

"That would be great."

"Okay," I said and touched his knee as I stood up. "I'm going to go get some work done. I'll be better behaved next time I meet one of your lady friends." I smiled at him and disappeared into my room.

CHAPTER 19

It was only 5:30. Emily wouldn't be home from work for at least another hour. I picked up my cell and dialed her home number before I could change my mind.

"Hello?" Jim said after a few rings.

"Hi, Jim, it's Keira."

"Oh, hey. Emily's not home yet. I'll let her know you called."

"Actually, I was hoping to talk to you. I was trying to follow your advice. But I'm worried I'm just going to be put in the friend zone."

Jim laughed. "If you're worried about that, then you're doing it all wrong."

I laughed too because I didn't know what else to do. I hoped he'd explain, but he didn't. "So, what do you mean by that?"

"You need to act like all you want is friendship. But at the same time you need to dress sexy and do sexy things."

"So like, hang out with his friends but dress like a whore?"

He laughed again. "Why don't you ask them all out to do something? And find some guy to flirt with all night instead. That kind of thing."

"Okay. I have an idea. There's this really cool music festival going on this weekend. Maybe I should casually talk about how I want to go all week leading up to this weekend when it starts. And then at the end of the week, let it drop that I've officially decided to go. Real casual like. And it won't seem weird because I've mentioned that I wanted to go all week long. And then ask Rory and his friends if they'd like to come cause I don't want to go alone. Or maybe say I'm going with some of my friends and ask if they'd like to go with us. A big group of friends thing? That definitely sounds better. And then talk to my friends the whole time about hot guys that we see at the festival. Maybe even talk to a few of them? All the while we'll be completely ignoring Rory and his friends. Maybe ditch them as soon as we get to the festival!"

"What?" Jim started laughing really loudly. "No. What the heck?" He continued to laugh. "That was completely ridiculous. You're overthinking it. And adding more women to the equation doesn't exactly help your situation."

Geez, I'm a situation. "So something simpler?" I bit my lip. "Oh, what about a bar?"

"Yeah. Much better. And be cool about it, Keira. Don't do that thing you always do."

"What thing?"

"That thing where you don't stop talking. And you keep saying weirder and weirder stuff until someone stops you. Like what you literally just did a second ago with that awful plan."

Right. That thing. Why did everyone always bring that up to me all the time? Was I really that awkward? I rolled my eyes at myself. *Of course I am.* "I don't do that."

"I'm not even going to try to argue with you about it...because it'll make you do it again."

I laughed. "Fine, maybe I talk too much sometimes."

He laughed. "Only sometimes."

"Thanks for your help, Jim."

"Should I tell Emily you called?"

"Don't bother. Have a good night!"

"You too, Keira."

I hung up the phone. That was what had been bothering me all afternoon. I was just acting super cool. And wearing sweatpants. I needed to step it up. I quickly stripped and wrapped a towel around myself. It was a little shorter than I had expected, but the more skin I showed, the better. Before I could chicken out, I went out of my room and knocked on Rory's door.

"Hey, Keira," he said and put his hand on the doorframe.

How did he always look so sexy? It took me a second to remember what I wanted to say. "Do you have my stuff from the other night?"

"Your stuff?" He raised his left eyebrow.

"My bra and thong."

"I'm sure I do somewhere."

I followed him into his room and sat down on his bed. The sheets smelled like him. I took a deep breath of the alluring smell.

"Are these yours?" he asked and held up a pair of panties I had never seen in my life.

Asshole. "Nope, try again."

"I'm just messing with you." He grabbed something off the counter. "I was gonna give them back to you, I just wanted to do it when you weren't around." He handed me my underwear.

"Why?"

"It's a little awkward." He sat down next to me on his bed.

"Not really."

He scratched the back of his neck.

"We're both adults, Rory. It was just sex, after all."

"Right. What are you doing tonight?"

I held up the bra. "I'm going out, and I needed this because it's my nicest bra."

He laughed. "It is really nice."

I gulped. *He's being flirtatious because that's who he is. He doesn't like you!* I let my towel slide down slightly to reveal the top of my breasts. "You can come if you want."

"Where are you going?"

"There's this cool new bar that just opened up. You should invite your friends," I added.

"Okay."

"I'm going to go get ready. Thanks for my bra back. You're the best!" I pulled my towel back up enough to make the bottom of my ass show as I left the room.

Much better. I went back into my room and dropped the towel. Now I just needed to find a newly opened bar.

***

I looked at myself in the mirror. I had bought the leather leggings on a whim a few years ago, but I had never worn them. They looked great with the loose fitting tank top. I just hoped it was sexy enough for Rory. I slid on a pair of red stilettos to match my red lipstick.

When I walked out of my room, I was surprised to see Rory sitting at the kitchen counter staring at his phone. I had heard him talking earlier and assumed Connor and Jackson were already hanging out with him.

"Where is everyone?" I asked.

"They couldn't make it." He looked up and his eyes traveled down my legs.

That's right, son. I got legs for DAYS. "Oh. Do you want to just go a different night?"

"Nah, let's just go together."

Together. The sound of my heels clicking on the wooden floor helped to block out the sound of my heart beating so quickly. *Is this a date?* "Oh, fun! I can be your wingman!"

He stood up. He was wearing a pair of suit pants and a button up shirt. The top few buttons were undone. I had never seen him look sexier. Except for when he was fucking me. I bit my lip.

"Sure, sounds good," he said.

"Okay, let's go!" I almost screamed. *Calm down.* I walked past him and opened up the door. We made our way outside and started walking side by side down the street.

"So, what about you, Keira?"

"What about me?"

"Why aren't you dating anyone?"

"I think I kind of suck at dating." I tucked a loose strand of hair behind my ear.

Rory laughed. "And why do you think that?"

The sound of him laughing was so sexy.

"Keira?"

"What? Sorry, I got distracted. I don't know, I've had three boyfriends and all three of them dumped me. They all said it was them and not me. But I'm pretty sure that means it's something I did, since they all said the same thing."

"I doubt it was your fault."

"Actually, it probably was my fault. I tend to overthink things."

"Hmm. You gotta learn to live in the moment, Keira."

"I think I did a pretty good job of that the other night." I smiled at him.

Rory put his hands in his pockets and looked away from me.

I hadn't meant to make our conversation awkward. I wanted to know more about him. "Did you grow up in Philly?" I asked.

"No, Bryn Mawr. It's like 20 minutes from here. But I've always preferred Philly."

"I know what you mean. I grew up in Wilmington. And after moving away for college, I couldn't picture myself going back to such a small town. So, I moved here."

He smiled at me. "Do you have any siblings?"

"A younger brother. That's actually why I'm so good at Nerf battles."

"I hate to break it to you, Keira, but you weren't all that great. I had you pinned down in less than a minute."

"Well, my brother and I didn't play that way." I lightly pushed his shoulder.

He looked away from me again. "So where is this new bar?"

"You know what, it's a little farther than I realized. Why don't we just go to Heritage?"

"Okay, cool, I've never been there anyway."

Thank God. For a second I thought he was going to question me. I hadn't been able to find any new bars nearby. And I had never been to Heritage either, but I had read that it was awesome. Maybe I was better at playing it cool than I realized. "What about you, Rory? Do you have any siblings?"

"No, I'm an only child."

"Are you close with your parents?"

"As close as any normal 26 year old, yes." He smiled at me.

"So, not close at all?'

He laughed. "I love my parents. But I don't really think they'd be thrilled with my lifestyle choices."

"Mhm." I tried to raise my eyebrow at him, but I couldn't. My face didn't work that way.

He laughed again. "Are you trying to give me a stern look? That's very cute."

Cute. I didn't want him to think I was cute. I tried to think of something provocative to say, but we had just arrived at the restaurant.

Rory opened up the door for me. *Such a gentleman.* When we walked into the restaurant, there were tons of people already dancing. A jazz musician was playing in the corner. I didn't know anything about jazz, but everyone seemed to be enjoying it. We went over to the bar and Rory ordered us each a beer.

I liked talking to him. I wish we could just sit down at one of the tables and talk all night. But that wasn't why he had agreed to come out with me. I had to stick to the plan. "So, who do you think is sexy?" I asked. *This is so awkward.* I so badly wanted him to look at me and say I was the only girl he noticed. But I knew I was far away from that happening.

"Well." Rory took a sip of his beer and looked toward the dance floor. "The blonde to the left."

My eyes wandered the dance floor until I found who he was talking about. There was a tall blonde with huge breasts. She was super tan and super fake looking. There was no way she was a real blonde. And she couldn't have looked more different than me. *Is that really the kind of girl he's attracted to?* "The one dancing with her friends?"

"Yeah."

"It's a good sign that she's not dancing with a guy. It probably means she's single. So what's the game plan?"

"I don't know, you're the wingman."

"But I've never done this before."

"Which is why I'm kind of curious to see what you come up with." He raised his left eyebrow at me.

Stop being so sexy! "Okay, I have an idea." I grabbed Rory's arm and dragged him over to the dance floor to dance with me.

His hands slid to my waist as the song suddenly changed to a slow paced one. "Shit, sorry," I mumbled. But I wasn't sorry at all. I loved the feeling of his hands on me. The smell of him was quickly engulfing me. This was the most intimate we had been since we had slept together.

"That's okay," he whispered. He looked over my head. He wasn't noticing me at all.

"So what is she doing?" I asked.

"She moved to the side of the dance floor and is just talking to her friends."

"Hopefully she'll come back out after this song."

"Yeah, or else you're a terrible wingman," he said and smiled down at me.

I heard a buzzing noise and Rory pulled his cell out of his pocket. There was a message from Connor that said, "Sorry I couldn't make it. Still good for poker night?"

I looked away from it. Any thought I had of this being a date quickly disappeared. That's what I got for eaves-dropping. Part of me was hoping that he had never even invited Connor and Jackson. I took a deep breath. *Stick to the plan.*

Rory put his phone back in his pocket without texting Connor back. His hand returned to my waist. I looked up into his hazel eyes, even though they weren't on me. He was so handsome.

As soon as the music sped up again, I turned around and put my ass against him. The blonde girl and her friends had returned to the dance floor, fortunately even closer than they had been before. I dipped low, pulling out my best dance move. Rory pulled my waist in closer. I smiled to myself and reached my hand up behind his neck. "Spin me," I whispered.

"I'm kind of liking this." His breath was warm against the back of my neck.

Me too. I closed my eyes tight. "Trust me," I said.

He grabbed my hand and twirled me. I pulled back more than he expected and ran right into the girl with blonde hair.

"Oh my God, I'm so sorry," I said.

She gave me a dirty look.

What a jerk. I literally just apologized to you. "Hey, have you met Rory?" I pointed toward him.

He gave the girl one of his dazzling smiles.

"No, hi," she said and held out her hand.

"Want to dance?" asked Rory. Before she could respond, he grabbed her hand and pulled her in close.

She laughed as he spun her around.

I realized I was awkwardly standing there staring at them. I quickly walked off the dance floor and sat down at the bar. Phase one was complete. However bad I was at being a wingman, I had successfully gotten him together with the girl he had picked out. Watching them together wasn't fun at all though.

"You're not a great dancer," a deep voice said.

I looked up at the man sitting down next to me. He was smiling at me.

"I'm actually a really good dancer. I was just helping out a friend." I used my beer to point at the blonde girl grinding against Rory. *Slut.* I downed the rest of my beer.

"Two more beers over here," he said.

"Thanks." I smiled at him. He reminded me a lot of my most recent ex. The same ex who got engaged several months after he dumped me, even though he had said he just wasn't ready to settle down. I hated men.

"Cheers to a fun night," the stranger said and held up his beer.

I picked up the beer that the bartender had just given me. Now it was time for phase two. "Cheers," I said and clinked my bottle against his. "So, what's your name?"

"Brian."

"It is nice to meet you, Brian. I'm Keira."

"So, Keira, do you usually wingman for your friend? What's her name?"

Of course he thought I was wingmanning for one of my girlfriends, not Rory. I didn't feel like explaining the awkward situation. I looked over at Rory and the blonde girl. "Jessica," I lied. "And no, I don't usually. But she's been having a rough couple days. Her boyfriend just broke up with her and she's desperate." Her hands were all over Rory. It was hard to watch.

Brian laughed. "She does look kind of desperate."

I smiled and peeled my eyes away from them. "So how about I prove to you that I'm actually a good dancer?"

"Sounds good to me." He put his hand on the small of my back and escorted me to the dance floor.

When he stopped, I grabbed his arm and pulled him over closer to Rory. I needed Rory to notice me ignoring him. I quickly turned around and wrapped my hands around the back of Brian's neck. He smiled down at me.

"So what do you think?" I said as he spun me around and grabbed my waist with one hand.

"You're right, you're not so bad."

"Not so bad?" I spun around again and let myself get lost in the music. It felt good to have someone's sole attention.

"You're so good that you're even stealing the attention from the guy you set your friend up with."

"Really?" I looked over at Rory. If he had been looking at me, he wasn't anymore. He was making out with the blonde girl. *Fuck you, Jessica!* I couldn't help but laugh at myself. I began to wonder what the odds were that her name actually was Jessica.

"Are you okay?" Brian asked.

I realized I had stopped dancing and was staring at them. "Oh, yeah, I'm fine. You know what though? I forgot that I have an important meeting tomorrow morning and I have to wake up really early, so I'm going to get going." I couldn't watch them kissing in the middle of the dance floor. I felt sick to my stomach.

"Do you want me to walk you home?" he asked as we both got off the dance floor.

Walk me home? I didn't usually hang out in bars. But it seemed like a walk home was synonymous with a one night stand. And I never wanted to have another one of those again. All I wanted was Rory. Over and over and over again. But part of my master plan to win Rory over was to go on a date with another man. I needed to make Rory jealous. But I definitely didn't want to lead Brian on. It would be better if I went on a date with a pretend man. "No, that's okay. It was really nice meeting you, though, Brian."

"You too, Keira. Hopefully I'll see you here again one night."

I smiled at him and disappeared through the crowd. The fresh air immediately calmed me down. When I was walking with Rory, I hadn't noticed how far away the bar was. But now that I was alone the walk seemed endless. My heels clicking on the sidewalk was starting to drive me crazy.

I wasn't sure how long I could play it cool around Rory. Seeing him with that girl was really hard. Two days into my plan and I was already feeling desperate again.

CHAPTER 20

Ouch. I had fallen asleep at my desk writing and my back was killing me. I yawned and rubbed my eyes. The paper in front of me was filled with notes about what I had tried so far. At the top was written, "How to Play with a Player." Ever since Rory had moved in, I hadn't been able to write. Until now. I had a feeling my editor was going to love it.

I opened up my laptop and typed up my idea for the article. The only problem was that my editor was going to expect me to follow through, and I wasn't sure if I could. Rory had made it clear that the one night we had spent together was all we'd ever have. I was quickly running out of ideas on how to be sexy and fun, yet unattached. All I wanted was for him to ask me out for a romantic dinner and sweep me off my feet.

I hesitated when I finished writing my pitch. The main point of the article would be about how dating was turning into meaningless hookups. And how I thought that maybe that could change, and my attempts to figure out how. I needed to believe that it could change. But Rory being a part of my story, even if he wasn't the focus, was a problem. It wouldn't really be about him, though. And I'd use a different name. I just wanted to see if it was possible to turn a one night stand into more. Because it should be more. *Maybe this is a bad idea.*

The sound of the front door opening pulled me away from the computer. Part of the reason I had fallen asleep while writing was because I had been waiting for Rory to get home. He was only just coming home now. Which meant he had slept over at the blonde girl's place. *Gross.* I sighed and sent over the email. A go-ahead and a deadline would surely motivate me. And maybe getting published would make me feel better about everything.

My cell phone started to ring. I looked down at the display and saw that my editor was calling. *That was fast.* "Hi, Judy," I said.

"Love, love, love the idea."

"Great. I have a ton of notes about different things I can try."

"What's the ultimate goal of the piece?"

To make him fall in love with me. "To get him to change his ways. To prove that women can change this new norm. One night stand are a terrible..."

"Not sexy enough," she said, cutting me off. "Get him to commit to being friends with benefits. The readers will love that. Friends with benefits is in right now."

"What?" That's not the direction I wanted to go in at all. It was the complete opposite of what I wanted to accomplish.

"Sex sells, hon. Make it happen."

"But I..."

"This will be great. Let's do a series of articles showing your progress. So we'll need something juicy by Wednesday."

"Okay." I searched through my notes. "I was planning on dressing up really sexy and going on a pretend date. I could do that tonight. Try to make him jealous..."

"Well, what is he doing right now?" she asked, cutting me off.

"Umm..." I pulled the phone away from my ear. The shower had just started. "I think he just got in the shower."

"Perfect! Join him."

"What?!" I shouldn't have told her about the shower.

"Just hop in and act like you shower with other people all the time. Ignore him completely. Our readers will eat this up."

"Judy, I can't do that." Was she high or something?

"You can. And you will. I know you heard the rumors that we're overstaffed. Well, they aren't rumors. Freelance writers are first on the chopping block. Don't make me bring your name up to the board. I expect the first draft by tomorrow morning." Judy clicked off.

What did I just do? Why did I pitch that idea to her? I couldn't write an article about seducing my roommate. Rory knew I wrote for The Post. He might read it. *Shit!*

But I couldn't lose my job, either. It had taken me three years to work my way up to actually getting to write. I didn't want to start over at a different newspaper. Rory probably wouldn't read it anyway. He wasn't even interested in me. And that was the problem. Regardless, I wanted that to change. I wanted him to notice me. But I never intended it to be like this.

I threw my phone down on my desk and walked out into the hallway. Before I could change my mind, I grabbed the handle of the bathroom door, but it was locked. Last time I had walked in on him in the bathroom I had freaked out about him needing to lock the door. He was actually being a really good roommate. I ran into the kitchen and started opening up drawers. The key to all the locks on the doors in the apartment was somewhere in here. *Shit, where is it?*

I pushed aside some of the items in the last drawer, but still couldn't find it. I laughed and ran into my room. Right before Rory had moved in I had hidden the key in my room. I had been so worried about living with a guy. Yet I was the one being insanely forward and awkward, not him. I grabbed the key out of my nightstand and ran over to the bathroom door.

I took a deep breath, unlocked the door, and walked in. The bathroom was full of steam. I was glad the mirror was foggy as I undressed. If I had to see myself stripping I was pretty sure I would chicken out. *I can't believe I'm doing this.*

I pulled the curtain back. "Hey, roomie, do you mind if I join you?" I asked and climbed in behind him without waiting for a response.

"Whoa!" Rory put his hand over his penis.

He looked so fucking sexy with his skin glistening from the water. Beads of water cascaded down his muscular abs and perfectly sculpted torso.

"What the hell, Keira?" He really didn't sound mad though. His eyes drifted to my breasts.

It was hard to focus on what he was saying when he was standing there naked. "I just really needed to take a shower. I have a meeting I have to go to." It was tempting to cover my breasts with my hands, but I resisted the urge.

"Can't you wait like five minutes?"

"Nope." I put my hand on his chest and made him move back slightly as I stepped under the water. I tilted my head and arched my back slightly, attempting what I hoped was a sexy pose under the showerhead. "There is no better feeling than a nice, *hot* shower. Don't you think?" I glanced over at him.

"Okay, I'm going to get out."

"Don't make this weird, Rory. I shower with my friends all the time. It's not a big deal. Can you hand me the shampoo?"

"Wait, do you really?"

"Of course." *No. Who the hell showers with their friends? Awkward.* "Besides, we've already seen each other naked. It's not a big deal at all."

He was still holding his hands over his junk. But he was barely covering his growing erection.

"Really, Rory, I'm not going to stare at you. " I grabbed his hand and pulled him back underneath the water. "Now please hand me the shampoo."

He grabbed the shampoo with his other hand, letting his erection spring free.

Fuck, he wants me. It was so tempting to reach out and wrap my hand around his massive cock. But that wasn't the plan. He had to come to me.

"Thanks," I said and took the shampoo from him. I turned away from him and arched my back again as I slowly lathered my hair. I moaned quietly, hoping that he could hear. When I stepped back under the water, his cock pressed against the small of my back. *Holy shit!*

"Oh, sorry," he said and moved away.

"It's okay. I should have warned you that I needed to get wet." I cringed at my own line. *That didn't even make sense.* I was starting to feel sweaty instead of clean. I wasn't sure if it was because I was so turned on or because the water was scalding. "Do you mind turning it down a little? It's just so hot in here."

"It is pretty hot in here."

I wasn't facing him, so I didn't know if he had turned it down, but the water still felt just as hot. I turned around to see him staring at me. "Excuse me, Rory," I said, and reached for the bar of soap. I let my hand slowly brush against his erection, but I kept my eyes focused on the bar of soap on the ledge.

He grabbed my breasts and pushed my back against the cool tile.

Everything below my waistline clenched. *Focus!* "What are you doing, Rory?!"

"If you wanted to fool around again, all you had to do was ask." One of his hands drifted to my ass.

"What? Rory!" I pushed on his chest to make him step back. "We're just friends. Oh my God, you just made this incredibly weird!" I picked up the soap and began to lather up my breasts, cleaning off where he had touched me.

"I made it weird?" he asked as he watched me.

"Yes! And stop staring at me! What are you doing?! Get out!"

He ran his hand through his wet hair. "Wow, I really misread the situation. I just thought when you touched my..."

"Get out, Rory!" I yelled, cutting him off.

He stepped out of the shower and closed the curtain. A second later I heard the door close. I sighed and leaned against the cold tile wall. I was so close to having him again. If I had wanted to, I could have let him fuck me in the shower. But I didn't want to just fool around with him. I wanted more. I needed more.

Shit, I'm falling for him. Screw the article. I needed to talk to him. I quickly turned the water off and wrapped a towel around myself. "Rory?" I called when I went out into the hallway. When he didn't answer, I knocked on his door. "Rory? I need to talk to you." I was greeted by silence. "Come on, Rory. I'm sorry about the shower." *This is ridiculous.* I opened up his door, but he wasn't there. *Damn it!*

I closed his door, walked back into my room, and sat down at my desk. I may have been falling for him, but he wasn't falling for me. I opened up my laptop and began writing as fast as I could. Everything just came pouring out. I wrote about how I had fallen for my gorgeous, unobtainable roommate. I wrote about how I couldn't stop thinking about him, and about how living with him was unbearable. I even wrote about our one night stand that didn't feel at all like a one night stand to me.

The more I thought about him, the more I realized how much more this was to me than a one night stand. It wasn't the game, or the chase, it was him. Despite what Emily thought, he was perfect for me. I looked down at article I had just written.

I wanted to learn how to play with a player. I came up with the idea to write about my experience, with all the juicy details, so that every woman out there could do the same. This new norm of one night stands is completely horrendous and unacceptable. What happened to gentleman callers and flowers? We all want more. And I wanted to fix it. But I'm not sure I'm the right person for the job anymore. Because I'm falling for the guy I thought I could play.

A few weeks ago, I put an ad in the paper looking for a new roommate. That's when Rory showed up. Rory is the kind of guy that you crush on from a distance but have never actually talked to. You know, the one with the perfect amount of scruff on his perfect face, with abs that you only see on movie stars, and a smile that makes your knees weak. Trust me, I've tripped over my own feet quite a few times around him.

But since he was my roommate, we had to talk. Which may have been worse than admiring him from a distance because I'm so awkward when I have a crush. I ramble and say stupid stuff I don't mean. Somehow we agreed to just be friends in this weird, twisted roommate pact, which I actually wanted nothing to do with. So I started acting even more awkward. Listening to his bed squeaking with different women screaming his name every night made me physically sick. I couldn't handle it. I completely hated that he was a player. Because I wanted him to want me, and only me.

But I knew that was impossible. He barely even noticed me. So my brilliant idea? I asked him for advice on how to have a one night stand. And then I pathetically followed his advice and used it on him. Never in a million years would I normally do something like that. I've only ever had sex with my boyfriends. With Rory though, I'd take what I could get. So I experienced my first one night stand. Despite the label, it wasn't a one night stand to me. A better label probably would have been "best sex of my life" or "best night of my life". I was completely and utterly hooked. All I wanted was more. And now all I can think about is more. So I failed my assignment. I can't play with a player because I've been completely played.

I'm falling for a guy who just wants to be my friend. So I have to listen to his bed squeak and other women scream his name. I have to sit next to him on the couch and pretend everything is fine. And I have to watch the guy I'm falling for eventually fall for someone else.

The article was basically just me saying that I was an awkward failure. But I didn't want to write about this now anyway. Not when I knew that I was falling for Rory. I pressed send before I could change my mind. Hopefully Judy would just reject it and I could move onto writing something else. I got up and went into the kitchen. I had been writing for hours, and it was almost dark. If Rory had gone to work, he would have been back by now. He was definitely avoiding me. I walked back into my room and slammed the door. The thought of eating made me feel nauseous. None of this was fun anymore. Any thought I had of it being a game had disappeared. I laid my head down on my desk and started to cry.

My computer dinging, signaling I had a new email, pulled me out of my pity party. It was from Judy.

"What the hell was that? I said sexy, not sappy and boring. There was nothing about how to play with a player.

Talk about what you've done. Do lists. Lists are hot right now. I've already pitched the idea to the top. Don't screw me on this."

-J

I laid my head back down on my desk. *Fuck me.*

CHAPTER 21

Rory never came home last night. I considered calling Emily and asking her what I should do, but that would involve confessing that I had taken her husband's advice instead of her own. She'd be so disappointed with me.

Rory's feelings wouldn't be hurt by this. He was playing me too. I bit my lip. He wasn't. He had warned me that a one night stand wasn't what I wanted. But I kept pushing him until he finally had sex with me. He had been trying to look out for me.

With each minute he didn't come home, the more I realized that none of this mattered. He had probably slept with another woman last night. *He might even be fucking her again right now.* He didn't want me. *Screw this.* I'd mix some lies in with the truth and use a different name. He'd never know it was him. I began typing furiously. I wrote down a list of things I had done to lead him on, trying to compile a step by step guide on how to play a player. After a lot of brainstorming I came up with five solid steps: give him a taste, remain unattached, flip the switch, turn up the heat, and make him jealous.

Step one was "Give Him a Taste." I described playing along with Rory's idea of a one night stand. Writing about it was actually fun. Just thinking about his lips pressed against mine sent a chill down my spine. I emailed my new article over to Judy along with the list of steps, presenting the idea that each part of the series would be a different step. This time I was confident that it was exactly what she wanted.

By the time I was done, it was almost 5 o'clock. Poker night was tonight, and even though Rory was avoiding me, I was hoping he'd at least be home for that. Which meant I needed to get ready fast.

***

I finished applying my mascara and looked in the mirror. My tight, lacy, crop top looked perfect with my super short skirt. I grabbed a necklace and put it on. It hung right between my breasts. Everything about this outfit screamed "whore." Fortunately I didn't actually have a date.

The boys had started playing poker in the living room a few minutes ago. They were laughing and cursing. I wasn't even sure if they knew I was home. Rory was definitely there. I recognized his laugh. I loved his laugh.

For some reason I was incredibly nervous to leave my room. I hadn't seen Rory since the shower incident. And now I needed to lie to him and say I had a hot date. Would they all be able to tell I was lying? "You can do this," I said to myself in the mirror.

I took a deep breath and walked out into the hallway. Rory, Jackson, and Connor were all sitting around the poker table.

"Hey, guys!"

All of their heads turned toward me.

"Damn, Keira, you look amazing." Connor pulled out the seat next to him. "I'll deal you in. We were wondering when you were going to show up."

"Oh, sorry, I can't join you guys tonight." I leaned against the armrest of the couch.

"But you were going to be our fourth. We're not stripping this time," Jackson added.

I laughed. "Well that doesn't sound nearly as enticing."

"We can play strip poker if you want," Connor said and winked at me.

"I'm really sorry, guys, but I completely forgot that it was poker night. I made plans."

"That's fine. Just invite them over here," Jackson said. "The more people, the more fun. Especially if we're switching to strip poker again. New meat!"

New meat? Sometimes the things Jackson said sounded awfully gay. "No, I mean I can't play."

"Why?"

"Actually, I have a date tonight." I smiled to myself, hoping that it would look like I was really excited to see the sexy man I was going on a date with.

"Well, a little heads up would have been nice," Rory said.

"I'm sorry." Rory seemed on edge tonight. He wasn't his usual calm, collected, self. But he was still sexy as hell. He looked cute when he was brooding. It actually seemed like he was jealous. He was probably just still uncomfortable from the shower incident, though. And he should have been. I still couldn't believe I had actually done that.

"Oh. Is he picking you up? Do we get to meet him?" Jackson asked. "I think we're all a little curious about what type of guys you usually date." He smiled at me.

"No, I'm meeting him at a restaurant downtown in a bit."

"He sounds like a dick," Rory said.

Connor pushed Rory's shoulder. "Chill, man." He had whispered it, but I still heard him.

Chill? Chill from what? "It's actually the guy I met at the bar the other night, Rory. Did you tell your friends about my awesome wingman skills?"

Rory laughed. But it wasn't his normal, cheery laugh. It was short and forced. "Yeah, you were okay."

"What? I was awesome! The last time I saw Rory that night, he was making out with the girl I introduced him to. And he didn't come home that night...so I can only assume that meant my services were a success."

Connor laughed. "You're awfully cocky. Next time Jackson and I will have to come check out your skills."

"And I'm extremely picky," Jackson said.

"I think I can handle it. I'm pretty much a pro now."

Rory laughed. This time it was his normal, captivating laugh. Whatever had been bothering him didn't seem like an issue anymore.

"Okay, well, I should probably head out. Sorry again, guys."

"Have fun, Keira," Jackson said.

"Don't play strip poker without me!" I said as I walked over to the door.

All three of them laughed as I closed the door behind me. Now I just needed to find something to do for a few hours.

***

I sat down in my favorite ice cream shop with a huge bowl of forbidden chocolate. My appetite had finally returned after reading in the park until it grew too dark to see. And this ice cream was the best. I needed to go on dates with myself more often.

I stared out the window, watching the people walk past on the sidewalk. Ice cream and people watching would definitely occupy me long enough. I wondered if they'd still be playing poker when I got home. It was silly, but I kind of wanted to play. I liked hanging out with them.

Rory and Connor appeared at the window of the ice cream shop.

Wait. What?

Rory turned and looked through the window as they walked by.

Shit! I quickly ducked down. *Please don't see me.* I got down on my hands and knees underneath the table. A few of the other patrons laughed. *Shut up!*

There was a ding as the ice cream shop's door opened, alerting the people at the counter that a new customer had arrived.

Please don't be Rory. Please oh please.

I saw two pairs of men's sneakers slowly approaching me. *Shit! Maybe I can crawl by them.* I'd be out of the door in no time if they were just heading to the counter.

"I could have sworn I saw her," Rory said.

Oh God, it's them. I felt my cheeks turn crimson. I cringed as one of the pairs of shoes stopped right in front of me. The familiar scent of cinnamon entered my nose. I had never noticed how big Rory's feet were before. Maybe that old saying about penis size and shoe sizes being correlated was actually true.

"Keira?" Rory said.

Part of me was hoping that he still couldn't see me. I closed my eyes tight, somehow thinking if I couldn't see them, they couldn't see me either.

"Keira, are you okay?" Rory put his hand down for me.

"Oh, hi, guys." I could feel my face turning an even brighter red. I grabbed Rory's hand and he pulled me to my feet. "I just dropped my earring." I laughed awkwardly.

Rory starred at me. "Both of them?"

"What?" I quickly put my fingers on my earlobes. *Shit, I'm not even wearing earrings.* "Yeah, I guess so. But they weren't on the floor. I must have lost them earlier at the park." *Why the hell did I just say that?*

"I thought you were going out to dinner?" Rory and Connor looked at each other.

"Right. I did. And then we went for a walk in the park. It was very romantic." I was completely flustered. I had been playing it so cool around Rory, but now I was spiraling out of control. I took a deep breath to calm my nerves.

"Does very romantic usually end with you eating ice cream alone?" Connor asked.

I laughed. "It's not like I was going to put out on the first date. I'm not a whore."

Rory pulled out the chair across from mine and sat down. "So you've never slept with someone on the first date?"

Why is he sitting down? I took another deep breath. I needed to keep my composure. "No."

His eyebrows lowered slightly. "Well now I'm curious. How many guys have you slept with?"

Connor sat down next to Rory. He seemed just as eager to know my number.

"A normal amount." I sat back down and took a huge bite of ice cream so I could think of something to say to change the subject. "Why aren't you guys playing poker anymore?"

"It's not as fun without you," Connor said and winked at me. "Seriously, though, how many?"

"Where's Jackson?" I asked, ignoring their question.

"Probably out making his number higher."

I rolled my eyes.

"He got a call and had to leave early," Connor said. "Poker isn't great with just two people. We were actually on our way to the bar down the street. Do you want to join us?"

I remembered the feeling of Rory's hands on my hips while we danced. His breath had lingered on my neck. I quickly crossed my legs. "Do you need a wingman or something?"

"Absolutely. You promised me that you were the best. But first tell us your number," Connor said. "Maybe we should be working on getting you laid instead."

I finished my last bite of ice cream. "Three." I said quietly. "I mean four. It's four." I locked eyes with Rory.

"Really?" Connor asked. "Only four?"

Rory was staring at me.

I could feel my face flushing. "Yeah, only four."

Connor glanced over at Rory and then back at me. "Okay, let's go."

"You guys can go ahead. I'm really tired from my awesome date."

"Come on, Keira." Connor stood up and put his hand out for me. "I'm a pretty good wingman too. And if I fail, I'll sleep with you myself." He winked at me again.

"I don't think she wants to come," Rory said.

I locked eyes with Rory again. He didn't want me to come. He seemed to dislike the idea of me potentially hooking up with a stranger. Or sleeping with Connor. Was Connor still trying to help me?

"No, I'll come," I said and stood up. Somehow my night had turned from getting caught not actually on a date, to possibly successfully making Rory jealous. I couldn't pass up this opportunity.

CHAPTER 22

We walked into the bar down the street. I had been there a few times before. It was always packed and always super loud. And it definitely wasn't a place I would normally go.

I wasn't sure if Rory and Connor actually believed my story about my date. I pretended to yawn and glanced over at Rory. He was staring at me.

"What's your poison, Keira?" Connor asked.

"Whatever you're having is fine."

"Scotch on the rocks?" Connor said skeptically.

I made a face. "A beer is fine."

"I'll be right back." Connor pushed through the other patrons to reach the bar.

Rory touched my shoulder and leaned in toward me. His touch gave me goose bumps. For a second I thought he was going to kiss me. But his lips moved to my ear. *Of course.*

"You don't have to stay," he almost had to yell over the band. "Let me take you home."

"I have to find someone else to take me home. Isn't that the whole point?" I tried to give him a challenging look. If he didn't want me to hook up with other people, all he had to do was say so. Even though I was trying so hard to hide it, I was pretty sure he could still tell I liked him. Why wasn't this working?

"You don't have to do this, Keira."

I laughed. "I want to. I think it's about time I let loose. Let's dance!" I grabbed his arm, but he didn't budge.

Connor came back over and handed me my beer. I took a long sip. I was supposed to be making Rory jealous, not mad. I was starting to regret my decision to go with them. *Maybe I should just leave.*

"So," Connor said. "Anyone spark your interest?"

I glanced over at Rory, but quickly looked away. "Umm..." I looked at everyone dancing. "I think I need more time to decide. Do you want to dance?"

"Absolutely." He set his drink down and escorted me to the dance floor. He grabbed my waist and pulled me in close. "You slept with Rory, huh?"

My face started turning crimson. "So he did tell you?"

"No. But it's kind of obvious. You've got him pretty worked up."

"I'm not so sure about that," I said. A girl had started talking to Rory and he seemed completely immersed in the conversation.

"I didn't say you no longer needed my help."

I looked up at Connor. "You still want to help me? What happened to pretending to be a bad boy?"

He shrugged. "Turns out I'm too nice."

I smiled up at him. "Well I'm glad you decided to be yourself. But I don't think there's anything you can do to help. Rory and I were just a one night thing."

"And that's what you wanted?"

"It's what I agreed to."

"You probably shouldn't have agreed to that."

"I know that now."

"Look, Rory's like a brother to me. But I feel like I should warn you...he's a fucking mess."

I laughed. "Said like someone who wants to get in my pants."

"No. I'm backing off. He wins. I'm saying this like someone who knows his friend has a thing for you."

"He doesn't."

"He does. He just doesn't know what he wants. But I know that he'll regret it later if you just become a one night thing."

"Yeah, right."

"Just give him some time."

"Time to fuck dozens of other girls? I can't live with time like that." I bit my lip. Time was killing me.

"Well, whatever you're doing is working. And the fake date? Genius."

"It wasn't fake."

"Um...yeah, it was."

"Stop getting in my head." I looked up at him. It was strange. I felt like we were friends now too. But I really didn't know anything about him. "What happened to your marriage?" I blurted out.

It looked like I had slapped him.

"I'm sorry, you don't have to answer that. It's none of my business."

"No, it's okay. We started dating in high school. Things were simple then. Same with college. We got married right after we graduated. I don't know. She just changed. Maybe I did too. We ended up not being as compatible in the real world as I thought we were."

"I'm sorry."

"Don't be. I wasn't happy."

"Are you happy now?"

"I'm happier. I'm figuring it out. I don't know how many more nights like this I have in me though. This isn't me."

"Me either."

"And I'm beyond pissed that you like Rory instead of me. I'm definitely the better catch."

I laughed. "You're fantastic. I just think we're too similar."

"It's for the best anyway. I think you're exactly what Rory needs."

"What he needs?"

"Yeah. A nice, sweet girl with a wild side."

"I don't have a wild side."

"I'm not sure if that's true. You play strip poker, wear lingerie around the apartment you share with a guy, pretend that you shower with all your friends, and you like being blindfolded in bed."

I could feel myself blushing. "I didn't... but you said Rory didn't tell you..."

"Rory's my best friend. Of course he told me he slept with you."

Oh my God. How much detail do guys go into?

"Which is why I thought you could still use my help," he added. "Especially after catching you on your fake date. You were very smooth," he laughed.

"Was it really that obvious?"

"It was to me. But Rory was so agitated after you left for your date that I'm not sure he did. You should play that up. Do it again tomorrow."

"I'm not sure lying to him is working out that well. Maybe I should just tell him how I feel."

"Trust me. Playing hard to get is the right strategy here."

"And why should I trust you?"

"I'm the nice one, remember?"

"Okay. So what should I do tonight?"

"I'm guessing you don't want to hook up with a stranger?"

"Not at all."

"Okay, so here's the game plan. See that guy at the bar over there? The one with the baseball cap right next to where Rory's standing?"

"Yeah."

"Go over to him. Talk for a few seconds and pull him onto the dance floor. When you're sure that Rory isn't looking, sneak out that back. I'll tell Rory you left with someone."

"Thank you, Connor. You're the best." I stood up on my tiptoes and kissed him on the cheek.

"Okay, game time." He lightly slapped me on the ass.

What the hell? I finally thought I was understanding Connor. These three guys were the most confusing people I had ever met. I pushed my way through the dance floor and walked right up to the guy with the baseball cap.

"Hey!" I said and touched his arm. "The Eagles?" I said and pointed to his hat. "I love them!"

He smiled at me. "You better love the Eagles if you live in Philly."

I could feel Rory's eyes on me. "You know what else I love? Dancing with handsome Eagles fans."

The baseball cap guy laughed. "Then it's my lucky night I guess."

I grabbed his hand and took him to the dance floor. We danced together for several minutes as Rory glared at me off and on. Connor knew his friend pretty well, because Rory definitely seemed jealous. When I finally got a chance, I excused myself, pushed through the people on the dance floor, and went out the back door.

CHAPTER 23

Rory had come home late last night. But he had been alone. There was no late night moaning and bed squeaking. I was beginning to think I had him right where I wanted him.

The sun was barely up, but I was completely awake. I hadn't felt so calm and happy ever since Rory had moved in. Everything was working out so well. I almost felt like whistling as I walked down the sidewalk.

I wasn't sure why Connor was purposely pushing Rory's buttons to help get us closer. It seemed like he was just a genuinely nice guy. Same with Jackson. But for some reason I had a thing for Rory instead of his nice friends. I always seemed to fall for the wrong guys.

I stopped at the closest newsstand and grabbed a copy of The Post. After paying the man at the cash register, I flipped to the editorial section that my article was appearing in. I stood frozen in the middle of the sidewalk. *Holy shit.* There was a picture of me next to my article. A huge picture. There was never a picture of me next to anything I ever wrote. *What the hell?*

My phone started vibrating in my purse. I quickly pulled it out and saw that it was Emily.

"Hey," I said. The optimism I had felt earlier had completely evaporated.

"You're making it in the big leagues, huh? You look hot in that picture."

"Can you tell it's me?"

"Um...of course you can. And even if someone couldn't, your name is right there for everyone to see. Keira, this is so awesome. Congratulations!"

"Did you just see it because you read everything I write?" I asked hopefully.

There was an awkward pause on the phone.

"I love you Keira, but no, I don't read everything you write. I was just flipping through the paper and saw your picture."

"Shit."

"Are you okay?"

"Do you think he's going to see it?"

There was another awkward pause.

"Emily! I'm so screwed. Rory's going to see it and freak out. He's going to hate me! And I already promised Judy that I'd follow through with the articles. What am I going to do?"

"Calm down. No one reads the paper anymore."

"But even if he doesn't, Jackson or Connor might. He's going to find out." I grabbed the rest of the copies of The Post from the newsstand and put them down on the counter. I put my hand over the receiver and said, "Can I buy the rest of these?" to the man at the counter.

"Are you buying all the papers right now?" Emily started laughing.

"You're not helping." I hung up the phone, handed the man some cash, and picked up the rest of the papers.

As soon as I got to a trash can I dumped all the papers into it and started running back to my apartment.

I bolted up the steps and stopped outside my door. *Please don't be up.* I unlocked the door and sighed. I had thought of an awful, terrible plan in my head on the run back to my apartment. There was no way it would actually work, but I was out of ideas. There was no going back on what had already been released in the paper. Rory would find out and hate me. But I at least needed to keep my job. So I just needed to get the rest of my information for my article as quickly as possible. No matter what. I had told myself that I could use this idea in case of an emergency. This qualified.

There was movement in Rory's bedroom. I grabbed a banana and sat down at the kitchen counter. A second later Rory came out. He looked surprised to see me. *Or does he look relieved?*

"Hey," he said and smiled at me. He was only wearing boxers.

"Good morning," I said and slowly peeled the banana. *I can't believe I'm about to do this.*

Rory ran his hand through his hair and walked over to me. "Did you have fun last night?" he asked.

"Eh." I shrugged my shoulders. "I actually couldn't stop thinking about my date from earlier. But now I'm incredibly nervous because we have another date tonight. And I'm worried we're going to get to second base. I want him to think I'm good at giving head."

Rory lowered his eyebrows slightly.

"Did you think I was good at giving head?" I asked as I finished peeling the banana and put my mouth around the top of it. *Oh God, I'm such a slut.*

His Adam's apple rose and then fell. "You were good," he said and sat down next to me.

"Really? Well, what did you like best? Is it better for me to go slowly..." I took my time sliding the banana all the way into my mouth. *Why the hell am I deep-throating a banana right now?* But it seemed to be working. His eyes were locked on me.

I pulled the banana out of my mouth. "Or maybe, licking the side?" I let my tongue slide up the banana as I looked down at Rory's growing erection.

He moved his hand over his boxers. "Both." His voice sounded tight.

"Oh my God, this banana is so good," I said slowly and batted my eyelashes at him. "Now I really want the real thing." I put my lips around the banana again and took a bite off. "Swallowing is the best part."

Rory's eyebrows lowered even more.

"Actually," I said and touched his knee. "It would really help me out if you'd let me practice on you." I dropped to my knees and let my fingers slide down his happy trail.

He stood up and the stool made a terrible squeaking noise on the floor. His eyes stayed locked on me. He wanted my lips around his cock again. And there was nothing I wanted more. I hooked my fingers in the waistband of his boxers and pulled down until his erection sprung free.

I hadn't stopped thinking about our night together. I'd never stop thinking about that night. I wrapped my fingers around the base of his thick cock and brought my lips to his tip. My eyes didn't leave his as I slowly took him into my mouth. I pressed my lips together as hard as I could as I slid down his length.

His hand gripped the kitchen counter.

I moved my lips up and down his erection. "Is that good?" I asked as I pulled him out of my mouth. I looked up at him as I licked the side of his cock and cupped his balls in my hand. He didn't need to answer. It was written all over his face. Pure bliss. And seeing him like that made me want him so badly. I pressed my legs together.

"Or maybe you like this?" I brought him back to my mouth and went all the way down, pressing his tip against my throat.

"Fuck, Keira," he groaned.

I smiled and moved my mouth faster, up and down his length. His fingers tangled in my hair as he started guiding me. He had done this before. With anyone else, it would have bothered me. But when he fucked my mouth, all I could do was beg for more.

He groaned again.

I loved that sound. I reached up and touched his abs. Everything about him was so sexy. I wanted to be back in his bed, blindfolded, begging for more. But that wasn't the plan. I pulled my hand back down.

His fingers tightened in my hair as he went faster and faster. I felt his dick pulsate and then his warm liquid shot into the back of my mouth. It was sweet yet salty at the same time. And I loved it. I was as addicted to his taste as I was to the smell of him. I drank him down greedily.

"So, how was that?" I wiped the side of my mouth with my finger and slid it into my mouth as I stood up.

He lifted me up, set me on the counter, and spread my thighs with his strong hands. Everything below my waistline clench. I wanted him so badly.

His eyes locked with mine as he moved between my legs and pushed my tank top up. The feeling of his fingers pressing against my skin made my head spin.

"Rory," I said and placed my hand on his chest. *Just say you want more. Say the words. Please.* I didn't want to have to play games anymore. *Say it!*

"Keira." He gave me one of his heart stopping smiles and put his hands on both sides of my face. He leaned forward to kiss me.

Stick to the plan. "Dude, what the hell?!" My own words made me wince.

"What?" He sounded confused.

I took a deep breath and tried to clear my head. "Why do you have to make everything so weird? I have a date tonight. I just wanted your opinion..."

"Screw your date." He leaned forward again.

"You think I should screw him on the second date? I was just going to give him head. That's why I was practicing on you."

"No, I meant skip it."

"Rory, I'm not sleeping with you. Like you said, one night stands aren't really my thing. You were completely right. I didn't realize what I was getting myself into. I need something more."

He didn't say anything.

Say something! I pleaded with him with my eyes. *Say something, damn it!* But he just stood there, with his hands on my face.

"So I'm going on my date tonight." I pushed his hands off the side of my face and pulled my shirt back down. "But first I have some work to do." I hopped off the kitchen counter and walked over to the front door.

"Can we at least talk about this?"

"There really isn't anything to talk about. I'm not going to sleep with someone who won't even take me out on a date." *Please get the hint. Ask me out. Please!* I wrapped my hand around the doorknob.

He ran his hand though his hair. "Where are you going?"

"To the office." It wasn't a lie. I needed to talk to Judy. She should have told me if my picture was going to be printed in the paper. "Thanks for breakfast," I said as I looked down at his cock. I bit my lip and quickly closed the door behind me before I could give in to my desires.

***

I sat down on a bench outside my office building and put my face in my hands. All Rory had to say was that it could be more. All I needed were those words. And more could have meant anything at this point. I just didn't want it to be one more time. Twice was just as bad as once. *No.* It was better. I needed him again. I wanted him to fuck me right there on the kitchen counter. I crossed my legs. It was impossible to think straight when I was this turned on.

Judy wanted me to somehow make it into friends with benefits. If he didn't want to be my boyfriend, maybe that could work. At this point none of it mattered. I needed him again. My mind was completely fixated. And I knew he wanted me too. He had tried to come onto me twice since our one night stand. Both times I had been incredibly forward, but that didn't matter. Friends with benefits. *That sometimes turns into love and marriage, right?*

I lifted my head out of my hands and stood up. Maybe Judy would be able to help me. I rolled my eyes at myself. Judy didn't care about me at all. She just wanted a good story. I walked into the office building that The Post was in and pressed the elevator button. The doors opened and I stepped on.

I got off on the seventh floor and walked toward Judy's office. "Hey, Liz, is Judy in?" I asked the receptionist outside Judy's office.

"Yeah, one sec, Keira." She lifted up the phone and pressed a few buttons. "Keira's here." She paused for a second. "Okay," Liz said and hung up the phone. "You can go ahead in."

I couldn't help but think that Judy didn't actually need a receptionist. Whenever I came to the office Judy never seemed to be busy. I knocked on the door and walked in. Judy was sitting behind her desk. She motioned for me to sit down across from her.

"Judy, why didn't you tell me that my article was going to have a picture of me next to it? I asked to be as anonymous as possible with all my articles."

She smiled at me. "Great news, Keira. The editor-in-chief loved your article even more than the original pitch.

And it's getting great buzz online. We'll need another one for tomorrow's paper."

She had completely ignored my comment. But the editor-in-chief had never said anything to me about my work before. That was really good news. The pit in the bottom of my stomach didn't allow me to enjoy it, though. "Can my picture please not be part of tomorrow's article?"

"Sorry, Keira. It's over my head. The editor-in-chief wanted our readers to be invested in the story. Seeing your face next to the article is important."

"Please, Judy. I..." I took a deep breath. "I know that all the readers have read about is my crush at this point, but it's more than that now. I'm falling for him."

"You should really keep your work and your love life separate. It's journalism 101."

"Judy, I'm begging you."

"There isn't anything I can do. It's over my head."

"But if he sees the article, there won't be any story left to tell."

"Then get everything you need for the story before he sees the article."

I sat there and stared at her. That's what I had tried to do earlier. But Rory wouldn't agree to more. He just wanted another casual hookup. I needed more time. Friends with benefits couldn't be the only conclusion to my article. I needed it to be more compelling than that, despite what Judy said. I wanted Rory to change. Not just for the sake of the story, but for the sake of my sanity. I swallowed but my mouth felt dry.

"What are you doing sitting there? Go get me my story."

I stood up. Every inch of me wanted to quit. I wanted to tell her to go screw herself. And I wanted to run home into Rory's arms and confess how much I liked him. But his arms weren't waiting for me. He didn't care how much I liked him. All he wanted was sex.

And this was my career. I needed to suck it up. "I'll send you the next article in a few hours." I walked out of her office.

CHAPTER 24

I sat down on my bed and pulled my computer onto my lap. My first article, Give Him a Taste, had been sexy and full of details about our one night stand. The second article wasn't nearly as fun to write. Step two was "Remain Unattached." Which was actually inaccurate because it was definitely all about pretending for me. I wrote about the importance of not sleeping in the same bed as him. Spending the night was basically a confession that you were in love. I remembered how strong the desire to kiss him in his sleep was. This was the painful article. This was the article that made it seem like I was going to fail at playing with a player. Hopefully the readers would like that. Because at this rate I was definitely going to fail.

Step three, "Flip the Switch," would be a little more fun. It was about flipping the switch on Rory and trying to be sexy. I started writing that one as soon as the one titled step two was done and emailed over to Judy. This article was about being fun and flirty, while still acting like all I wanted was friendship. I wrote about befriending his next one night stand and being his wingman in a bar. And I went into great detail about our shower together. I bit my lip as I remembered how sexy he looked with beads of water dripping down his six pack. Maybe Connor was right. It did seem like I had a wild side.

The front door closing made me jump. I heard some pots and pans clinking in the kitchen. Rory must have been making himself dinner. I didn't have any ideas left. I had played all my cards. After giving him head in the kitchen, I expected him to at least lie in order to have sex again. All I could do was look as sexy as possible for another fake date.

I hooked on my best pushup bra and pulled on the new dress I had bought on the way home from the office. It was black lace with a tan slip underneath. But the color of the slip matched my skin, so it basically looked like the lace was see-through. There was a deep V neckline and virtually no back. The lacy fabric ended right below my ass. The dress was way too tight to wear underwear. I thought about the girl that had played strip poker with us. Rory had apparently thought that going commando was very sexy. I looked in the mirror.

I pulled on the new black, platform stilettos I had bought with the dress. I could barely walk, but if Rory asked me to stay, then I wouldn't be wearing them for long. Well, maybe I'd be wearing them, but I'd be flat on my back so it wouldn't really matter how tall they were. This was definitely the sexiest outfit I had ever worn.

I turned on the YouTube tutorial I had found earlier. I had stumbled upon Phoenix's Fashions and knew that if I could pull off the look she had in the video, I wouldn't have any problem getting Rory to commit. I'd have to give her vlog a shout out in my article if this went well. I put on the inappropriate amount of eyeliner, mascara, and black eye shadow that she recommended and looked in the mirror again. Everything about the way I looked screamed slut. Hopefully it would make Rory realize what I was going to do tonight on my fake date if he didn't stop me.

I pushed my breasts together once more before opening the door. The kitchen smelled amazing. It was definitely something Italian. The aromas of garlic and parmesan made my stomach rumble. Rory had his back to me, and was stirring something at the stove. He was wearing a pair of jeans with a blazer. Why was he so dressed up? I looked over at the kitchen counter. There were two place settings and several candles lit. It looked so romantic.

That's why he didn't want more. He already had more with someone else. I blinked hard. My tears were imminent, but I couldn't cry. I was wearing too much eye makeup. I turned around to run back into my room.

"Keira."

I winced and pretended to close the door to my room when I was actually reopening it.

"Hi, Rory," I said and put on a fake smile. "It smells really good in here." I walked into the kitchen and leaned on the counter. *Don't cry. Hold it together for just one more minute.*

"I hope so."

"What's the special occasion?" I looked over at the table setting for two.

Rory poured a glass of wine and handed it to me. "I was just in the mood for *more*."

The way he said it made me gulp. That's what I had said I wanted instead of a one night stand. It was vague, and I didn't actually know what it meant, but more was what I wanted too. *Is all of this really for me?* I took a big sip of my wine. I didn't want to jump to any conclusions. I needed him to say it.

Instead, he took a sip of wine from his own glass and turned back to the stove.

I stood there awkwardly until I finished my glass of wine. It was hard not to admire his ass in those jeans. And he was wearing his usual v-neck t-shirt under his blazer. I could see every muscle in his chest. He looked so sexy. But it didn't seem like he was being sexy for me. I set my glass down on the counter next to him. Maybe he just meant he was hungry for more food than he usually had. "I have to get going. I'm going to be late."

"I think you should skip your date." His fingers brushed against my wrist. "Stay here tonight."

"What did you want to do?"

He lowered his eyebrows slightly. "You."

Holy shit.

"Wine, dinner, dessert." He locked eyes with me when he said dessert. "I think that counts as a date, right?" He lifted up my glass and poured me some more wine.

"Yes," I said breathlessly.

He grabbed a pan off the stove and walked over to the counter. He put pasta down on each plate and then the sauce, which is what I thought smelled so wonderful.

"Let me just make a call," I said. I pulled out my cell and scrolled through my contact list. Instead of clicking on anyone, I held the phone to my ear. After a few seconds I said, "Hey, Brian. I'm really sorry, but I have to cancel tonight." I paused for effect. "Something important." I looked up at Rory.

He smiled at me.

"Sorry again. Bye, Brian." I pretended to hang up. I put my cell back in my purse and dropped my purse on the counter. I walked over to Rory and he pulled out one of the chairs for me. This had to be a dream. *How had this really worked so well?*

Rory grabbed something out of the oven and kicked the oven closed with his foot. My mouth started watering. It wasn't the sauce that smelled so good. It was the chicken. He put a piece on each of our plates and sat down next to me.

"Rory, this looks so good."

He smiled at me as I took a bite.

"Oh my God. This is literally the best thing that's ever been in my mouth."

He laughed. "You mean one of the best." He raised his left eyebrow.

I swallowed hard. *Is he referring to his cock?* If he was, he wasn't wrong.

"So, just four?" he asked as he twirled some pasta around his fork.

"Yeah, four."

"Four is a pretty good number."

"It is a pretty good number."

"Maybe it should stay there then."

He's asking me out. I took another bite of chicken. *No, he's asking me not to sleep with anyone else. Is there a difference?* "What is your number?"

"More than four." He smiled at me.

"You've slept with more than four women since you've moved in."

He laughed. "Yeah. Well, it's been harder living with you than I anticipated."

What did he mean by that? Did he really mean that living with me made him horny all the time?

"You look amazing in that dress, by the way."

"Thanks." He had subtly changed the subject, but I didn't care. I didn't need to know his number. All I needed to know was that he wanted me. For real now. "So, I'm hard to live with?" I smiled innocently at him.

"I'm used to having guy roommates."

"I'm used to having girl roommates."

"So this is kind of uncharted territory for both of us." He took another sip of wine. "What else don't I know about you?"

"Well, what do you want to know?"

"What's the most embarrassing thing you've ever done?"

"What makes you think it wasn't something I've done since you moved in?"

He laughed. "Because you get embarrassed really easily. You're blushing right now."

I could feel my cheeks flushing. "Actually, there was this guy I really liked in high school. And I was hoping he'd ask me to prom. A few days before prom I walked outside and he had written on my car with this foam stuff, asking me to be his date to prom. And I freaked out. I ran over to him and threw my arms around him and told him how I had a crush on him all of high school."

"That's not embarrassing. That's just a cute story."

"I didn't get to the embarrassing part. So he pulls back from me and asks who I am. And I'm thinking, weird, we had a bunch of classes together and you just asked me to prom. So I say I'm Keira and I point to my car. And he says, I'll never forget it: 'Shit, sorry Carrie, I must have gotten the wrong car. Do you know which car is Ashley's?' He didn't even know my name after I told him."

Rory started laughing. "Okay, that is embarrassing. And horrible."

"I was a total geek in high school. You know, frizzy hair, glasses, the whole thing. No one was ever going to ask me to prom."

"So you went alone?"

"I went with my friends. That's how I like to put it."

"Hmm. Well, it's his loss. Frizzy hair, glasses, and all. There's no way Ashley was as hot as you." He sipped his wine as his eyes fell on my breasts.

"Were you always super sexy? Even in high school?"

He looked back up at me. "Super sexy huh?" He put his hand on my thigh. "Is that what you think?"

He hadn't answered any of the questions I had asked him. But all I could think about was his hand on my thigh. I didn't want his fingers to stop moving. "I think I'm done with dinner," I said breathlessly.

"I agree. I think it's time for dessert." He pushed his plate away.

The way he was looking at me made me blush again. I had barely eaten anything. But I wasn't really that hungry anymore. I only had one thing on my mind now. I wanted him so badly. "I'm pretty full."

"Well, maybe I'll just indulge myself then. It's something I've been craving since this morning."

I was super curious about what he had made. If it was something chocolate then I wouldn't be able to resist trying it. He was an amazing chef. I watched as he pushed the rest of the dishes to the side to make room for the dessert. But instead of walking over to the oven or fridge, he grabbed my waist and lifted me onto the counter.

His hands slowly spread my thighs.

"What's wrong?" I asked when his hands stopped moving. My voice sounded needy, but I didn't care. I wanted him right that second. *No.* I needed him.

"I'm waiting for you to storm off and tell me I'm reading this situation wrong." His hand dipped to my inner thigh.

I grabbed the collar of his blazer and kissed him.

There was no hesitation in his response. He grabbed both sides of my face and kissed me back. No one had ever kissed me like that. Intense, passionate, leaving me powerless. If I wasn't sitting on the kitchen counter, my knees would have been too weak to stand.

One of his hands moved back to my inner thigh and his fingers brushed against my wetness.

There was a low noise in his throat, almost like a growl. "You're not wearing any underwear." He pulled my ass to the end of the counter and spread my legs even farther apart. Before I could respond, he bent down and placed a long, slow stroke against my aching pussy.

I moaned and leaned back on my elbows.

His tongue swirled around all my walls, acting like I truly was the dessert he'd been craving all day.

He pushed my thighs farther apart as his tongue went even deeper.

"Yes!" I groaned and tilted my head back. For days I had been waking up in the middle of the night panting, remembering what it was like for him to be inside of me. The real thing was so much better than my dreams. He was going to put me over the edge in a matter of seconds.

But instead of keeping his steady, torturous pace, his lips moved to my clit and his finger entered the void.

"Rory, please," I moaned.

"You've been teasing me for days, Keira. I'm not letting you come that easily."

What?!

He moved his fingers faster. It felt amazing, but somehow wasn't what I needed to find my release.

"Rory," I moaned again.

He placed another stroke against my wetness. "You taste even better than I remembered."

Fuck. His naughty words made me even hornier. I couldn't even think straight anymore. He pulled away from me and took off his blazer. He grabbed his t-shirt by its collar and pulled it off, revealing his perfectly sculpted torso.

He wrapped his hand around my waist and pulled me off the counter. "Turn around."

I didn't care what he did to me. I turned around. All I needed was his cock deep inside of me. And hopefully he wouldn't make me wait much longer.

"Hands on the counter." His breath was hot against my neck.

I placed my hands on the counter and arched my back.

He pushed the bottom of my dress up over my ass. His hands pressed against the small of my back, making me arch my back even more. "Close your eyes."

"Rory, please. You're killing me."

"Then next time you shouldn't tease me so much. Close your eyes."

I gulped. *What is he going to do to me?* I closed my eyes and felt his hands leave my back. A moment later I felt something cold against the back of my thigh. *What the hell is that?* My whole body shivered.

"Stay still." The cool item traveled up my thigh and across my ass. It was definitely something metal.

"Rory." My voice was airy and needy. I hated how he made me beg.

The metal object left my skin and I felt a sharp slap on my ass.

Shit. Why do I like that?

"If I remember correctly, you're kinkier than you look."

"I'm not..."

He slapped my ass again. *Fuck.* The metal object slid down my ass and slipped between my legs, pressing against my wetness. I gripped the counter tightly. I was so aroused, and the coolness of the metal felt relieving against my aching pussy. "Oh God."

Rory laughed and moved the object back over my ass. "No you don't. You're not coming until I say you can." He slapped my ass even harder.

"Please fuck me."

"You know, I've been wanting to spank you ever since I met you," he said, ignoring my plea. He slapped my ass again and slid the metal object back between my legs, pressing hard against my clit.

My knuckles were turning white as my fingers pushed against the counter.

"When you want me, you really should just tell me." He spanked me again.

"I want you, Rory. Please, I need you!"

He slid the object back between my legs and pressed it hard against my wetness. And then suddenly the pressure was gone. The stool beside me squeaked against the floor. I opened my eyes and saw Rory sitting down next to me.

"All the best desserts are eaten with spoons. Don't you think?" He put the metal spoon into his mouth and licked off my juices.

Holy shit. I could hear myself panting.

He tossed the spoon and it clanged against the counter. "I thought I preferred you blindfolded and naked on your knees. But this just might be better."

I was suddenly very aware of my whore makeup and my exposed ass. My back was arched, just waiting for him to enter me. And all I could hear was my heart racing in anticipation.

He stood back up and caressed my ass where he had spanked me. I closed my eyes and tried to lose myself in the sensation. I had never been so aroused in my life. Every touch almost sent me over the edge.

He leaned over behind me and nipped my shoulder blade. The sound of my whimpering made me wince. How was he doing this to me? I pushed my ass against him. I could feel his erection through his jeans.

Rory groaned and grabbed my hips, pulling me away from the counter. He kissed the back of my neck as he pushed my dress up my waist and over my breasts. I lifted my arms in the air. He slowly pulled the lacy fabric off of me and dropped it to the floor. His hands ran back down my arms and he unhooked my bra. I quickly pulled the straps down my arms as his fingers slid down my stomach, stopping right below my bellybutton.

I whimpered again.

He kissed the back of my neck. "You like pushing my buttons. But it just so happens that I like punishing you." He bit my earlobe.

Punishing me?

His hands left my stomach and I heard the zip of his jeans.

Thank God.

He pushed me forward and I gripped the counter again. I heard the squeak of the stool again and looked over at him. He was completely naked, his erection even bigger than I remembered. He leaned back and put his elbows on the counter behind him.

"Rory..."

"I'm trying to decide how I want to fuck you. And where." His eyes lingered on my ass.

Where? It seemed like he was probably talking about somewhere in the apartment, but there was another possibility. I closed my legs slightly.

"I don't think you're ready for that, Keira," he said while still staring at my ass.

"I'll never be ready for that." My voice wasn't convincing. I was so horny I'd let him do anything he wanted to me. I stared down at his erection. *Please fuck me.*

He smiled. "Challenge accepted. But not right now."

I gulped.

"No, right now, I just want to fuck you senseless." He stood up and walked behind me again, trailing his fingers down my spine. "Until you can't take any more." His hand dipped between my thighs as he pushed them back apart.

I heard the rip of foil and closed my eyes. *Please be done teasing me.*

And as if answering my needs he grabbed my hips and thrust his thick cock deep inside of me.

"Yes!" I moaned.

Last time he had been slow and gentle at first, letting me adjust to having his massive cock inside of me. But not this time. He was fucking me hard. And I loved every second of it. His hips moved faster and faster as his fingers dug into my hips. It felt like a lifetime ago that I had him inside of me. It was all I ever wanted. Him so deep inside of me that it hurt.

He tilted his hips so that his erection hit a spot inside of me that only he could find.

"Rory," I groaned.

He grabbed my hair and tilted my head back, making me arch my back more. He was fucking me relentlessly, harder than I had ever been fucked. I pushed against the countertop, trying to prevent myself from collapsing on top of it.

His other hand slid down my stomach and his fingers brushed against my swollen clit. "You can come now, Keira."

And I shattered. *Finally.* "Rory! Oh God." I had never felt such relief. All of his teasing. All the days of wanting him. I clenched around him, waiting for his own release. But it didn't come. He continued fucking me, harder than ever.

"I'm not even close to being done with you yet," he said and pulled out of me.

I wasn't sure how much more I could take. I was completely spent. He grabbed my arm, spun me around and pulled me into his chest. His erection was pressed against my stomach. And somehow it no longer mattered that I had just orgasmed. The way he was looking at me made everything below my waistline clench again. He had such control over me.

He leaned down and kissed me as he grabbed my thighs and lifted me up. I wrapped my legs around him and let my fingers run through his hair. He was carrying me back to his bedroom. He slammed my back against his door and reached for the doorknob. It reminded me of the first time we had slept together.

I placed my hand on his cheek and turned his face back to me. "Here," I said. My voice was laced with desire.

"Here," he repeated. He pulled my hips back and shoved his length back inside of me.

Fuck. I turned my head, pressing my cheek against the cool door. I gripped his hair.

He grabbed my wrists and pulled my hands away from him, pinning them against the doorframe. I tried to move my arms, but they were immobilized. I was completely at his mercy. And I loved when he was in control of me.

With each thrust my ass banged against the door, reminding me of where he had spanked me. Somehow it aroused me even more. I moaned as he made the desire build and build. His fingers tightened around mine as I felt myself tightening around his cock.

"Keira," he groaned as I came again. He bit my lower lip and turned my face back toward his. He kissed me hard as he came. He groaned in my mouth as he continued to slide his length in and out of me. I clenched around him one last time and let my head fall back against the door. He pulled out of me and released his grip on my hands. My back slid down the door until I was sitting on the floor. He smiled down at me.

"Now I just want to tease you even more often so you'll do that to me again." I smiled up at him.

His eyebrows lowered slightly. "I'll do that to you whenever you want."

"Deal," I sighed and closed my eyes.

He laughed and picked me up in his arms. "Your bed or mine?"

"I want to sleep with you."

"Okay."

I heard his door open and close. He placed me down on his sheets and his familiar cinnamon scent completely engulfed me. He slowly took off my high heels and dropped them on the floor. As soon as he lay down beside me, I put my head on his chest. No more one night stand nonsense. Rory was all mine. I fell asleep with his arms wrapped around me.

CHAPTER 25

When I woke up, Rory wasn't lying next to me. I closed my eyes and took one more deep breath of his cinnamon scented sheets. This was where I wanted to spend every night. I felt like the luckiest girl in the world.

I slowly climbed out of his bed. The only thing in here that was mine were my high heels. I grabbed one of Rory's t-shirts off the ground, pulled it on, and looked in the mirror. My makeup was smudged, but fortunately it looked sexy instead of horrendous. I hoped Rory was out there. I picked up my shoes and walked out of his room.

Rory wasn't in the kitchen. I looked at the counter and felt myself blushing. Eating there would never be the same. I walked past the kitchen, turned the corner to go into the living room, and ran right into someone.

"Oh, shit," I said and dropped my high heels as two strong hands grabbed my arms.

"Hey, Keira." Connor was smiling down at me. He let go of my arms and looked at his watch. "You must have had a good night," he said.

I pulled back. "Yeah, actually." I tucked a loose strand of hair behind my ear. "What are you doing here?"

"I had a meeting downtown and needed a quick lunch."

"Is Rory here?" I tried to peer around Connor.

"No, I think he's at work."

"Wait, so how did you..." I looked up at him. "Do you have a key?"

"Um...no."

"Oh my God, Rory gave you a key to our apartment?"

"Here, I'll give it back to you." He reached into his pocket and pulled out the key.

"No, it's okay. If he gave it to you, that's fine. I was just surprised to see you." I crossed my arms in front of my chest.

He put the key back in his pocket. "You look great in just a t-shirt, by the way."

I couldn't help but smile. "Thanks, Connor. And I definitely owe you one. Your advice worked really well."

"So you two are together now then?" He ran his palm along the scruff on his chin.

"I don't really know. I think we're in a good place. But we haven't really talked about it. He asked me not to sleep with anyone else, though."

Connor frowned slightly. "I can talk to him if you want."

"Oh, geez, no. We're good. I don't want to freak him out. I'm so happy, I don't want to mess anything up."

"Okay." Connor scratched the scruff on his chin again. "I'm glad that you're happy, Keira. I'm gonna go. I just need to go to the bathroom real quick."

"Oh, yeah, of course." I stepped out of his way.

I had a slight sinking feeling in my stomach. Rory had asked me not to sleep with anyone else, but he had never said he wouldn't. I went into my bedroom and closed the door.

The dress I had worn last night was folded at the foot of my bed, and my bra was laying next to it. *Oh God, he's been in my room?* My eyes locked on my laptop in the middle of my bed. *Shit.*

I jumped on my bed and swiped my finger across the touchpad. The makeup tutorial I had been watching came up. My documents describing in painful detail my blossoming relationship with Rory weren't open. I sighed and looked back at the dress on my bed. There was a note on top of it.

"I'll be home at five. You better not be wearing underwear."

I gulped as I ran my fingers across the note. *He wants me again.* I glanced back at my computer screen. It was already past noon. I needed to finish my article.

***

If this was going to be how my days went from now on, I wouldn't complain. Writing for a few hours while looking forward to having sex with the hottest man I had ever laid my eyes on was pure bliss. Judy had even sent me an email full of compliments about my latest installment. And there really was buzz about my articles. The online version of The Post had tons of comments underneath both my articles that had already been published. The best part was that it didn't seem like Rory or anyone he knew read The Post. So I could just focus on us and not put so much pressure on myself.

I pulled on a white tank top and jean shorts, but skipped the bra and thong. It was cold in the apartment and my nipples were clearly visible through my shirt. I quickly changed into a loose fitting v-neck t-shirt. *Much better.*

My hair was still wet from my shower, so there wasn't much I could do to it. I applied a little extra mascara and went out into the hallway. I wasn't sure what to do. Waiting by the door seemed pathetic. I went into the kitchen and poured myself a glass of water.

Rory came in a second later. He pulled off his t-shirt as he walked over to me.

I swallowed hard as I looked at his abs. As soon as he reached me, he took the glass of water out of my hand and set it down on the counter. I thought he was going to kiss me, but instead he put his hands on the counter on either side of me and looked down at me. It felt like my heart was beating out of my chest.

"So you got my note?" His eyes trailed down my body.

"Yes." I hated how eager my voice sounded. *How was I this turned on without him even touching me?* Whatever we had wasn't official yet. I needed to calm down.

"Let me shower real quick. I'll be right back." He let go of the counter.

What? "Don't." I ran my hands down his six pack.

"It'll just be a second. I went to the gym after work."

"I like the way you smell." He smelled like cinnamon and sweat. To me, that was the smell of sex. Just his scent made me wet. And I didn't want to wait. I had been waiting all day. "I want you right now, Rory." He had told me to just tell him whenever I wanted him. But it seemed weird to say. I could feel my face blushing.

"I could get used to this." He grabbed my ass and lifted me up. I quickly wrapped my legs around his waist and kissed him.

He didn't hesitate to kiss me back. He squeezed my ass and began walking somewhere, but I didn't care where he was taking me. I buried my hands in his hair and deepened the kiss.

He set me down on the edge of the couch and pushed my shirt up the sides of my torso. I lifted up my arms as he pulled my shirt off the rest of the way. He tossed it behind the couch and leaned down to kiss me again.

I ran my hands down his abs and traced his happy trail with my fingertips. He moaned softly in my mouth. That was my new favorite sound. I decided to take advantage of the fact that he was wearing athletic shorts, and let my hand dip beneath them and his boxers. He was already fully erect. I wrapped my hand around his cock. He groaned again.

But then there was a creaking noise. Rory stepped back and looked over his shoulder. "Oh, shit," he mumbled. "Get dressed."

"What?"

The front door began to open. *Fuck!* I ducked down behind the couch and grabbed my shirt. I had just pulled it on when Connor and Jackson walked in. *I should have taken Connor's key when I had the chance.* "Hey, guys," I said and slowly rose. I ran my fingers through my hair.

Jackson looked back and forth between me and Rory.

"What are you guys doing here?" Rory asked. He didn't have his shirt on and there was a visible bulge in his shorts from his erection. I could feel myself blushing.

"It's the second Thursday of the month," Connor said.

Rory just stared at him.

"It's Throwback Thursday, man," Jackson said and lifted up a case of beer.

"Oh, right." He scratched the back of his neck. "Sorry guys, I forgot."

The four of us just stood there in silence for a second.

"What is Throwback Thursday? Do you guys like look at old pictures and drink beer?" I asked, trying to break the silence.

"No, we just drink beer and watch whatever game is on T.V." Connor walked in and sat down on the couch.

"Isn't that just Thirsty Thursday?"

"Well we used to call it that. But Jackson always gets really drunk and starts talking about all his exes."

"I don't do that." Jackson laughed and sat down in the chair next to the couch. "It's called Throwback Thursday because we literally throw back tons of beer. No reminiscing."

I looked up at Rory.

"Sorry," he mouthed silently at me. He sat down on the opposite side of the couch as Connor.

"Okay, well I'll let you guys watch your game or get super drunk or whatever it is you actually do." I was so horny. I couldn't just sit there next to Rory. I wish he had just told them to leave.

"Oh, no, Keira, you can join us," Rory said. "There's a Phillies game on. I know you like watching all those sexy players." He smiled at me.

"I um..."

Connor turned around and handed me a bottle of beer.

It would have been weird if I hung out in my room. Especially when I had skipped out on poker night. "Okay." I grabbed the beer, walked around the couch, and sat down between Connor and Rory.

Rory turned on the game and then put his arm behind me on the couch, without touching me.

Jackson looked back and forth between us again instead of turning toward the game. Jackson smiled at me. "Okay, I just have to ask. Is something going on between you two? Because you know I hate feeling like I'm out of the loop. And Keira's basically part of our group now. If two people in our group are hooking up, I feel like everyone in the group should know."

Rory moved his arm off the couch behind me. "Keira's not really in our group. She hasn't even had the induction yet or anything."

Connor laughed.

"Yeah, that doesn't really answer my question," Jackson said.

"What is the induction to your group?" I asked, hoping to change the subject.

"There isn't really..."

"You have to blow one of the group members," Connor said, cutting Rory off.

I could feel my face blushing. *Haven't I already been inducted then?*

"I knew it," Jackson said. He clapped his hands together but missed slightly. It seemed like he had already had a few beers before coming over.

"Whatever, guys. You all just admitted that you're gay," I said.

"No, we just tricked you into admitting that you and Rory are hooking up," Connor said. "Obviously original members don't have to do the initiation. Just new female members. So really just you. And maybe we should change it to blowing two group members." He raised his eyebrow at me.

I pushed his shoulder. "But you didn't trick me. You already knew," I said.

"Damn it, Rory. Why do you always tell Connor everything before you tell me?!" Jackson said.

Rory started laughing. "Calm down, Jackson. I'll tell you first next time."

Next time?

The only noise in the room was from the T.V.

Next time that he hooks up with me? Or next time as in a new girl? I felt sick to my stomach. He must have meant next time he hooks up with me. There was no way he meant with the next girl he hooks up with. I knew we hadn't talked about what we were, but I didn't think he was going to move on that quickly. And why would he say that in front of me if he meant a different girl?

Connor cleared his throat.

"Connor!" I almost yelled, trying to change the subject. "I actually thought of the perfect girl to set you up with. I was good friends with her in college, but we kind of lost touch when I moved to Philly. But she just moved here, so I texted her this afternoon and told her all about you. And she really wants to meet you. Maybe if you're lucky you'll get to induct her into the group."

"Oh, wow. Okay. I can't argue with that. Actually that would be great. I was about to sign up for Tinder or something. It seems like the same girls have been at the bars every time we go."

"Grindr?" Jackson asked. "I'm on that."

I laughed. *Wait, is Jackson actually gay?*

"You do know that Grindr is like a gay version of Tinder?" Rory asked.

"I meant Tinder. I'm on Tinder." Jackson turned toward the T.V.

What the hell is happening right now? "Let me see your phone," I said to Connor, again trying to change the subject.

He handed it to me. I quickly added in my friend's number and tossed it back to him. "Her name is Julie. And I happen to know she's free tomorrow night. So you should text her."

"Thanks, Keira."

"So if you two are together now and Connor has a date, what about me?" asked Jackson. "Do you have any more single friends, Keira?"

Rory shifted in his seat.

I tried not to read into his body language too much. He wasn't comfortable admitting we were together. That was fine. We hadn't really discussed it yet anyway. And I knew he had issues with his past relationship. It would take him time to trust me. "I'm sorry, Jackson. All of my closest friends are married or engaged. Oh crap." I quickly stood up. I had completely forgotten about a wedding I was supposed to attend on Saturday.

"You okay?" Rory asked.

"Yeah, sorry, I'll be right back." I walked over to the fridge and pulled the invitation off. I had RSVP'd that I would be bringing a date. *What is wrong with me?* It was always so hard putting an X through the line of my plus one. Even though I had RSVP'd months ago, it was still rather optimistic of me.

"Hey, sorry about tonight."

I looked up at Rory, leaning against the fridge. *God is he sexy.* "It's fine." I smiled at him.

"Are you sure everything's okay?"

"Yeah, it's just...it's stupid really. It's not a big deal at all. I just completely forgot about this wedding I'm supposed to attend this weekend. One of my friends from college is getting married. At least I'm not a bridesmaid this time." I laughed awkwardly. I wanted to ask him to be my plus one. But he had just acted so weird around his friends. I didn't want to put him in an awkward position.

"Oh." Rory lowered his eyebrows slightly as he looked down at the invitation. "Who's your plus one?"

"I don't think I'll bring anyone. I mean...it's probably going to be boring. I don't want to subject anyone to all that." The invitation suddenly felt heavy in my hands. It would have been so nice to bring a date. And Rory had been the one to bring it up. If he really liked me, then he wouldn't want me to go with anyone else. "Unless you want to go," I said. "But you definitely don't have to."

"When did you say it was?"

"This Saturday."

"I'll be your date if you want."

"Really? That would be fantastic."

"Yeah, of course. Now let's go watch the game. You can point out all the players you think are the hottest."

I laughed and followed him back into the living room.

CHAPTER 26

The smell of cinnamon completely engulfed me. I took a deep breath, opened my eyes, and immediately snapped them shut. I had fallen asleep on Rory's lap on the couch. My cheek was directly on top of his crotch. And he was definitely semi-erect. *Hopefully he's dreaming about me.* I slowly opened up my eyes again.

His bare feet were up on the coffee table, his right ankle crossed over his left. His legs were really hairy. I wasn't sure why I found that so insanely hot. There was just something so masculine about hairy legs. I pulled up his athletic shorts slightly so I could look at his knees. *How are knees sexy?* I bit my lip.

Rory's body shifted slightly and I heard him yawn. I closed my eyes again so he wouldn't realize I was awake yet. I wasn't ready for this moment to end.

He put his fingers through my hair and then ran his thumb along the back of my neck.

I gulped. *He likes studying me too.*

His fingers wandered over my shoulder and traced my collarbone. I could feel him getting more erect beneath my cheek. I smiled to myself. I wanted for us to continue where we had left off the night before, so I pretended to yawn. Rory immediately pulled his hand away.

I rolled onto my back and looked up at him. He had more scruff on his face than usual. Probably because I hadn't let him shower last night. And his shirt was still off, revealing his perfect abs. It took every ounce of restraint in me to not trace my fingertips along the lines of his six pack.

"Hey," he said and smiled down at me.

"When did we fall asleep?" I asked.

"You fell asleep right after Ryan Howard hit a home-run. You said something along the lines of seeing what a guy can do with a baseball bat isn't nearly as fun as seeing what he can do in bed."

"I did not," I said and sat up.

Rory laughed. "No, you did. And then you said if skills in the bedroom were somehow related to baseball, that I'd be hitting homeruns in every game."

"No. In front of your friends?"

"You become very honest when you've had too much to drink. You passed out after your confession."

"But I didn't even drink that much." I put my arm over my eyes and leaned back against the couch.

Rory put his arm around my shoulders. "Yeah, I know. I'm just messing with you."

"Rory!" I shoved his chest. But I didn't move my hand away. I let it wander down his chest and abs.

"I'm in serious need of a shower. You are welcome to join me though." He stood up and put his hand out for me.

I quickly grabbed it and he pulled me to my feet.

"None of that friendship shower shit, though." His eyes were smoldering. Whenever he looked at me with his hazel eyes I got completely lost.

"Sorry, what?"

He laughed and picked me up over his shoulder.

"Rory!"

He spanked my ass and carried me into the bathroom, closing and locking the door behind him.

"Rory, put me down!"

He spanked me again and turned on the water.

"Rory I haven't even brushed my teeth."

He slowly lowered me down, keeping my torso pressed against him. "If you insist." He let go of my hips and grabbed his toothbrush. I looked down at his erection pressing against his athletic shorts. I quickly grabbed my toothbrush and began brushing my teeth. He looked at me in the mirror and smiled.

I turned around and rested my ass against the sink. He was staring down at me with even more intensity. I put my hands down on the counter and lifted myself up so that I was sitting on the sink, and continued to brush my teeth. He spit into the sink and placed his toothbrush back into the holder.

But I wasn't done yet. It was fun making him wait. I spread my thighs. With my free hand, I traced my fingers up my inner thigh

"Okay, that's it." He grabbed my waist again and lifted me over his shoulder.

"Rory! I'm not done!"

"Too bad." He slapped my ass as he pulled back the shower curtain. I tossed my toothbrush in the sink as he stepped into the shower. I was still fully dressed and he was still wearing his shorts.

"Rory!" I screamed and started laughing as the water fell on my back.

He lowered me down again once I was completely soaked. "Now this is a good look on you." His eyes wandered away from my face.

I looked down and saw that my nipples could be seen clearly through my wet, white t-shirt. "Someone told me that I shouldn't wear underwear. I wasn't sure if that included a bra or not."

He looked so sexy with droplets of water falling down his face. Beads of water were even forming on his eyelashes. It made me want to kiss every inch of his face.

"It did," he said, grabbing the side of my shirt and pulling me against him. Our lips met under the cascading water. And he kissed me like he never had before. It was like he missed me and hadn't seen me in weeks.

I ran my hands through his wet hair. It was hard to breathe under the water but I didn't care. I didn't seem to care about anything but him anymore.

He pushed my back against the cool tile wall and unzipped my jean shorts. "I don't like when you make me wait. Especially when I need to be at work in twenty minutes." He slid my shorts over my ass and down my thighs.

Oh crap. Not getting him last night had been torture. I didn't want to wait all day. "So there's no time..."

"I never said that." He grabbed his wallet out of his shorts, pulled out a condom, and tossed the wallet out of the shower.

"So what...are you going to punish me or something?" I swallowed hard. That's what I wanted. It was fun getting spanked with a spoon, but I wanted to know what it felt like to have the handcuffs on his bedpost attached to my wrists.

He grabbed my waist and thrust himself deep inside of me.

I groaned and pressed my cheek against the tile. I wasn't ready for him. *Fuck*. But I was so aroused that after a second it didn't matter. I didn't need foreplay with him. I just needed him.

He grabbed my chin and tilted my face back to his. "I am going to punish you." He tilted his hips, making my back slide up the shower wall. "But I only have a few minutes. And since you've been really bad, I need a lot more time than that." He slammed his cock into me again, harder than before, pressing my ass firmly against the tile. A quiet groan escaped from his lips. "So right now, I'm just going to make you come faster than you ever have before."

Holy shit. I bit my bottom lip to prevent it from trembling.

He moved his hand to my thigh and started fucking me even harder. Harder than he ever had before.

And I loved it. I loved that he was rough with me. He knew how much I could take, and he wasn't afraid to push me to my limit.

His fingertips dug into the sides of my thighs. "If you don't come in thirty seconds, I'm going to leave you here, wanting me all day."

"Rory," I moaned. "Please don't stop."

He pulled out of me and then slammed into me deeper still. "This is one of the many places that you teased me, you know. I'd love to leave you dripping wet right here."

"Rory, please." I grabbed a fistful of his hair. I was so close.

His hips began to move faster. With each thrust my back slid slightly against the sleek wall.

"You have ten seconds, Keira."

Oh God. I could feel myself climbing higher and higher.

"I want to feel your tight pussy clench around me." He lightly nipped my earlobe. "Come for me, Keira."

His words were my undoing. "Rory!" I squeezed his strong shoulders. I had been so wound up all night. To finally find my release was the best feeling in the world. My toes curled as I came crashing down.

"Fuck," Rory groaned as he slammed into me again.

I felt his cock pulse inside of me. He leaned down and kissed me hard. I never wanted this kiss to end. He grabbed my ass and pulled me off the wall, letting the water fall down on us. With him still deep inside of me, I could feel myself wanting him again, wanting to feel that release over and over again. No one had ever made me feel like this. He groaned into my mouth and slowly pulled out of me. My body slid down his. I was still wearing my t-shirt, and it clung to my rock hard nipples as I stared up at him.

He didn't say a word as he quickly washed his hair and poured body wash into his hand. But he was staring at me. Just his eyes on me made me want him all over again. It felt like my heart was beating out of my chest.

His eyes landed back on my breasts. He stepped back under the water and rinsed off all the soap suds.

"I'm looking forward to you punishing me properly." I held my breath. I hadn't meant to actually say that out loud.

His eyebrows lowered slightly. I watched his Adam's apple rise and fall.

"I really wish I didn't have to leave right now," he said.

The way he was looking at me made me feel like I was the only girl he had ever liked. I swallowed hard. I was in way deeper than I realized. If it was up to me I'd stay in bed with him all day, talking about stupid stuff and rolling around in his cinnamon scented sheets.

"When will you be back?" My voice sounded needy. *What is wrong with me?*

He ran his hand through his wet hair. "I have plans after work tonight. What time is the wedding on Saturday?"

I hoped he couldn't see the disappointment on my face. "The ceremony is at five. And it's about half an hour from here." It was weird having a conversation with a guy in a shower. Especially a naked guy who I was crushing on, who was starting to get another erection. I peeled my eyes away from his groin.

"Okay." He smiled at me. "In the meantime, you should think of all the different ways you think you deserve to be punished." He leaned forward. "And don't worry, I already have a few ideas of my own," he whispered in my ear. His warm breath and naughty words made me shiver.

I watched him and his perfect ass step out of the shower and close the curtain.

CHAPTER 27

"What's wrong?" Emily asked as she opened the door.

"Why do you always assume something is wrong when I visit you?"

She stepped aside to let me in. "Because whenever you show up unannounced, something is always wrong."

I sat down on her couch and tucked my feet beside me.

"Seriously, Keira, you're freaking me out. What's wrong?"

"Really, nothing. I just finished my last two articles for the How to Play with a Player series."

"What steps were those again?"

Emily seemed to love hearing about my risqué articles. "Step four was 'Turn up the Heat'. You know, being super sexy and all." *And giving Rory head and pretending I was practicing for my date.* Emily didn't need to know that though. Fortunately she already confessed that she never read my articles, so hopefully she just wanted to hear about it and wouldn't read it. It was actually really fun to remember all the crazy stuff I did to get Rory's attention. "And step five was 'Make Him Jealous'. It was just about going on a fake date. So I'm officially done now."

"Well, that's great. Now you can just put that behind you and hope that Rory never sees it."

My stomach churned. "Yeah, I know. The last one will come out in Sunday's paper and then hopefully the whole thing will just blow over. But..." I looked down at my hands in my lap. "It's just...when I was writing, I felt..." I sighed and put my face in my hands. "I've never felt this way before," I said into my hands.

"Keira, I can't even understand what you're saying."

"Even when I'm not with him, just thinking about him makes me...ugh, what am I going to do?"

"I seriously can't understand anything you're saying right now."

I lifted up my head. "I think I'm in love with him."

"Wait, what?"

"No, I know I'm in love with him. Because I thought I loved David. And it killed me when he dumped me. And I couldn't stop crying when he got engaged to the next girl he dated. But I never felt this way about him. I've never felt this way about anyone before."

Emily smiled.

"I'm completely addicted to him. Why are you smiling at me? Stop smiling like that. You look like you just murdered someone, you psychopath."

"Whoa! Calm down for one second. I'm smiling because I'm happy for you."

"You can't be happy for me! I wrote a whole series of articles about how I tricked him into sleeping with me. I'm a monster."

Emily laughed. "You're not a monster. Just think of all the things that he's probably done to get women into bed with him."

"I don't want to think about that. Besides, that's different. He didn't do any of that with me. When he finds out about my articles, he's going to hate me. His last girlfriend completely fucked him up when she cheated on him. That's why he acts like a slut and is afraid of commitment. He's going to think what I did was a huge betrayal."

"You don't know that."

"Wouldn't you?"

Emily paused for a second. "What made you write the articles in the first place? I've been reading along and all these things you've done...it's not like you."

Crap, Jim. "I just got some advice about how to make Rory want me again. And the article just kind of accidentally happened. I pitched a pretty different idea to my editor and she wanted it to be sexier."

"Who the heck gave you the advice to be more risqué instead of being yourself? That's terrible advice."

"Just another friend."

"Well don't listen to them anymore. They're the worst."

I couldn't help but laugh. It was pretty funny that she was making fun of her own husband. I sighed. "What do you think I should do?"

"Maybe you should just tell him about it. Laugh it off early. It's not a big deal."

"But we only just started dating, or whatever it is we're doing. We haven't even had that conversation yet."

"I think you should probably tell him. Especially if it's bothering you this much. When you hold things back you always act really weird."

I laughed. "Yeah, just when I hold things back."

She smiled and stood up. "I actually have to finish getting ready to go. I'm meeting Jim at that new Thai place downtown for dinner. And I'm already running late. Do I look okay?"

I hadn't even noticed how dressed up she was. More guilt was added to the pit already forming in my stomach. "You look amazing, Emily. What's the special occasion?"

Emily bit her lip. "Well...we actually are celebrating tonight."

"Right, I got that. But what are you celebrating?" Their anniversary wasn't for another couple months.

Emily smiled. "No one but Jim knows yet, and I'm not supposed to tell anyone else for a while, but I can't even stand it. I'm pregnant!"

"What?! Oh my God, Emily!" I stood up and hugged her. *Pregnant?* How could she be pregnant? I thought about Rory's housewarming party and the other day when I had come over and we had wine with lunch. *No.* She only had water at the party. And she had poured herself a glass of wine the other day, but she had never drank any of it. It had just sat there on the table. How could I have not noticed that? I suddenly felt like a terrible friend. I was always so concerned with my own problems that I didn't even realize all the signs pointing to my best friend being pregnant. "I'm so happy for you guys. You and Jim are going to be the most amazing parents."

Emily laughed. "I'm so excited. I can't even stop smiling. That's probably part of the reason why I looked like a murderous psychopath earlier. Or maybe I just have an evil monster baby that's taking over my mind."

"You don't. Stop it. You look amazing." I let go of her embrace. "You don't even look pregnant at all."

"I'd hope not, I'm barely a few weeks along."

"Geez, I can't even believe it. I'm so happy for you. Why didn't you tell me you were going to start trying?"

"I just...you were busy with everything with finding a new roommate. And then all the issues with Rory..." her voice trailed off.

She felt sorry for me. Here she was, married and pregnant with her first child. She already had everything I had ever wanted. And I just kept losing roommate after roommate as everyone around me got engaged and married. But never me. I had thought all my closest friends getting married was hard. Watching them all have babies suddenly seemed a lot harder. I was falling further and further behind. And after I tell Rory about the articles I had written about him, I'd be back to square one again. The thought of losing him actually made my heart hurt. And not only would I lose the guy I was in love with, he'd probably move out and I'd need to find another roommate on top of my heartbreak. I wanted to be happy for Emily. I so badly wanted to be happy. But I was jealous. I was jealous of my best friend for being pregnant. *What is wrong with me?* I shook the thought away. *Stop being so dramatic. Be happy for her.*

"I'm so happy for you," I said with as much enthusiasm as I could muster.

"Thanks, Keira." She hugged me again. "But I seriously have to finish getting ready. Jim hates when I'm late. And this is probably the last time I'm going to look this good for a while." Emily laughed and pulled away.

"Okay, okay. I'm going. Congratulations, Emily."

***

It was hard to separate my feelings for Rory from the fact that I was falling behind all my friends. I suddenly felt old and desperate. *Do I just think I'm in love with him because I so badly want to be in love?* I shook my head. I didn't think so. I really hadn't felt this way with anyone else before. But what did I really even know about him?

I stood up and started pacing back and forth in my room. I had to tell him about the articles. Thinking about how I felt was just going to make it harder when he said he no longer wanted anything do with me. *How I felt. Oh my God!*

I ran to my computer and opened up my email thread with Judy. I scrolled through the emails until I came across the one she had deemed boring and unsexy. And there it was. Everything that I had wanted to say to Rory but couldn't. It was more now. Because I wasn't just falling for him anymore. I had already fallen...toppled down the stairs head first for this boy. And this explained all of that. The piece that got rejected. I quickly printed it out, slipped it in an envelope, and wrote Rory on the front of it.

No matter how much closer we got, I was still awkward around him. He still made me nervous every time I saw him. I wasn't sure if those butterflies would ever go away. I sighed and sat down on my bed. Somehow letting him know what I wanted to write made the whole situation seem better. Even if the original words were full of confessions about falling for him. I'd feel so much better after he knew the truth. And if he didn't care, really didn't care, and forgave me right away...he really could be the one. He was funny, and smart, and sexy. God was he sexy.

I heard the front door open and close. *This is it.* I didn't want it to wait until morning. I wanted to do it right now. And then do him. *Oh please God don't let this morning be the last time he looks at me like that.* I glanced in the mirror. *You can do this.* Everyone did stupid shit. Writing about him was a mistake. And I was done. The segment was done. *People don't usually do shit this stupid.*

I gripped the envelope in my hand and left my room. Rory wasn't in the kitchen. I turned the corner and screamed. There were two people making out on my couch.

"Oh, Keira, shit." Connor stood up.

"Oh my God, it's just you. Connor, you almost gave me a heart attack." I took a deep breath to calm down. But then I realized that I shouldn't have to. He shouldn't just keep showing up like this. "What are you doing here?"

Connor laughed. "I am so, so sorry. I didn't realize that you'd be home." He scratched the back of his neck. "You remember Julie."

I had been too scared to even realize that my friend from college was the one he was making out with.

"Oh, geez, Julie. Hi, it's been forever."

"Hi, Keira. I'm sorry, Connor said no one would be here. We may have had a little bit too much to drink. And..."

"And decided to bang on my couch?"

"Rory's couch," Connor said. He looked embarrassed. "And we were only kissing."

"I'm really sorry to break this up, but I'm going to need that key back Connor. All you've been using it for is scaring me to death."

"I really am sorry, Keira. I wouldn't have come if I thought you were going to be here."

"Why do you keep saying that? Of course I was going to be here. It's my apartment, not yours." I was so full of emotions tonight. I just felt like exploding. I was jealous of Emily, yet so happy for her. And I was worried about what Rory was going to say to me when we talked. And my heart hurt already. Because most of all I was full of love. And I was terrified of losing that feeling. Everything was just too much for me to handle. I couldn't deal with Connor right now.

He just stared at me.

"Seriously, why did you think I wouldn't be here?"

"I don't know..."

"Connor." Something was wrong. He looked so guilty. What was he hiding from me? "Connor, tell me!"

"Rory said he was going on a date tonight." Connor's voice was soft. "I just figured he meant with you."

I looked down at the envelope in my hands. *Of course.* His plans were with another girl. *The next girl.* The one he'd tell Jackson about first. I had tried to play with a player and failed miserably. Instead of making him change his ways, I had fallen in love with him. And he was probably sleeping with someone else right now.

"Keep the key, Connor," I said. I walked over to the front door and opened it. "I'm not going to be needing it anymore."

"Keira?"

I walked out of the apartment.

"Keira, wait!"

I slammed the door behind me.

PART 3

CHAPTER 28

I looked down at the envelope that was still clutched in my hand and slowly opened it. It was dated at the top, two days before my articles about Rory had started being published in the paper. I began reading what I had felt then.

I wanted to learn how to play with a player. I came up with the idea to write about my experience, with all the juicy details, so that every woman out there could do the same. This new norm of one night stands is completely horrendous and unacceptable. What happened to gentleman callers and flowers? We all want more. And I wanted to fix it. But I'm not sure I'm the right person for the job anymore. Because I'm falling for the guy I thought I could play.

A few weeks ago, I put an ad in the paper looking for a new roommate. That's when Rory showed up. Rory is the kind of guy that you crush on from a distance but have never actually talked to. You know, the one with the perfect amount of scruff on his perfect face, with abs that you only see on movie stars, and a smile that makes your knees weak. Trust me, I've tripped over my own feet quite a few times around him.

But since he was my roommate, we had to talk. Which may have been worse than admiring him from a distance because I'm so awkward when I have a crush. I ramble and say stupid stuff I don't mean. Somehow we agreed to just be friends in this weird, twisted roommate pact, which I actually wanted nothing to do with. So I started acting even more awkward. Listening to his bed squeaking with different women screaming his name every night made me physically sick. I couldn't handle it. I completely hated that he was a player. Because I wanted him to want me, and only me.

But I knew that was impossible. He barely even noticed me. So my brilliant idea? I asked him for advice on how to have a one night stand. And then I pathetically followed his advice and used it on him. Never in a million years would I normally do something like that. I've only ever had sex with my boyfriends. With Rory though, I'd take what I could get. So I experienced my first one night stand. Despite the label, it wasn't a one night stand to me. A better label probably would have been "best sex of my life" or "best night of my life". I was completely and utterly hooked. All I wanted was more. And now all I can think about is more. So I failed my assignment. I can't play with a player because I've been completely played.

I'm falling for a guy who just wants to be my friend. So I have to listen to his bed squeak and other women scream his name. I have to sit next to him on the couch and pretend everything is fine. And I have to watch the guy I'm falling for eventually fall for someone else.

The words blurred in front of me. Judy had rejected the article, which definitely made sense. It didn't read like a proper editorial piece at all. The words were just my heart and soul on paper. And it was incredibly painful to read, because I wasn't falling for Rory anymore. I had fallen. I loved him and he was currently fucking some other girl. Writing the articles had helped me cope a little the past week, but now that they were done, all I felt was pain. Rory really was the type of guy you admired from a distance. I should have never let him move in with me.

But that would have been worse. Even just getting to be with him a few times was better than never. Because now that I knew he would never feel the same way as me, I realized how final never really was. I crumbled up the paper, tossed it on the table, and looked down at my bowl of ice cream. It had completely melted into dark brown goo.

That's how I felt, like a melted, destroyed version of myself. I wanted to be mad at Rory, but I couldn't be. He had warned me that he wasn't what I wanted. He tried to keep me away with that pact. But I just kept pressing him. It was my fault. Not his. I was just mad at myself for falling for someone who would never love me back. I had probably chosen the most emotionally unavailable guy in the whole freaking city.

"I thought I might find you here."

I looked up at Connor. I wasn't sure when it had happened, but somehow he had become one of my closest friends. Just seeing him made the tears start to stream down my cheeks again. "Connor," I said between sobs. I stood up and wrapped my arms around him, pressing my cheek into his chest.

"I'm so sorry, Keira." He hugged me back.

I felt safe in his arms. Connor was so sweet. He had tried so hard to help me with Rory. But of course it didn't work. Because Rory was Rory and I was just me. I could feel Connor's shirt getting damp from my tears.

"I might have misunderstood what he said, you know. Maybe he didn't say date," Connor said.

"Don't, Connor. Please don't defend him. I know he's your friend, but if that's what you're here to do, then please just leave." I pushed on his chest so he'd release me from his hug as I wiped away my tears.

"That's not why I'm here, Keira." His expression was pained.

I didn't know what to say. I wiped my eyes with the back of my hand.

"I was worried about you." His words hung in the air. He had left his date to track me down. That was probably the sweetest thing a guy had ever done for me.

"I'm sorry that I ruined your date."

"I don't care about that."

Our eyes locked together. "Connor, I'm really glad that I got to meet you."

"You're acting like you're not going to be seeing me anymore." He gave me a small smile.

I sighed and sat down. "I'm going to move out."

He sat down across from me. "It's your apartment, Keira."

"I can't live there anymore." Rory only wanted sex from me. And I couldn't wait around hoping he'd change his mind. It hurt too much to think about him on other dates. And now everywhere I looked in the apartment would remind me of him. I bit my lip. I didn't want to start crying again.

"I'm sorry that I tried helping you make things happen with him. I should have known he'd screw it up."

I laughed. "He didn't screw anything up. He told me all he wanted was a one night stand. And when it became more than that, we never talked about what we were. There's no reason why he shouldn't be out screwing someone else right now."

"There is a reason. You."

I could feel my tears welling in my eyes again. "Me? That doesn't seem to be enough, does it? I'm never enough for anyone." I thought about my past three boyfriends breaking up with me. No one ever wanted me back.

"For the record, I would never do that to you." He reached out and put his hand on top of mine. "You deserve better."

"Better than your best friend?"

"I love him to death, but he's clearly an asshole."

I laughed.

Connor rubbed his thumb along my palm.

Suddenly the reason why Connor had run after me was apparent. And it hurt me that I was about to hurt him. "I'm in love with Rory," I whispered.

Connor immediately removed his hand. "What?"

"I am." I shook my head. "I was. I thought I was?" I took a deep breath. "I am. But it doesn't matter now." I put my hands in my lap.

Connor looked like he was in pain again as he searched my face. "I didn't realize. Honestly, I was still hoping I had a chance." He gave me a small smile.

"Maybe you can call me in a few months." I wanted to believe that I'd be over Rory by then. I wasn't sure I'd ever be, though.

He sighed and ran his hand through his hair. "I really want to take you up on that offer. And I hope I don't look back on this and realize it was the biggest mistake of my life. Because I think you're absolutely amazing. You're beautiful and funny and smart. And you get along with my friends. A little too well." He smiled. "But I think you should give Rory one more chance."

"It's not that I'm not willing to give him another chance. It's that I know he doesn't want to be with me. He's made that perfectly clear. Over and over again. So what's the point?"

"You know, I never actually got to cash in on that favor you owe me."

"Are you sure you don't want me to just sleep with you?"

He laughed. "Yeah, I'd certainly like that more. But I'm going to ask you to give my best friend the benefit of the doubt. Like I said, maybe I misunderstood what Rory said he was doing tonight. Besides, aren't you two going to a wedding tomorrow?"

"We were supposed to."

"So go. Weddings are romantic. Just give him one last chance to make the right choice."

"I'm not sure I'm what he wants."

"You are. I know him better than anyone. He's been screwing around waiting for someone like you."

"I don't understand why you keep trying to help me."

"Because you're my friend and so is Rory. I want you to both be happy."

"You're the sweetest guy..."

"Yeah, don't say anything else. Because you'll make me change my mind about the favor you owe me. And I don't think the owners of this place would be happy when I started fucking you on this table."

I swallowed hard.

"I see that I've still got it." He winked at me. "Let me walk you home." He lifted up the crumpled up letter to Rory. "What is this?"

I had completely ruined it with tear stains. I'd have to print out another one anyway. If we ever even got to that discussion. Right now I just needed to see how our date went without any extra problems. "I don't need it anymore. It's just trash."

"Okay." Connor grabbed the crumpled up paper, the envelope, and my melted ice cream and walked over to the trash can.

He put his arm around my shoulders as he walked me home.

CHAPTER 29

I had avoided Rory all morning and afternoon. I wasn't sure when he had come home, but no screams of pleasure had woken me up. So I was hoping that meant he hadn't actually been on a date. I didn't realize how much being in love was going to hurt. In the movies it always looked so wonderful. But my chest hurt. And I felt anxious. And I was so nervous about going to the wedding with him. It was like we had just met all over again.

I looked through the dresses in my closet. There were five bridesmaid dresses in it, all equally hideous, and all taking up a ridiculous amount of room. I wasn't sure why I had kept all of them. For a while I thought maybe it was because I wanted to remember how fun the weddings were. I was usually sentimental. But that wasn't it. The weddings all sucked. I was happy for my friends, but their weddings had just ended up with me getting drunk and going home alone or making out with one of their distant cousins and never hearing from them again.

I stared at the hideous dresses in the closet. *No.* I held onto all of them because I was terrified that being a bridesmaid was the closest I'd ever get to the altar. I was so pathetic. I pushed them to the side. I needed to look great tonight. Because I needed to hear that he wanted to be with just me. And if he didn't feel the same way I did, I was going to run away and hide in a new apartment all the way across town.

I sighed and pulled out one of my favorite dresses. It wasn't one that fit Rory's criteria of being sexy. But for some reason it was the one I felt like wearing. Somehow I had lost a little bit of myself ever since Rory had moved in. Just because he made me feel butterflies in my stomach and could make me want him with just a smile didn't necessarily mean he was my forever. I barely even knew anything about him. The idea of not being with him made me feel sick to my stomach, though.

The dress was a red silky material. It was the dress I had bought for my very first date back in college. I sat down on the edge of the bed. *Justin.* I had said yes right away when he had asked me out. I was such a nerd in high school, and I jumped at the chance to have a boyfriend. But he always had better things to do than hang out with me. And then there was Mike, who I wanted to date in order to get over my first heartache. He was probably even worse than Justin. We weren't compatible at all. I just didn't like feeling alone. My last boyfriend, David, I had met in Philly. He was charming and seemed so much more mature than the boys I dated in college. I thought he could be the one. But he thought I had gotten too serious too fast. He wasn't ready for commitment. But he was ready to propose to the girl he started dating right after me. They hadn't even known each other for a year. And David had broken up with me over the phone right before our one year anniversary dinner. I had to hand it to David. He had been right. I didn't love him. I just loved the idea of being in love.

I was so sick of making mistakes. And I was even more sick of having men make me feel worthless. The way Rory looked at me didn't make me feel that way. He was definitely the sweetest guy I had ever dated. I sighed. But we weren't really even dating. I so badly wanted that to change.

I ran my fingers along the silky dress. It was definitely appropriate for a wedding. The hem landed right above my knees, although there was a slit up the side. The top wasn't low cut but somehow still accentuated my breasts. It was super tight and still made me feel sexy even though it was modest. I applied my makeup and finished with red lipstick. I smacked my lips together and looked in the mirror.

I was so glad that Connor had convinced me not to run away. I didn't want to hide from how I was feeling right now. Yesterday before I had discovered Rory was on a date, I had been so happy, despite the weight of telling him about the newspaper articles. And I didn't want to miss out on that feeling just because I didn't have the guts to tell Rory how I felt yet.

There was a knock on my bedroom door. "Keira?"

Even his voice gave me that now familiar pull in my stomach. I slipped on a pair of black heels before opening my door.

"Wow, you look amazing." He leaned forward and placed a soft kiss against my lips.

He had never kissed me like that before. There was something gentle and loving about it. When he pulled away I felt like I could see it in his eyes. He was looking at me like he had missed me. All those doubts from last night seemed so ridiculous when he was right in front of me.

He held up a tie. "Do you know how to tie this?" Just seeing him holding a tie reminded me of being blindfolded with one in his bedroom. He smiled at me, as if he could tell what I was thinking. "I've been thinking a lot about all the ways you might want to be punished. It should probably involve this, don't you think?" He handed me the tie.

I swallowed hard and took the tie from him. "I think you know what I like better than I do." I slipped the tie under the collar of his white shirt. He was wearing a dark gray suit and I had never seen him look more handsome. His suit was fitted and seemed to show off all his lean muscles. I pulled the end of the tie through the knot I had made and tightened it. His eyes locked with mine as I adjusted his tie.

He took a step forward, pressing my back against the doorframe. "Are you sure you don't want to just stay here?"

"As tempting as that is, I already told them we were coming."

He pretended to pout.

"Come on, Rory," I grabbed his tie and lightly pulled it, directing him to the door. "It's going to be fun."

"It'll be fun to dance with you all night." He slapped my ass.

"Rory!" I laughed. "You're going to try to embarrass me tonight, aren't you?" We stepped onto the elevator.

"I do like making you blush. But no, I'll be on my best behavior." He raised his eyebrow at me.

"You don't have to quite be on your best behavior." I pinched his ass.

He laughed and grabbed my hand as we walked along the sidewalk in search of a taxi. I looked down at our intertwined hands. He wouldn't be holding my hand if he didn't like me. This was the first time we were going on an actual date outside of our apartment. I couldn't help but wonder when the last time he had gone on a real date was. Was it his girlfriend from college? Or was it with someone last night? I didn't want to think about last night, but something seemed different about him today. If he had been on a date, it must have been an awful one, because he was acting like he was as smitten with me as I was with him.

Rory hailed down a taxi and opened up the door for me. He was being such a gentleman. Did a sweet, nice guy exist somewhere under his player façade? I didn't need to ask myself that question. I knew it did. Because I had witnessed him being sweet and nice. He was all those things on top of being sexy, and that was why I had completely fallen.

He sat down next to me and wrapped his arm around my shoulders. "So, what is your friend's name?"

"Becca. And the lucky guy is Jeremy."

"How do you two know each other?"

"We were in a journalism club together in college."

"You really are a huge nerd, aren't you?" He smiled at me.

I shrugged. "I was worried about getting a job after graduating. Journalism club was just something else I could add to my résumé."

"Isn't actual experience better than some club?"

"Yeah, but how was I supposed to get my first job? That's the problem. Everyone wants someone with experience, so it's hard to land your first gig. I was worried. Weren't you? Culinary arts is really competitive, isn't it?"

"It is." He shifted slightly in his seat, but kept his arm around me. "I never actually finished, though."

"Wait, you didn't graduate?" I never would have guessed that. Everything that he had made for me was delicious and he had a really good job.

"Is that a deal breaker for you or something?" His thumb had dipped below one of the straps of my dress. There was something comforting about the way he always wanted his hands on me.

"No, not at all. I was just surprised. Why didn't you finish?"

"I just figured that actual experience was better than being critiqued over some dish I had no desire to ever make again in my life."

"So you just quit? How close were you to being done?"

"I finished two out of four years."

Two years. That was how long he had dated his last girlfriend. That couldn't be a coincidence. "What do you want to do?"

He looked back at me and traced his fingers along the back of my dress. "You know what I want to do," he said in a low voice.

"No, Rory," I laughed. "I mean what do you want to do in the future? Like five years from now what do you want to have accomplished?"

"I don't really like thinking that way. I just want to be happy. And thinking about the future all the time isn't the way to get there." He turned and looked out the window.

The way to get there. So he's not happy now? I wanted to be the one to make him happy. "So what did you do after you dropped out?"

"After crashing in Connor's dorm and driving him crazy, I went to Italy and got a job at this amazing restaurant. I learned way more in those few months than I did in two years at Penn University."

"If you liked it so much, what made you come back to Philly?"

"I loved Italy, but I was homesick. It was more running away from something than actually wanting to be there."

"Your ex?" He was even more like me than I realized. I always wanted to run away from problems too. That was why I had told Connor I was moving out last night. I couldn't help but think that it was bad that we were both flight risks. But being with him was a risk I was more than willing to take.

"Yeah." He scratched the back of his neck. "So what about you, Keira? What's your master plan for five years down the road?"

I'd like to be with you. "Being happy seems like a pretty good goal. That's what I want too." *Give me a chance to make you happy.* I leaned against his shoulder and was happy when he didn't flinch.

CHAPTER 30

I grabbed another glass of wine off one of the trays that waiters were carrying around.

"What do you usually do at weddings when you don't have a date?" Rory was smiling at me.

"Honestly? I usually drink too much and try to make out with someone in a closet." I lowered my glass of wine.

He laughed. "Well, I guess it's good I came with you then. Because I wouldn't mind making out with you in a closet at all." He wrapped his arm behind me and let his hand rest on my hip. "By all means, keep drinking."

"You don't have to get me drunk if you want to kiss me, Rory."

"But what if I want to do more than kiss you?"

I could feel my face flushing. I had never done anything like that before in public. But for some reason the idea excited me.

"From the look on your face, you probably don't need to be drunk for that either." Rory glanced behind him. "There's a closet right over there if you're interested."

Holy shit.

"Oh my God, Keira, is that you?!"

I turned my head to see another girl from my journalism club. "Hi, Ella. Wow, it's been so long." I gave her a quick hug. We had never really been friends. I probably wouldn't have even said anything to her if she hadn't approached me. She always talked too much and tended to annoy me. The only thing I ever wanted to listen to when I was writing was music, not Ella's endless chatter.

"And is this your boyfriend?" Ella stuck her hand out to Rory and gave him a big smile.

Shit don't use that word, Ella! You freaking bitch! I took a deep breath. I was completely on edge tonight. I almost wanted to laugh at my reaction. *Calm down.*

Rory coughed. "We're just friends," he said and stuck out his hand.

"Oh, sorry. You just..." she let her voice trail off and let go of his hand. "It was nice seeing you, Keira." She quickly walked away.

My reaction hadn't been that inappropriate. That was completely awkward. But I didn't want to dwell on it. Rory and I still hadn't had that conversation. I might have said the same thing if one of his friends had asked. It definitely wasn't worth ruining our night over. Besides, I had never seen Ella shut up so quickly. It was probably good that Rory had acted weird.

Rory put his hands in his pockets instead of putting his arm back around me.

Damn it. "Do you want to go find our seats?" I asked. The cocktail hour was winding down and the doors had been opened to the banquet hall where the reception was being held.

"Is that a rain check on the closet?"

"I'll probably need another drink before that."

"Then let's go find our seats and get you another drink." He put his hand on the small of my back and escorted me over toward the reception room.

I wanted to sigh with relief. His hand on my back made me feel like we were back to where we had been before Ella had almost ruined everything.

Rory pulled my chair out for me and sat down beside me. "So, are you going to know any of the other people at this table?"

"I'm not sure. I wasn't super good friends with Becca. We were in that club together but never really hung out beyond that. But since I'm a huge nerd...we saw each other a lot."

Rory laughed. "I like that you're a nerd." He put his arm behind me on the chair and scooted a little closer to me. "How many weddings have you been in?"

"Five. I was a bridesmaid four times and I was Emily's maid of honor. What about you?"

"Just one. I was Connor's best man."

"How long have you two known each other?"

"Since fourth grade."

"That's adorable."

Rory laughed. "I'm not adorable."

"I hate to break it to you, but you're super adorable."

He leaned toward me. "I thought you said I was super sexy?" he whispered in my ear. "I prefer that over super adorable."

I turned toward him. Our faces were only a few inches apart and I could smell the aroma of cinnamon wafting off of him. "I think you're super sexy and super adorable. I like that you're both." The way he was looking at me made it hard to breathe.

"I'm pretty sure the things I've done to you aren't adorable."

"No. But the things you do with your wolf pack are. You guys are quite adorable."

Rory laughed. "Is that what you call us? I like that so much better than what Jackson calls us...a threesome of big strong men."

I couldn't help but laugh. "I'm so sorry, but I have to ask. Is Jackson gay?"

"What? No."

"Are you sure? Because sometimes he says...well, the gayest things."

It was Rory's turn to laugh. "Geez, he really does, doesn't he? But no, he's just like metrosexual or something. Trust me, he likes women."

"Okay," I said skeptically.

"Keira, just because he doesn't have a crush on you like the other members of the wolf pack doesn't mean he's gay." He gave me one of his smiles that made my knees weak.

I swallowed hard. *Rory has a crush on me? Rory has a crush on me!* That was all I needed to hear. I put my hand on his knee. "Well, thank you for making me an honorary member of your weird wolf pack metrosexual group." I looked down at his lap.

"I should really be thanking you for that."

"Have there been any other honorary members of your group?" I kept my hand on his knee. I wasn't sure why I wanted to know the answer to that. I was basically asking him if any girl that had sucked his cock had ever gotten along with his friends before.

"Really just Connor's ex wife."

I tried not to sigh out loud. I was the only girl that he liked that had gotten to know his friends. For some reason that made me feel better. It also meant that his ex girlfriend hadn't gotten along well with his friends. I wondered if that had something to do with their break up. "What was Connor's ex wife like?"

"She used to be really cool. I was always third wheeling with them, ever since high school. Cindy was one of my best friends too. I still don't get what happened. One day she just started being really cold. Connor put up with it for as long as he could. I know he wanted to make it work." Rory shrugged.

"That's sad."

"I think you're a better honorary member anyway. But maybe that's just because you're mine."

Mine? Is that how he thinks of me? I so badly wanted to be his. Maybe I already was. I didn't need him to say anything else. That was all the commitment I needed. Him calling me his and admitting he had a crush on me was the best feeling in the world.

"Well, you'll be happy to know that you're my favorite member of the group," I said.

"You're becoming my favorite too."

I just stared into his hazel eyes. That was it. He liked me just as much as I liked him.

"I'm sorry, I don't mean to interrupt you guys."

We both turned to the girl next to Rory. She was sitting next to a guy that looked like he'd rather be anywhere else in the world. *Awkward.*

"But you two are like the cutest couple here," the girl said. "Besides for Becca and Jeremy, of course. How long have you two been dating?"

Rory pulled his arm off my back, picked up his wine glass, and took a big sip.

I wanted to cut in and tell her we weren't official or anything, but I was curious to see what Rory would say. He had just said such wonderful things to me. Maybe his response would be different this time.

"Oh, no," Rory said and laughed awkwardly. "We're actually..."

"Aw, are you engaged? Congratulations!" the girl said.

What the fuck is everyone's problem here?

Rory coughed and spit his wine back into the glass. "Oh, God no." He set his glass back down on the table. "We're not even dating."

The girl made a strange face and I looked down at my lap. Rory wasn't just acting like he was scared of commitment. The tone he was responding to people in made it seem like I was the problem. As if he just couldn't possibly see a future with *me*. He almost sounded repulsed every time someone asked if we were a couple. And even if that wasn't what he meant, it still embarrassed me every time he said it.

I didn't even know that girl. It would have been cute and funny to just pretend we had been dating for years. What was Rory's problem?

"Now, for the first time ever, Mister and Misses Rogers!" said the DJ into his microphone.

I stood up and clapped as my friend and her new husband walked into the room. And I felt like crying. The first few weddings I had gone to after college were okay. They were actually fun. But four years later, it wasn't fun anymore. I was falling so far behind. And Emily was having a baby. Her kid would be like ten before I had my first one. We had always talked about our children being best friends too. I took a deep breath.

"How about we go find that closet," Rory said as he wrapped his arms around me.

He seemed to be thinking along the same lines I was. Not about falling behind, but about how he hated weddings. Although he probably hated them because he hated commitment and he hated me. I rolled my eyes at myself. I was being dramatic. Rory didn't hate me. But I still didn't want to give in to him. Despite our conversation earlier, I was still worried that sex was all he wanted from me. Maybe sleeping with him so soon had been a mistake.

He pushed my hair to the side and kissed the back of my neck, sending chills down my spine. I may have slept with him too soon, but I definitely didn't regret it.

I tilted my head back. "They're about to serve dinner. And I'm starving." I removed his hands from me and sat back down. I hated that this was somehow still a game between us. All I wanted to do was tell him how I felt. But if strangers asking if we were dating freaked him out, I didn't want to know how he'd react to me telling him that I was in love with him.

CHAPTER 31

The music started before I had even finished my overcooked dinner. I turned to Rory. "Everything you've cooked for me has been so much better than this."

He smiled at me. "It's harder to cook in large quantities. Everything I've cooked for you was made specifically for you." His thumb ran along the back of my neck.

"Well, you could totally cook for a place like this." I still wanted him to confess his ambitions to me. Maybe he just needed a little push.

"I really like my job right now. It gives me lots of free time."

The way he was staring at me made me blush.

He stood up and put his hand out for me. "Let's dance."

A slow song had just started. I put my hand in his and let him lead me toward the dance floor. He grabbed my waist and pulled me close.

The anger I had felt earlier seemed to completely disappear when he looked down at me. I wanted him to stare at me like this forever. Like I was the only girl he saw in the entire room. Like I was the only thing in the world that mattered to him. I clasped my hands behind his neck and smiled at him. I so badly wanted to tell him how I really felt. "I'm glad you came tonight," I said instead.

The scruff along his jaw line brushed against my cheek as he brought his lips to my ear. "Keira, you haven't made me cum tonight. I think it's about time we changed that." His hands drifted to my ass.

I laughed and moved his hands back to my waist. "You seem awfully eager." My voice didn't hide my own eagerness at all. I wanted him so badly.

"Well, I'm pretty sure I was promised that I'd get to fuck you in a closet if I agreed to be your plus one."

I laughed again. "You agreed to come with me two days ago. I only just told you that I've made out with guys at weddings a few hours ago."

"Hmm. I remember it differently."

The music changed to a faster paced song, but Rory kept his body pressed against mine. I wouldn't be able to resist him much longer.

"Keira!"

Becca and Jeremy had just walked over to us.

"Congratulations, Becca!" I said and gave her a hug. "You look so beautiful. That dress is gorgeous."

"Thank you! You remember Jeremy," Becca said and gestured to her new husband.

"Of course. It's great to see you again. Congratulations." I shook Jeremy's hand.

"And is this your boyfriend?" Becca asked. "It's nice to meet you." She put her hand out for Rory to shake.

Rory laughed. "Everyone at this wedding really likes to jump to crazy conclusions. We're really just roommates."

What the hell? Just roommates? It felt like he had slapped me. I could feel myself gaping at him. I turned back to Becca. "Congratulations again." My voice caught slightly.

"I'm so happy for you guys." As I hugged Becca, I could feel the tears welling in my eyes. "If you'll excuse me." I quickly walked off the dance floor and past the tables full of happy couples. I felt so stupid. I walked out into the foyer where the cocktail hour had been. *Where is the bathroom in this stupid place anyway?* I just needed some time to regroup. Or a place to climb out a window and run away.

"Keira!" Rory had followed me out of the reception hall. When he reached me he was smiling.

Why the hell was he smiling? Couldn't he tell that he had been hurting my feelings all night? *Just roommates?* I wanted to punch him.

"Your friends are all so ridiculous."

"Ridiculous? You're my date to a wedding. Why is them assuming we're dating so ludicrous? Is it really that horrible for people to think I'm your girlfriend?"

He laughed. "It's really no one else's business what we are or aren't."

"It's not funny, Rory. Every time someone asked if we were together you made it seem like you didn't like me at all. Am I really that repulsive?"

"You know I don't think that. You're..."

"I'm what, Rory?" I asked, cutting him off. I hated the way my voice cracked. And I hated the way he was staring at me. It was like somehow I had hurt him instead of the other way around.

"You're..."

"What? Your friend? Oh no, wait, don't let me jump to any crazy conclusions." I poked him in the center of his chest. "You're just my roommate, right?" *Fuck you.*

He gave me a pleading look.

"Exactly. We're just roommates. Goodnight, Rory." I stormed off toward the exit. But before I could reach the door, he grabbed my wrist.

"All I was going to say was that you're overreacting."

"Seriously? Rory, we're sleeping together and all you see me as is your roommate. Don't you see how that kills me? You know that I like you. Obviously I like you. I don't think I could have made it any more clear."

He ran his hand through his hair. "This is all I know. I told you that I wasn't what you wanted. I didn't want you to get hurt. But you didn't listen to me."

"Then why did you say you wanted more? I'm like everyone else in there." I pointed to the reception hall. "I thought more meant more than just sex."

"It does." He let go of my wrist and ran his hand through his hair again. "I agreed to come to this wedding with you, didn't I?"

"Well thanks for the favor, Rory. I really appreciate you coming here and insulting me all night."

"God, you're driving me crazy."

"I'm driving *you* crazy? Look, stay. Hook up with some random girl. I'm going home."

"I don't want to hook up with anyone else, Keira."

"Really? You were just on a date last night, weren't you?" I had been wrong last night. I was so mad at him. I was mad at him for leading me on, when it was clear he never wanted more than just sex.

His eyebrows lowered slightly. "How the hell do you know that?"

"So you're not even going to pretend to deny it?" *What an asshole.*

"What, did Connor tell you or something?"

"Fuck you, Rory."

He grabbed my wrist again before I could turn away. "Yes, I was on a date, okay? I agreed to go before we started whatever the hell this is. And you'll be happy to know that I had a horrible time. It was the fucking worst."

"What, do you want me to feel sorry for you or something? Fine. I'm sorry that she didn't put out on the first date. I'm sorry she wasn't slutty enough for you. I know how much you like easy women. Better luck next time, roomie."

"Would you just let me finish?!"

"I don't want to hear what you have to say. I can't do this anymore." I tried to walk away from him again.

"Damn it, Keira." He pushed my back against the wall so I couldn't move. "The date sucked because I couldn't stop thinking about you."

For the first time since we had come out here, I locked eyes with him. The only sound in the room seemed to be my heart pounding out of my chest. He seemed just as upset about this fight as I was. I didn't like seeing him hurting. I loved him more than I even realized. "I can't stop thinking about you either," I said breathlessly. I grabbed both sides of Rory's face and kissed him.

He pressed my body against the wall and deepened the kiss. I didn't care that we were in public. All I wanted was more of him. But he pulled away far too soon.

"I know that we're more than just roommates, Keira."

"So...friends?" I smiled at him.

"Come with me."

I'd follow him anywhere. I slipped my hand into his and followed him to the closet we had found earlier.

He pulled me inside and quickly closed the door. All I saw was a mop and a bucket before darkness engulfed us. Instead of finding the light, Rory pressed my back against the door. "Let me show you how I feel in the best way that I know how." He kissed me again, slower and more passionately than before.

I liked his version of what more was.

He grabbed my ass and lifted my legs around him. He walked over to a table in the corner and gently placed me on the edge. "You don't realize how hard it's been for me, living with you." He moved his lips to my neck.

"I do." I moaned when he lightly nipped my earlobe.

"All the teasing. You've been torturing me." He kissed my shoulder and slowly left a trail of kisses down my arm. He placed a kiss on my palm and then moved to my other shoulder. "I find everything about you irresistible."

Each kiss down my arm made me want him more and more. My whole body seemed to shiver when he kissed my opposite palm.

"So if you want more, I'll give you more." He kissed the inside of my ankle.

With each kiss he placed up my leg, I felt the familiar pull in my stomach that only he could seem to give me. That desire so deep down that it was all I could focus on. God I wanted him. I had never wanted him so badly.

He slowly repeated the process with my other leg, torturing me. He pushed my dress up and kissed the inside of my thigh.

"Rory," I panted.

He stood up and put his hands down on either side of me on the table. "One day I'd like to own my own restaurant. Definitely Italian cuisine. I don't know if that'll be in five years or twenty, but eventually it would be nice. That's what I really want."

I smiled at him, even though he couldn't see it in the dark. "I knew you had dreams."

"And what do you really want, Keira?"

For you to love me back. "I want to write articles that are actually meaningful, instead of fluff pieces. I want to inspire people to change and take action. But I like the idea of working toward happiness, like you said before." I took a deep breath. "You make me happy, Rory."

He didn't say anything for a few seconds. "You make me happy too."

It was like he was confessing that he wanted me to be a part of his future. I grabbed his tie and brought his lips back to mine. He was kissing me like he loved me back. I buried my hands in his hair. I didn't care that there was a wedding going on outside or that we were in a custodial closet. All I cared about was him.

He pushed my dress the rest of the way up my thighs. I lifted up my hips as he hooked his thumbs in the sides of my thong. I could just make out his hazel eyes in the dark. They were the only eyes I ever wanted to look into again.

His fingers traced the insides of my thighs as he slowly pulled my underwear down my legs. "Maybe we should go to a hotel." He kissed me along my clavicle bone. "The smell of bleach isn't very romantic."

"No." My voice sounded so needy. "I want you to fuck me right here."

He pulled the zipper of my dress. "Keira, I'm not going to fuck you."

What is he going to do to me then? The straps of my dress fell off my shoulders and his experienced fingers quickly unhooked my bra in the dark.

He pushed something off the table behind me and it clattered to the floor. The smell of fake lemons filled my nose. It smelled like the cleanser I used to mop my floor. His lips on mine brought me back to him. He let one of his hands slide to my breast and he squeezed it as he lowered my back down on the table. His lips wandered from my mouth, down my neck, and onto my other breast. I felt his teeth lightly tug my nipple, and it was as if the sensation was somehow reflected in my groin.

"Rory," I moaned.

"I love when you say my name like that." His fingers brushed against my clit, making my whole body shiver. "And I love how wet you always are for me." The tip of his index finger slipped inside of me, making me moan again.

I wanted more. *No.* I needed more. My hips rose, trying to meet his hand, but instead, his hands fell from me. I was about to protest when I heard the rip of foil. A second later he spread my thighs and brushed his fingers against my clit again.

"Rory," I panted.

He grabbed my ass and pressed the tip of his massive erection against my wetness. "And I love how tight you are." He slowly began to slide his length into me. I wasn't sure what I had been thinking last night. There was no way I could ever quit him. I loved every single inch of him.

He leaned down and kissed me again, soft yet passionate. I reached up to touch his chiseled abs, but he was still wearing his shirt. My fingers fumbled with the buttons until they met his happy trail. I ran my hands along the contours of his six pack as he slowly thrust in and out of me.

I waited for him to move faster as he continued to kiss me, but he kept his slow pace. I loved when he was rough with me. I didn't think there could possibly be something better than him fucking me, pushing me to my limits. But this was better. He was being slow and gentle and intimate. *He's making love to me. Oh my God, he's making love to me!*

I grabbed both sides of his face and deepened our kiss. When he said he wasn't going to fuck me, I hadn't realized what he meant. He loved me back. And it was the best feeling in the whole world. I wanted all of him. I ran my hands down the back of his suit jacket and grabbed his ass. I needed more.

He groaned into my mouth as he thrust himself deep inside of me.

"Yes!"

His hand slid up the side of my thigh and stopped on my hip. "God you're sexy." He leaned back and looked down at me as he began moving his hips faster. "One night of you would never have been enough."

I could feel myself clenching around him. If possible, his words affected me just as much as him inside of me. He tilted his hips, hitting me in that spot that only he could.

Oh God. I turned my head as the sensation of him completely consumed me.

But he grabbed my chin and tilted my face so that I was staring directly into his eyes. "Come for me, Keira."

"Rory!" I moaned as his words pushed me over the edge.

He stared into my eyes as he found his own release.

My heart was racing as I stared up at him. This boy loved me. And I had never felt this way before. Everything was different with Rory. Somehow with him, everything seemed so much more real. I reached up and ran my palm along the scruff on his jaw line. And so perfect.

He leaned forward and placed a soft kiss against my lips.

"I like more."

"Mmm." He slowly pulled out of me.

I didn't like the empty feeling. The smell of lemon scented cleaning supplies suddenly came back to me. We must have spilled a bottle because it smelled even stronger than before. "Every time I mop the floor now I'm going to want you to do that to me."

"I think I can arrange that." He grabbed my hands and pulled me to a seated position. He kept my hands in his as he looked down at me. "I don't like fighting with you."

"I don't like fighting with you either."

"I'm..." his voice trailed off. He ran his thumbs along my palms. "I'm not good at this."

"I'm not good at relationships either. It's one of the many things we have in common."

Rory laughed and then was silent for a moment. "The last thing I want to do is hurt you. I don't like seeing you upset."

"Then don't hurt me."

He leaned forward and ran the tip of his nose down mine. "You really shouldn't be with me."

"I want to be with you." I unwound my fingers from his and grabbed the sides of his face. "Rory, I've wanted to be with you ever since you first stepped into my apartment. Please don't give up on this before we've even started."

"I'm not. I'm just...worried that you want what's out there." He pointed to the door. "I'm not there yet. I'm not even sure if I'll ever want those things."

How had we gone from being un-exclusive to talking about marriage? How did he know that I felt like I was falling behind my friends? What he didn't seem to understand, though, was that I didn't care about any of that when I was with him. I didn't feel the clock ticking when I looked into his eyes. Getting married in one year or ten years didn't matter if he was going to be beside me. I just wanted to be with him.

"Rory, you're exactly what I want." I ran my fingers between his naked torso and his silky tie.

"Okay."

"Okay?"

He turned away from me and looked around for the light switch. When he found it, the sight of him took my breath away. His hair was mussed up in that way that it could only be after sex. He had already zippered up his suit pants and hinged his belt back in place, but his shirt was still unbuttoned. His tie hung loosely around his neck and was pressed against his naked torso. I couldn't help but wonder why men ever wore shirts. Just a tie seemed to work fine.

He smiled at me. "Okay, let's give this thing a shot."

I wanted to clap my hands and yell and dance around the closet. Instead, I slid off the table, walked over to him and wrapped my arms around his neck. "Does that mean if people ask if you're my boyfriend you won't freak out? Maybe I could even say yes?"

"Hmm." His hands slid to the small of my back. "Maybe you should say it a few times so I can get used to it."

"So like...no we're not just roommates, this is my boyfriend, Rory." *My boyfriend, Rory.* I wanted to say it a million times.

"It sounds pretty good actually."

"It does." I smiled up at him.

"We should probably get dressed so we don't spend our first night as boyfriend and girlfriend in jail."

"That would just make a great story."

"Yeah, but I think we could make better use of our first night back home in bed, don't you?" He let go of the small of my back and lightly slapped my ass.

I laughed and turned around to search for my bra. I quickly grabbed it off the table, put it back on, and zipped my dress back in place. I looked around the small closet in search of my thong, but I couldn't seem to find it anywhere.

"Are you looking for this?" Rory pulled my thong out of his pocket and let it dangle from his index finger.

"Thanks." I reached for it, but he pulled his hand away.

"I thought I told you not to wear underwear."

"I didn't realize you meant never again. I thought you meant just that one night."

"I like having easy access to you. So I'm keeping these." He put them back in his pocket.

"Rory, it's part of a lingerie set."

"Maybe you can convince me to give it back to you later." He raised his eyebrow at me. "You're pretty good at convincing me to do things I wouldn't normally do."

I laughed and straightened his tie. "You mean like breaking our roommate pact?"

"That roommate pact was doomed from the start. Especially since neither one of us really wanted it."

"I thought you did want it?"

"I wanted the pact solely because I thought it would make you more comfortable with our living situation. But I always intended to sleep with you." He gave me one of his panty dropping smiles.

"Rory," I said and pushed on his chest.

He grabbed my hands. "And when you kept flirting with me, I knew you wanted me too. It was only a matter of time before you begged me."

"You're the worst!" I said playfully. I already knew he had been stringing me along. That's what he did. He was a player. I had known that from the start. I just never realized how much he wanted me too.

He scratched the back of his neck. "But I never expected to like you this much."

"Thanks, I guess?"

He laughed. "You know what I mean. I'm not used to girls being so down to earth. I like that you can hang out with my friends and talk about sports and play poker. I find that very sexy."

The way he was talking made it seem like he wanted me again. "Well, I find everything you do sexy."

"Then maybe we should go home and do more sexy things to each other. I have a few things in mind." He grabbed my hand and led me out of the closet.

CHAPTER 32

Making love in his bed was even better than making love in a closet. I had thought that my ex-boyfriends had loved me, but now I was certain that they hadn't. Because none of them had made me feel like this before. And if I hadn't written an article about playing Rory, then I'd be the happiest I had ever been.

Instead, I was starring at his beautiful face after he had fallen asleep, worrying about telling him the truth. My last article was coming out in the morning. It was the last step, "Make Him Jealous," which involved going on a fake date. And about how it worked. How Rory said he wanted more. How we had become friends with benefits. I had written it the way my editor wanted me to. But it wasn't true. My original goal of the piece had worked, though. I had gotten a player to stop playing. I had gotten him to break his norms of one night stands and settle down with me. I had tricked him into falling in love with me.

I sat up in his bed. That was the problem. I tricked him into liking me. Maybe he would find the whole thing funny. *God. How would anyone find that funny?* I needed to know more about his ex. I needed to know what went wrong. If it was just betraying his trust then I was completely screwed.

I pulled on one of Rory's t-shirts and tiptoed out of his room. My purse was sitting on the kitchen counter. I grabbed my phone out of it, scrolled through my contact list, and found Connor's name. It wasn't even 8 a.m. I wasn't sure what Connor's normal weekend schedule was like, but I hoped I wouldn't be disturbing his sleep too much. I pressed the call button and drummed my fingers against the counter as it rang.

"Hello?" Connor sounded awake. But he also definitely didn't realize it was me calling.

"Hey, Connor. It's Keira."

"Is everything okay?" He sounded concerned. Like he thought that last night had most likely gone horribly, horribly wrong.

"Yeah, everything's great." I sat down on a stool. I knew what I was about to do was awkward, but I needed to know. "I was actually just calling to ask you a favor."

"What do you need?"

"I was wondering if you could tell me what happened between Rory and his ex?"

Connor was silent for a second. "Shouldn't you just ask him about that?"

"He doesn't seem to want to talk about it." I stopped tapping my fingers against the counter. "Please, Connor, it's important."

"I'll be right over."

"Oh, no, you don't need to come over. We can just talk on the phone."

"I'm already on my way." Connor clicked off.

"Wait, Connor?"

The line was dead. I looked down at my phone. *Weird.* I walked over to my bedroom so I could get changed, but there was a knock on the front door. *What the hell?* I walked over to the door and peered through the peephole. Jackson was standing there.

Shit. I was only wearing one of Rory's t-shirts. Did that matter? Rory had already told him that we were sleeping together. But the t-shirt was kind of see-through.

Jackson knocked on the door again.

Crap. I opened up the door a crack.

Jackson's eyes immediately fell on my legs. "I'm guessing things are going well with Rory?" He smiled at me.

"Mhm. What are you doing here?"

Jackson pushed the door open the rest of the way and walked in. He was holding a fruit tray. "Is Rory still asleep?" he asked, ignoring my question.

I crossed my arms over my chest. "Yeah. It's a little early, Jackson. What are you doing here?" I repeated.

"It's Sunday Brunch Day." He held up the fruit tray. "I brought the fruit."

Of course you did. "I feel like you guys are just making stuff up so you can hang out here as much as possible."

"You two do have the nicest place. But we actually do this every second Sunday of the month. And Rory has to host because he's the chef." Jackson sat down on one of the kitchen stools. "He's super annoying in other people's kitchens. He's always complaining about dull knives and crap like that."

"Okay, but brunch is supposed to be closer to lunch time, isn't it? It's 8 a.m., Jackson."

Jackson shrugged. "We usually make it an all day thing. I mean, we used to all just crash at Rory's the night before. But he was a little busy last night, wasn't he?" Jackson winked at me.

I could feel my face turning red. "Well, I'll be right back. I need to change."

"Don't do it on my behalf. You're fine."

I rolled my eyes at him and began to retreat to my bedroom when there was a second knock on the door. "Do you mind getting that, Jackson?"

"Stranger danger," he said and popped off the lid of the fruit tray.

"I'm sure it's just Connor."

"You never know. Besides, if it is Connor, I'd love to see his reaction to your outfit."

Why was he torturing me on purpose? I sighed. It didn't really matter. Connor had already seen me in just one of Rory's t-shirts before. I walked over to the door and opened it.

"Hey...Keira." His eyes landed on my breasts for a second, but then immediately snapped back to my face. "I brought coffee." He held up the tray of coffee and smiled. "Is Rory up yet?"

"No, he's still sleeping."

Connor peered over my shoulder at Jackson. "Hey, Jackson."

"Hey, Connor."

Connor looked back at me. "Sorry, I rushed over," he whispered. "I thought I could beat Jackson here. Are you sure everything is okay?"

"Yeah, everything's fine. I just..." my voice trailed off when I saw the newspaper tucked under Connor's arm. *Shit, is that The Post?* I couldn't tell from the angle. I looked back up at Connor. "Thanks for bringing coffee. Can I help you with that?"

"Oh, yeah. I didn't know how you liked it. Cream and sugar okay?"

"Yeah, that's perfect."

"Here." Connor picked a cup out of the tray and handed it to me.

"Thanks." *Crap.* I had been hoping he'd hand over everything to me.

Connor walked past me, placed the tray of coffee on the counter, and tossed the newspaper down next to it.

It was The Post. I took a deep breath. It's not like any of them read my articles, though. They had never said anything about them. And they definitely didn't sit around the kitchen reading the newspaper out loud. That would be so weird. But they were weird. *Oh God.* It was probably a brunch reading session.

"Do you still want to talk about what you wanted to talk about?" Connor asked.

"That sounds ominous," Jackson said. He lifted one of the coffees out of the tray. "I'll let you two talk." Jackson winked at me again and walked over to the couch.

"Why does Jackson keep winking at me?"

Connor sat down on one of the stools. "I may have crashed at his place Friday night and confessed to him that I have a crush on you. Maybe." Connor shrugged.

"That's a lot of details for maybe. How did you like Julie?" I wanted him to be happy. He was such a nice guy.

"I actually had a really good time. But I think I probably blew it when I ran after you."

"I'm sure you didn't blow it."

"No, I did. I mean, I seriously just ran after you. I didn't even say anything to her."

"She knows we're friends, Connor. I can explain what happened to her. I can fix it."

"I should have already apologized. I just felt like such an ass."

"You're not an ass. That was the sweetest thing a guy has ever done for me."

Connor looked down at his coffee. "Maybe we should just talk about what you wanted to talk about, Keira. What do you want to know about Rory's ex?" He took a sip of his coffee.

I hated that I always seemed to be hurting him. I sat down on the stool next to his. "What happened between them? And what was she like? Anything you can tell me, really."

Connor looked back up at me. "She was like the exact opposite of you. I really don't even know why Rory liked her. Probably cause she was a freaking ten." I must have made a face, because Connor quickly said, "Not that you aren't, Keira. That's not what I meant at all. You know I think you're an eleven." He looked back down at his coffee cup.

"What do you mean by the complete opposite of me?"

"Super high maintenance. She was just always a bitch. And she didn't like when Rory hung out with his friends instead of her. She really hated Jackson and me. We didn't see him that much when they dated. And when we did get to hang out, he was always texting her. I'd never seen him like that. He was completely whipped. It was so bizarre."

I couldn't imagine Rory being whipped. He was always so in control. Especially in the bedroom. I could feel myself blushing. Maybe that was why. Maybe he resented her for being so bossy. Nothing Connor said so far was a concern at all. I loved Rory's friends. He could hang out with them whenever he wanted. And I would never try to control him. I was a complete pushover. I was barely good at making decisions for myself.

"I think he thought that she was out of his league or something. Like she was the best he could ever do. And he completely lost it when he found out she cheated on him. He crashed at my place for months and then just disappeared. He didn't even tell me he was going to Italy. When he came back, he seemed completely back to his old self. Except for his desire to fuck every girl in the city. It was like he was taking it out on every girl he met."

I winced.

"Sorry, Keira."

"No, it's fine." I ran my thumb along my coffee cup. For some reason that information was unsettling. I thought about how he was always so in control again. Did he like dominating women to somehow get back at his ex? That was really messed up. Was he actually thinking about her when we were having sex?

"Keira, I wasn't trying to upset you. Rory is a good guy."

"But he's super fucked up, right? Isn't that what you said?"

"I shouldn't have said that before."

"It doesn't make it untrue." I swallowed hard. "Do you think he still loves her?"

Connor laughed. "No. I don't think he ever loved her. He just liked the idea of her."

Because she was out of his league? I felt a pit forming in my stomach. "Do you think he's settling for me?"

"You're not the type of girl someone settles for, Keira. You're a reacher."

"A reacher?"

"Yeah. A girl that someone reaches for." He smiled at me.

I was overthinking this. Rory wanted to be my boyfriend or he wouldn't have asked. And yes, he liked being in control in bed, but I liked that about him. And last night he wasn't being dominant. He had made love to me. Twice. There was definitely a difference there. We were more than whatever it was he and his horrible ex were. And he hated her for more reasons than her just cheating on him and lying to him. He'd forgive me for the article. He had to. Besides, he and his friends definitely weren't going to sit around in a circle reading boring articles all morning. Everything was fine. I still had time to figure out the best way to tell him.

"So I'm assuming if you're asking these questions that last night went pretty well?"

"It did. Thank you for encouraging me not to run away."

"Well, that's what friends are for." He lifted up his cup.

I tapped my cup against his. "You're a really good friend, Connor."

"I still don't know how I wound up in the friend zone in this situation."

"Because you're the nice one."

"I hate being the nice one."

I laughed.

"Wow, you really are comfortable around my friends," Rory said as he walked out of his room. He was wearing athletic shorts and no shirt. It was hard not to drool over his abs. Rory looked down at the t-shirt that I was wearing. "And that looks a lot better on you by the way."

I could feel my face turning red. "Sorry, I didn't realize anyone was coming over. I need like a schedule or something to keep track of all this stuff." I stood up. I needed to go to my room to change, but I also didn't want to leave the newspaper unattended.

"I send email memos," Jackson said as he got up off the couch and walked back over to us. "Are you two done with your top secret conversation yet?"

Rory lowered his eyebrows slightly.

"Yeah, we're done talking about you, Jackson," Connor said.

Jackson laughed. "I'm flattered."

"Maybe you can put me on that email list?" I asked Jackson, hoping to change the subject.

"Well, that depends. It's only for committed members of the group." He glanced at Rory and then back at me. And then he looked at Connor.

Connor gave him a dirty look. I hoped that Rory didn't see it.

I stayed silent. It wasn't my place to tell Rory's friends that we were a couple now. Jackson seemed to purposely be pushing everyone's buttons this morning. Maybe he was still mad at me for not setting him up with someone. I was starting to think he'd be a great fit for my editor, Judy. She loved pushing people's buttons too.

"Well." Rory walked over to me and put his arm around my shoulders. "I think as my girlfriend she's probably allowed on that list." He smiled down at me.

God I love the sound of that.

Connor coughed and spit a mouthful of coffee back in his cup.

"And since you are my girlfriend now, it would make me a little more comfortable if you were wearing a little, well...more." He grabbed my hand and pulled me toward my bedroom.

I laughed as he pushed me through my door and closed it behind us. He immediately pulled me to his chest.

"Good morning," he said and smiled at me.

"Good morning."

"Maybe you can just let me see you like this from now on. I don't like the idea of sharing you."

"You don't have to share me." I ran my hand along the scruff on his jaw line. "I'm all yours."

"Hmm. I like the sound of that." He pushed the t-shirt up my torso. I lifted my arms in the air and let him pull it off the rest of the way. "Maybe we should just stay in here the rest of the day."

"Your friends are right outside, Rory." It was hard to protest when I was completely naked and he was staring at me like that. "And they're waiting for you to make breakfast."

"There's only one thing I want for breakfast." His eyes wandered down my body.

I gulped. Even his words made me wet. I could never resist him. He could have me whenever he wanted.

"But you're probably right. You'd be too embarrassed to face my friends ever again after they heard you yelling my name repeatedly. It is very tempting though."

"You're such a tease."

He leaned down and kissed me hard. "It's just a rain check. There's no way I can resist you all day." He tucked a loose strand of hair behind my ear. "What did you want for breakfast?"

"I'm sure I'll love anything you make."

"How about crêpes?" He pulled on the t-shirt he had stripped me of. "I was looking for this, by the way."

I laughed. "Crêpes sound very fancy."

"Yeah, well, I'm trying to show off for my new girlfriend." He slapped my ass and walked over to the door. He opened the door a crack and slid out, ensuring that his friends didn't see a glimpse of me.

I quickly put on a pair of yoga pants and a tank top. I couldn't leave them alone with the newspaper for even a minute. I needed to find a way to throw it out without anyone noticing. Or set it on fire. Or flush it down the toilet. I would tell Rory eventually, but right now was too soon. Right now that paper needed to be destroyed.

Before I grabbed the handle, I heard hushed voices outside. It was wrong to eavesdrop. I bit my lip. But that had never stopped me before. I pressed my ear against the door so I could hear them.

"Girlfriend, huh?" Jackson asked. "I'll be the first one to say that I did not see that one coming."

"And why is that?" Rory sounded annoyed.

"I thought you two were just sleeping together."

"We were."

"So what makes this different than the past hundred girls you've slept with?"

"Jesus, Jackson, would you keep your voice down?"

Gross. I knew I shouldn't be listening, but it was hard to stop. Had he really slept with over a hundred women? How many women had he slept with since he had moved in? I tried to stop my brain from doing the math. I didn't want to know the answer. Luckily Jackson's voice derailed my train of thought.

"I'm just saying..."

"Well it's different."

"Why?"

"If you're not careful I'm going to spit in your crêpe, Jackson."

"Dude. Chill. I just think if you're not really serious about her, then you probably shouldn't have asked her out. She clearly adores you. It's just going to get super messy when things go south. I mean, she is your roommate after all. Do you even know how to be in a relationship?"

"Why do you just assume I'm going to fuck this up? I am serious about her. I wouldn't have asked her to be my girlfriend if I didn't want to be with her. She's different. You know she's different. She's nothing like Harper."

Harper. That must have been his ex's name. It sounded so pretentious.

"Well thank God," Connor said.

They were all silent for a moment.

"Look, Connor," Rory said. "I'm sorry if I..."

"Keira's a catch," Connor cut in. "You would have been crazy not to take the next step. I think she's perfect for you. Congrats, Rory. You win."

"Thanks, man. See, Jackson. That's why I tell Connor stuff first."

"Yeah, whatever. You and Keira make a cute couple. Yadda, yadda. Happy now? Feed me please."

"I still might spit in your crêpe."

"As long as it has extra Nutella I don't even care. And I am happy for you. I just knew that Connor had a crush on Keira too. I don't want this to tear us apart."

"Is that why you're acting so weird this morning?" Connor laughed. "Look, like I said, Rory won. I've officially bowed out of this thing. Keira and I are just friends. That's it. You're being a little dramatic, Jackson."

"I just don't want this to break us up," Jackson said.

Geez, Jackson was so sensitive. I didn't want to hear anything else about how I was ruining their friendship. I wouldn't ever let that happen. They had all become my friends too. I opened up the door and stepped out. All three of them turned to me.

"So what does Sunday Brunch Day usually entail?" I asked.

"Usually we're too hung over to do anything fun," Jackson said. "But since we didn't have a late night last night, maybe we can play a game or something."

"Yeah? I have a whole bunch of games in the closet in my bedroom. What do you guys want to play?" I asked.

"I'm thinking we should just play Never Have I Ever." Jackson smiled at me.

"We're definitely not playing that," Rory said. "What do you want in your crêpe, Keira?"

"Whatever you recommend." I slid into the stool next to Connor.

"That just means you have a lot to hide, Rory," Jackson said. "Actually, I think it would be good for your budding romance with Keira if you both aired out your dirty laundry."

"Jackson, cut it out," Connor said.

"If Jackson wants to play Never Have I Ever, I'll play. It could be fun," I said.

"See, Keira wants to play." Jackson opened up the freezer and pulled out a bottle of vodka.

"It is a little early for shots though, don't you think?" I asked.

"It's never too early on Sunday Brunch Day."

"You're definitely just making stuff up now."

I watched as Jackson poured four shots and handed them out.

"I'm sitting this round out," Rory said. He expertly flipped a crêpe in his pan.

"Nope," Jackson said and placed one of the shot glasses next to the stove. "Okay, I'll go first. Never have I ever had a threesome."

"Sorry, how does this work again?" I asked. "Do we drink if we have done it?"

"Yeah, so I have never had a threesome, that's why I said it. So if you've ever had a threesome before, it's shot time!" Jackson looked at me.

"Why are you looking at me like that? I've never had a threesome."

"I was just curious." Jackson shrugged.

Connor and I didn't touch our glasses. I hesitantly looked over at Rory. I was afraid I already knew the answer. I wasn't at all surprised when Rory picked up his glass and downed his shot. He didn't look back at us. He just placed his glass quietly back on the counter and continued cooking. I wasn't sure if he was hoping I wouldn't notice, or if he was just trying to focus on cooking. This game was not going to be very fun for me.

"Your turn, Keira," Jackson said.

"Umm..." I looked back over at Rory. "Never have I ever cheated on someone." I wanted him to know that. I wanted him to know that I'd be faithful to him. I was relieved to see that no one touched their glasses. They were all good guys.

"Okay," Connor said. "Never have I ever slept with a man."

Oh my God, Jackson. I looked over at him. He was looking at me. We stared awkwardly at each other for a few seconds.

"Why are you looking at me? You have to drink, Keira," Jackson said. "We all know you're fucking Rory."

Rory started laughing.

"Oh, right, sorry." I downed my shot and tried not to choke. I hated the feeling of the burn down my throat. I couldn't help but be surprised that Jackson didn't drink. For some reason, I really thought he was gay. I guess Rory was right, though. He was just metrosexual.

"You're up Rory," Jackson said.

Rory folded up one of the crêpes and walked over to me. "Your crêpe, mademoiselle."

"Why thank you, monsieur."

"You two are so cute. But you're up, Rory," Jackson repeated.

"Never have I ever punched one of my friends in the face. Yet." He slapped the back of Jackson's head and walked back over to the stove."

"Ow, man. Keira wanted to play. Okay, my turn then. Never have I ever slept with someone in a public restroom."

Connor picked up his shot glass and downed it.

"Seriously?" I asked.

"Getting divorced is rough."

I heard the clink of a cup against the counter. I looked over and saw that Rory's glass was empty again. *What hasn't he done?* I knew it was my turn, but I was starting to feel uncomfortable. Maybe it would be better if Rory and I just talked about these things in private. Or if I just never knew about them. Jackson and Connor were both staring at me. "Umm...never have I ever slept with someone within half an hour of meeting them."

All three of them drank their shots.

"You guys are the worst."

Connor cleared his throat. "Never have I ever slept with another member of the wolf pack. By the way, I love our new name."

Why is Connor trying to get me drunk? I downed my second shot. Maybe he was just saying that so that Rory knew nothing happened between us. Things had gone too far between Connor and me after strip poker that night, but Connor and I hadn't gone past second base.

"Never have I ever felt up and made out with two members of the wolf pack," Jackson said.

Oh my God. Connor must have told Jackson about what had happened. I cringed and downed another shot. I really needed to talk to Rory alone.

Rory turned toward us. He looked down at my empty shot glass and slammed down a plate in front of Jackson. "It wasn't even your turn, asshole."

Jackson looked down at his crêpe and then back up at Rory. "Did you actually spit in this?"

"I don't remember."

"It's not like I'm the other guy she made out with in this room."

Rory glared at him. "Never have I ever cried during sex."

"I told you that in confidence," Jackson mumbled and downed his shot.

"Do you guys maybe want to play charades or something instead? I don't mind going first." I was starting to feel a little dizzy. Vodka was so much stronger than wine and beer.

"Actually, now I'm kind of curious to see what else you want to know about me," Rory said. I could tell he was feeling the alcohol too. He had drank the most shots of anyone.

I stared at him. I didn't want to know anything else about all the other women he had slept with. "Never have I ever loved any of my exes."

Rory smiled at me and turned back to the stove.

Connor and Jackson both drank their shots, but Rory's glass stayed on the counter.

Rory hadn't loved Harper. Maybe he thought he had at the time. I thought I had loved my exes at the time. But I knew I didn't love them now that I knew what it was like to be with Rory.

Rory turned off the stove and set a plate down in front of Connor and one down next to me. He slid into the stool beside mine and put his hand on my knee. "Aren't you going to try yours?"

I had completely forgotten about my crêpe. I quickly cut into it and took a bite. It was light and crispy and filled with strawberries and Nutella. "Rory, this is amazing."

He squeezed my knee and started eating.

"Never have I ever had an STD scare," Connor said.

Rory gave Connor a dirty look. He sighed and downed another shot. "I swear I'm clean, Keira."

For some reason I started laughing. I had definitely had too much to drink. "Ew. Did you not wear a condom or something?"

"I always use a condom. It broke." He looked back at Connor. "Thanks, man."

"I just thought that might be something Keira would be happy to know. She knows you have quite the sexual history. And now she doesn't have to worry about it."

"Right. Well, never have I ever attempted anal sex and failed," Rory said.

I started laughing again. I began to laugh even harder when Connor took a shot. "Wait, I need to hear that story."

"That is the whole story. It's not easy to do. Stop laughing at me, Keira!"

"Never have I ever slept with an average of two women a week for the past six years," Jackson said.

Rory laughed and took a shot. "I hate you."

This time no one stopped me from doing the math. For some reason I thought it would be close to the 100 women Jackson had thrown out earlier when I was eavesdropping. But it was so much worse. It was over 100 women a year. "That's over 600 women." I dropped my fork. "Rory, have you seriously slept with over 600 women?"

"What? No. God, no." He scratched the back of his neck.

"But you said you only ever did one night stands. So that's...624 women. Give or take depending on how lucky you were."

"They weren't all one night stands."

"Then why did you tell me that? So you have been dating other people between Harper and me?"

"No. Wait, how do you know about Harper?"

My stool made a terrible screeching noise as I stood up. I felt like I was going to throw up. "Rory, can I talk to you in private for a second?"

As soon as we were in my bedroom, I thought I'd start freaking out, but I didn't even know what to say to him. I just wanted to cry. That was too many women. I wasn't sure if I had ever even talked to 624 men.

"They weren't all one night stands, but I wasn't serious about any of them. They were just booty calls, Keira. They didn't mean anything."

"So you had a few girls you'd call up randomly just to have sex with you?"

"A few dozen girls, yes."

"Dozens? So, they're like...in your phone right now?"

"It's not like I'm going to call them anymore."

"They might call you."

"I won't answer. Here, delete them if you want. Seriously, Keira, none of them mean anything to me."

I looked down at the contact list in his phone. There were so many girl's names in his phone. And they all had stars next to them. "You rated them?"

"Oh, shit." He scratched the back of his neck. "I forgot about that. Don't look at me like that. You knew I'd slept with a lot of other women."

"So if it's not 624 women, what is your number?"

"I'd say closer to 100 or something."

"So some of these women you've had sex with several times then?" I looked back down at his contact list. There were only a few girls that had five stars next to them. "Like, Tiffany Five Stars?"

"I've slept with Tiffany a handful of times, yes."

"I don't have a rating. Did I not even rank? Am I that bad or something?" Why did men always seem to be able to make me feel so insecure. Why did I so desperately want to know how I compared to these other girls. I felt so gross.

"Damn it, Keira, why are we even talking about this?" He grabbed his phone back and shoved it into his pocket. "You don't get a rating because you're my girlfriend. You're a freaking ten okay? I can't get enough of you. You know that."

"Rory, I figured you'd had threesomes. I figured you'd slept with women after only knowing them for a few minutes. Sex in a public restroom? Sure, why not. I figured that too. But 100 women is a lot of women. I'm not sure I'm the kind of girl you're looking for, Rory. I don't have a lot of experience. I don't ever even want to have a threesome. It seems complicated and gross."

Rory laughed. "I'm done with those things. I don't want to share you with anyone else. Not even another woman." He smiled at me. "And I like that you're inexperienced."

I didn't know if it was the alcohol or the tension of the situation somehow evaporating, but I started laughing. "You're such a slut, Rory."

"I *was* a slut. I'm not going to cheat on you, Keira. Actually, the more I find out about you, the more I like you. Well, except for the fact that you rounded second base with Connor. I kind of wish that didn't happen."

"I'm so sorry." I was still giggling.

"You find that funny, huh? You're so drunk." He started laughing too.

"What is Jackson's problem? Why is he trying to get us to fight?"

"I think he's actually trying to help. He's worried that you're going to ruin all of our friendships or something. Obviously you know that Connor liked you too. So it's been a little awkward between us recently. But I guess Jackson thinks that if everything is out there, then there's nothing to be upset about down the road or something."

"He's such an ass."

Rory started laughing even harder. "It was so funny when you thought he was going to drink when Connor said he'd never slept with a man. I told you he wasn't gay."

"I really thought he was going to drink."

Rory stopped laughing and looked down at me. He tucked a loose strand of hair behind my ear. "Okay, let me clear the air here before we go back out there. I don't want you to get upset again. I've only ever had one other girlfriend. Her name was Harper. I don't know who already told you about her, but I don't care. All you need to know is that I was young and stupid. I thought she was so perfect. And when she broke up with me, it completely blindsided me. I thought that I was in love with her. I thought that she was it. But I was so dumb. She wasn't a good fit for me at all." He rubbed his palm along my cheek. "You're on a whole other level, Keira. Harper means nothing to me anymore. None of those girls in my phone mean anything to me. They never did. So that's it. That's all my dirty laundry. Well, and I have some pain in the ass best friends. But you already knew that."

I laughed and clasped my hands behind his neck. If that was everything, that wasn't so bad. In a weird, twisted way, it was flattering that after sleeping with 100 women he wanted me. I took a deep breath. Now was the time to tell him about the articles.

"So, I've had three boyfriends, which you know. And besides for you, they're the only other people I've slept with. But none of them ever made me feel the way that you make me feel."

"You mean they sucked in bed?" he laughed.

"No. Well, yes." I smiled at him. "What I was trying to say was that they didn't make me feel like I mattered at all. You make me feel special."

"You are special."

"But I've done a lot of dumb stuff too. I'm still young and stupid I guess."

"I don't care about anything that you've done in your past. I'm sure I've done worse. Maybe it would be better if we just move forward instead of looking backwards?"

"I love that idea. But there is one thing that I need..."

A knock on the door interrupted us. "Lovebirds!" Jackson shouted. "Are you done with your make-up sex yet? Connor and I are still hungry!"

Rory laughed.

Crap.

"It appears as though they kept drinking," Rory said. "Come on, I'm still hungry too." He opened the door before I could protest.

CHAPTER 33

"So did you guys have fun banging it out?" Jackson said.

Connor laughed.

"We were just talking about all those lovely things you revealed about me," Rory said. "And now I think we wasted time, because make-up sex sounds pretty great." He leaned down and kissed me.

"Gross. But I helped, right?" Jackson asked. "Now you know all the bad stuff about each other. Although, I don't know why anyone would want to be with someone who's had over 100 sexual partners. Keira must be more messed up than we realize."

"Okay, just stop talking. Yes, you helped. Geez," Rory said and lifted up the bottle of vodka. It was almost empty. "Sunday Brunch Days aren't usually this crazy, Keira."

"Are they always this delicious? I think this is even better cold." I started giggling again. "I'm sorry, I'm so drunk." I didn't think I had ever had so many shots before.

"I love that it's only 10 a.m.," Connor said. "I don't even remember the last time I was drunk before noon."

"I'm so glad that we're all equally immature. Okay, I want to make a toast." Jackson stood up. "Here's to new friends."

"Thanks, Jackson," I said.

"And don't break my friend's heart," he added. "Because we will kick you out of this group so fast, you won't even know what happened."

"I'm not going to break his heart. I'm in love with him." *Holy shit! Did I just say that out loud?* I put my hand over my mouth. I really hated drunk me.

"Shit!" Rory pulled his hand away from the stove and put his finger in his mouth.

"I'm going to shove him. I said I'm going to shove him. I'm really abusive in relationships. Shoving is the worst I'll do, though. I definitely won't break his heart." *What the hell am I saying?*

"Fuck," Rory said as he pulled his finger out of his mouth.

"Are you okay?" I ran over to the sink and turned on the cold water. "Rory, give me your hand."

He walked over to the sink and I put his hand under the water.

"What, were you that surprised that I wasn't planning on breaking your heart?" I leaned against the kitchen counter. I tried to act cool but my face was bright red and I was starting to feel all sweaty. Clearly he had burnt himself when I had confessed that I was in love with him.

"No." He laughed. "I was just trying to focus on what you were saying instead of cooking. I think I'm a little drunk too." He laughed again. "No, I'm super drunk. I should not be cooking right now. This is extremely hazardous."

"I think I have some aloe in the bathroom. I'll be right back." I quickly walked toward the bathroom. It felt like I had just ruined everything. Confessing that too soon freaked guys out. Rory already had commitment issues. He was probably running out the front door right now.

I pulled the bottle out of the medicine cabinet and looked over as I heard the door close. Rory walked over to me. For a second I thought he was going to kiss me, but instead, he hoisted himself up onto the bathroom sink. He was staring down at me expectantly. And it didn't look like he was waiting for me to put aloe on his finger. I glanced over at the door and then down at the bulge in his athletic shorts.

"That probably would make my finger feel better."

I looked up at him. He didn't say anything about the fact that I just confessed that I loved him. Maybe he hadn't heard me. Or maybe he was just pretending like he hadn't. Either way, I wasn't sure if it was the alcohol or the way he was looking at me, but I no longer cared that his friends were in the next room.

"I never realized how much the thought of sex in public turned you on." He raised his left eyebrow.

"It doesn't." *Does it?*

"Really? Because I bet you're soaking wet right now. I bet you'd let me bend you over this sink and fuck you without even hesitating. You wouldn't care at all if Connor and Jackson knew that I was fucking you. And trust me, they'd know. They probably think you have my cock in your mouth already. The thought of them hearing me fucking your brains out turns you on even more. And you like knowing that they could walk in on us any second. The door isn't even locked."

Holy shit, he's right. Why is the thought of getting caught so hot?

"I had almost forgotten that you said you get super horny when you're drunk. It's so much fun teasing you." He put his hand out in front of him.

I wanted him right now. I picked up his hand and slid his burnt finger into my mouth.

His lips parted slightly as he watched me slide his finger in and out of my mouth. After just a few seconds, I had successfully turned his shorts into a very structurally sound teepee. I loved turning him on. There was nothing more satisfying than him wanting me as much as I always wanted him.

"Fuck, Keira."

When I put my hand on the waistline of his shorts, he immediately lifted his hips. I pulled off his shorts and boxers, freeing his massive erection. I immediately abandoned his finger for the real thing. I wrapped my lips around him and took him all the way to the back of my throat.

He groaned quietly.

I loved pleasing him. I slowly slid him in and out of my mouth. His hands gripped the edge of the counter. I tightened my lips, and moved my mouth faster. I suppressed my gag reflex and took him into the back of my throat again.

"I want you." He grabbed a fistful of my hair and pulled my head up. He tilted my head back even more as he stared down at me.

I realized I was panting as I looked up at him. I swallowed hard.

He pushed himself off the counter and walked behind me, trailing his fingers along my waist. He pulled my yoga pants and thong down my thighs and pushed the front of my hips against the cold counter. "How long does it take to apply aloe?" He reached down and pressed his thumb against my clit.

My whole body seemed to tremble. I stared back at him in the mirror. His eyes were smoldering.

"How long, Keira?"

"I don't know." I couldn't focus on anything but his fingers. "Only like a minute."

"That's a shame. We've already been in here for over a minute." He ran his hand over my ass. "This will just have to wait."

What? "Rory, please."

He sunk his finger deep inside of me.

Oh God.

"Connor and Jackson are going to know what we're up to." He pressed his thumb against my clit again.

"I don't care," I moaned.

"They're going to know I'm fucking you." He moved his finger faster. "They'll be able to hear us."

"Please, Rory."

"They're going to know that you like it rough. Because I'm going to fuck you harder than I ever have." He hooked his finger inside of me.

Oh God. "Fuck me, Rory. Please fuck me."

"Don't make a sound, Keira." He grabbed my waist and thrust himself deep inside of me.

I couldn't suppress the moan that escaped my lips. The alcohol coursing through my body somehow made the sensation of him filling me even more intense. I pressed my hands against the mirror and pushed myself back on him.

He responded by gyrating his hips. All I could feel was pleasure. I liked when he was rough with me. And I liked that he knew how to make me orgasm within a matter of minutes. I was already close. Looking back at him in the mirror was almost enough to take me over the edge. He was the sexiest specimen that I had ever laid my eyes on. And he was staring back at me with so much intensity.

Rory thrust forward, locking me between him and the cold countertop.

I moaned again.

He tilted my head to the side and kissed me, silencing my moan. His lips fell from mine and he placed a hard kiss on my neck. "If you want them to hear you, I can make sure they do," he whispered and bit down on my earlobe.

"Rory!" I moaned.

"You're so responsive." His voice was a bit airy. He grabbed a fist full of my hair and tilted my head back, kissing my neck again. He began to thrust faster and faster, making my hip bones dig into the edge of the sink.

Yes! I pressed my hands against the mirror again, making him go deeper still.

He groaned and his kiss on my neck grew harder.

Oh my God. Is he giving me a hickey?

He sucked on my neck once more and then pressed down on my back, pushing my torso against the counter. He grabbed the sides of the sink and began fucking me even harder. With each thrust, the counter dug deeper into my hip bones.

"Come, Keira." It was a demand.

And I was completely at his mercy. My orgasm was intense, making me moan louder still.

"Say my name," he said as he slapped my ass.

"Rory!" I could feel his cock pulse inside of me as he found his own climax. "Oh God, Rory!"

He continued to slide his length in and out of me as my toes uncurled. With one last thrust, he pulled out of me. I felt completely spent.

"Who knew living with your girlfriend could have such perks?" he said as he ran his hand along my ass.

I looked at his reflection in the mirror. He was staring at my ass. I turned around to look at him but he didn't make eye contact with me. Instead, his fingers lightly drifted over my hip bones.

"I'm sorry," he said gently.

"What?" I looked down. There were red lines where my hips had been pressed against the counter. I quickly pulled my yoga pants back up. "There's nothing to be sorry about, I liked it."

"Hmm." He knelt down in front of me and pulled the top of my yoga pants down slightly. He rubbed his thumbs along the red lines on my hips. He kissed one of my hip bones and then the other.

There was something so intimate about what he was doing. I wanted to bring up the fact that I said I loved him. But it seemed like maybe he really hadn't heard me. Or if he had, he was pretending he hadn't. So it was probably better not to press it.

"You know, I think you get horny when you're drunk too," I said. "And by the way, I said I get corny, not horny."

"Yeah right." He laughed as he stood up. "I think living with you makes me horny all the time. It has nothing to do with the fact that I'm completely wasted." He flashed me a smile as he sat back down on the sink. "And I can't even apologize for that, because I did that on purpose." He lightly touched the side of my neck.

I tilted my head to see my reflection in the mirror. "Oh my God!" There was a huge hickey on the side of my neck. "Why would you do that?" I put my hand over the hickey to hide it.

"I don't know, I'm drunk." He ran his hand through his hair.

I shoved his arm. "Rory, I won't be able to leave the house for like a week."

"Yeah, but you work from home." He raised his eyebrow at me.

"But I still go places."

"You can't be mad at me." He put his hand out. "I'm hurt."

I laughed and picked up the bottle of aloe. I squirted out a small amount of aloe and then gently ran it along the small burn mark on his finger. "Does it still hurt?"

"Now that my distraction is over, yes."

"Well, that should help." I wanted him to confess that he loved me too. But instead he just smiled back at me. "Do you think they heard us?"

"They definitely heard you." He leaned forward and placed a soft kiss against my lips. "You were very, very loud."

I could feel myself blushing. "I can't go out there." I put my hand back over my hickey.

"Are you embarrassed that you're having sex with me?"

I laughed. "No, you're the best thing that's ever happened to me." I swallowed hard. I was completely losing it. When I had been writing the article it almost seemed like I was playing the part of this super cool, confident person. But now I was just me again, saying stupid things like I love you to the sexy guy I only just started dating.

"I thought I wasn't even the best sex you've ever had." He put his elbows on his knees and leaned toward me.

"I may have lied about that."

He smiled at me. "Thank you for taking care of me," he said and looked down at his finger.

"Of course. That's what girlfriends do." I put my hands on his knees.

His lips parted slightly when his eyes met mine. But he didn't need to say anything. I could tell by the way he was looking at me that his ex-girlfriend had never taken care of him. It took every ounce of resolve in me to not repeat saying that I loved him.

"I'm really glad I answered your ad," he said. "And that you said yes."

"Yes to you moving in or yes to being your girlfriend?"

"Both." He pushed himself off the counter and placed a soft kiss against my lips.

CHAPTER 34

As soon as I walked out of the bathroom I almost screamed. Connor had The Post spread out on the counter and was flipping through the pages. *No, no, no!* "What are you guys doing?" I said way too loudly.

Jackson looked over at us. "Not banging in the bathroom when you should be entertaining your house guests. You could have at least let us watch."

Connor laughed but didn't look up at us.

I could feel my face turning red. "Do you really want to see Rory naked that badly, Jackson?" I hoped my inappropriate joke would distract them as I inched closer toward the newspaper.

"Um...no, Keira. I've seen Rory naked plenty of times." He smiled at me.

"Okay," Rory said. "That's enough. New group rule. I think that now that Keira and I are official, you guys can't flirt with her anymore."

"I wasn't flirting with her," Jackson said.

"You just implied that you wanted to see her naked."

Jackson laughed. "I've never really seen you jealous before. Is that why you gave her a hickey? To mark your territory?"

Shit. I put my hand on the side of my neck. Connor looked up at me. I could tell he was trying to not look hurt. He gave me a small smile.

"Do you mind if I see that?" I asked, gesturing toward the paper. "One of my friends had an article that was supposed to come out and I wanted to read it."

"Yeah, sure. What section?"

"I don't remember where she said it would be. Could I just see the whole thing real quick?"

Connor gave me a strange look and slid the paper toward me. "What section are your articles posted in, Keira?" he asked while I looked for the editorial section. "I actually bought the paper so we could check out some of your work."

"None of my articles have been picked up ever since you guys moved in. I've been too distracted to write anything good. Plus hanging out with you guys takes up a surprisingly large amount of time. Besides, I don't know how much I like writing for The Post anymore. They've been really annoying recently. I think I might look for a new job. And then you can read all the new good stuff I write." I found the editorial section and pulled it out. I pushed the rest of the paper back toward Connor. When I looked up, Rory was staring at me.

"You're totally lying," Rory said.

"What? No I'm not." I put the editorial section down by my side.

Rory laughed. "Yes you are. You always ramble when you're lying."

"I wasn't rambling. I'm just talking like a normal person. Everyone has work problems. Let's discuss that. Who wants to go first?"

"And you get this cute little worry line on your forehead whenever you lie."

"No I don't." I put my hand on my forehead. *Am I seriously getting wrinkles already?*

"And you're blushing."

"Okay, right, well I'm blushing because now I think I have wrinkles." I slowly moved the paper behind my back.

"Give it to me." Rory held out his hand.

"Give you what?" I clutched the paper as tightly as I could and backed away from him.

"I just want to see what kind of stuff you write."

"I don't write anything worth reading. Really, Rory, you don't need to read it."

"So you do have an article in the paper today?" He smiled at me.

I sighed. "Yes, okay? Can we please do something else now?"

He smiled at me. "I don't think so." He reached for the paper, but I dodged him. I started to run away but he grabbed me and started tickling me.

"Oh my God, Rory, stop!" I laughed as I tried to fight him off. "I can't breathe!"

Rory easily grabbed the paper and held it up in the air and backed away from me.

"Rory!" I jumped and tried to grab the paper but he was so much taller than me. "Seriously, give it back."

Rory tossed the paper to Jackson.

Oh God. "Come on guys. It's boring and lame and let's do something else, please."

"What, are you writing about us or something?" Jackson asked as he started scanning through the editorial section.

I ran into the kitchen and tried to snatch the paper from him. "No, you guys are weird. No one wants to read about you."

"Harsh."

I leaned forward. My hand slipped onto his thigh as I reached for the paper.

"I'm pretty sure you have to worry about Keira getting fresh with me, not the other way around," Jackson said.

I quickly pulled away. "I'm not."

"I know." He laughed and tossed the paper to Connor.

Damn it! "Connor, give me the paper."

"Sorry, Keira. I'm curious too." He dropped the part of the paper that didn't contain my article onto the floor.

"What is wrong with you guys?" I grabbed Connors arm to try to get the paper, but he put his hand on my shoulder to hold me back.

"You're being ridiculous, Keira," he said. "Oh, here it is. There's a picture of her and everything!" He tossed the paper to Rory.

"No!" I ran over to Rory and jumped on his back. I covered his eyes with my hands so he couldn't read the article. But it prevented me from knocking the paper out of his hand.

He started laughing as he easily peeled my hands off his eyes.

"Rory, I need to talk to you. Please don't read that." My heart was beating so fast that it felt like it was going to explode. I slid off his back and reached for the paper again.

Rory hopped up on the counter to avoid me and then cleared his throat. "How to Play With a Player. Step 5:

Make Him Jealous." The smile on Rory's face quickly faded. His eyes darted back and forth as he began to read the article.

"Rory stop."

"What the hell is this?"

"I can explain."

"Is this about me?" He looked so mad.

"Rory please get down. I can explain," I said again.

He just stared at me. I was wrong, he didn't look mad. He looked hurt. And that was so much worse. Rory's look alone was enough to make me suddenly feel cold. But Connor and Jackson's eyes on me seemed to make my whole body shiver.

"Please can we talk in private?"

"Now you think privacy is important?" He held up the paper.

"Rory, I'm so, so sorry. I came up with the idea after our first night together. I never wanted a one night stand. When you said that was it I didn't know what to do. It killed me. I couldn't let it be one night."

"So you wrote an article about how to mess with my head?"

"No." *Shit. Kind of.* "That wasn't the premise, Rory. And I never wanted to just be friends with benefits either. My editor made me change it. I just wrote what she wanted. Not everything in the article is even true. Some of it's just made up."

"Why didn't you just talk to me?"

"I tried to tell you how I felt. You made it very clear that you didn't want anything past that one night."

"What are you talking about? I asked you to be my girlfriend."

"That was after I wrote the articles."

"Then what was the original premise, Keira?"

"I wanted more. I wanted you to love me back."

"Stop saying that you love me! You don't love me." He jumped off the counter and tossed the paper at me. "Obviously you don't love me."

He did hear me before. "I do love you, Rory. I love you so much."

"Stop. This whole thing was stupid anyway. I never should have asked you out. Nothing good lasts forever."

"What are you talking about?"

"If Connor and Cindy didn't last, no one's going to last with me. They were perfect together. I'm a mess. How could you possibly love someone like me?"

I wanted to cry. It wasn't just my article that he was upset about. *Does he really not think that someone could love him? How can the man that I love so much feel that way?* "You're not a mess. I think that you're perfect, Rory. And I think we're perfect together."

He laughed and grabbed his keys off the counter. "I trusted you, Keira. How could you do this to me? After everything we've been through?"

"Everything we've been through? Are you kidding me? You mean the obstacles of getting you to stop fucking random women? Because that's what I've been through, Rory. Not you. That's my obstacle, not yours."

"Oh come on."

"And it was after one of the many times you crushed me that I came up with the idea for the article in the first place."

"So this is all my fault?"

"No, that's not what I meant." I took a deep breath. "I know I messed up. Right after I pitched the idea to my editor I realized it was a mistake, but it was too late. My editor was already running with it."

"So you thought you could just hide this from me forever? What did you expect would happen when I found out?

"I don't know. I was so scared to tell you because I knew it would hurt you."

"Well congratulations, you were right." He ran his hand through his hair. "I can't do this anymore, Keira."

"This? What do you mean you can't do this? I made one mistake. But you had no problem hurting me ever since you moved in. You knew that I liked you. You hurt me over and over again. You're a fucking hypocrite, Rory!"

"Yeah, I'm definitely done." He opened the front door.

"Where are you going?"

"Out."

"Rory! Please can't we just talk about this?"

"You can't change people, Keira. So screw you and your articles. And you know what? I'm glad I didn't let you delete those numbers from my phone."

"Seriously? That's what you're going to go do? You said you'd never cheat on me."

"What does it matter? I don't even know you, Keira. This whole thing was just a game to you. You used me. Come on, guys, we're leaving."

"Rory, I don't think..." Connor said.

"Fine. Don't come."

I couldn't let him leave. I couldn't lose him like this. "Rory, you told me that all you care about is being happy. Do I not make you happy?"

"You do. I love being around you." His words hung in the air.

"I love being around you too."

He stared at me for a second. His lips parted slightly like he was about to say something. Instead he shook his head. He stepped out of the apartment and slammed the door.

The apartment was eerily quiet. I could feel Connor and Jackson's eyes on me, but I just stared down at the paper on the counter. I felt numb. Rory had just dumped me. He was out looking for some girl to hook up with. Or calling one of the five stars on his phone. I felt so empty.

"That wasn't what I wanted," Jackson eventually said. "We should probably go after him."

"Okay," I said. I didn't want Rory to go sleep with someone else. I needed to stop him. If he would just talk to me. I had explained it all wrong. Or maybe I had explained it right. Maybe his reaction was totally justified. *I'm a monster.* I picked my purse up off the counter.

"Not you, Keira. He needs to blow off some steam."

"Yeah, blow off steam. That's an elegant way to put it." I could feel the tears welling in my eyes.

"He's drunk," Connor said. "He didn't mean any of that."

"He did."

"He didn't." Connor walked over to me and hugged me.

"He did." I let the tears run down my cheeks. "I messed up. I messed everything up."

"Yeah, you did," Jackson said.

"Jackson," Connor said. "She's already upset."

"I just mean that you shouldn't have written an article about your relationship. But honestly, whatever you did fixed him. And if it was writing the article that somehow made you help him realize he was being a dick for the past six years, then it's good that you wrote it. He really likes you, Keira. He hasn't dated anyone in forever. If he asked you out, then he has it bad."

"He hates me. He just broke up with me." My voice cracked when I said it. "And I handled it all wrong. I'm mad at him for being mad at me. He never apologized for hurting me. I didn't realize how angry I was."

Connor put his hand on the back of my head. There was something so comforting about the gesture. Again it felt like the last time I'd ever see him. I didn't want it to be the last time. And I definitely didn't want Rory and me to be over.

"I need to go find him," I said.

"Jackson and I will find him."

"Please don't let him sleep with someone else, Connor. Please..."

"I won't." Connor released me from his hug. "Let's go, Jackson."

"If you can just get him to talk to me again..."

"I'll explain it to him," Connor said and walked over to the door with Jackson.

"But you don't know what..."

"I'll handle it."

I didn't care what Connor told him. I just wanted Rory to come home.

CHAPTER 35

"Why won't any of them answer me?" I stared down at my cell phone.

"Keira, stop, you're driving yourself crazy." Emily picked up my phone and moved it out of sight.

"Do you think they still haven't found him?" It had been several hours since Rory had stormed out. I thought Connor or Jackson might text me once they found him, but I hadn't heard from either of them. And Rory wouldn't pick up whenever I tried to call him. I rubbed my forehead. I had a terrible hangover from drinking shots in the morning. I was physically and emotionally spent.

"I'm sure they found him. They're probably just hanging out. That's what guys do."

"They always hang out here. No, he's definitely sleeping with someone else right now. They can't find him because he's at some tramp's house."

"He's not."

"Emily, he's slept with an average of two women a week for the past six years."

"Yeah, that's disgusting."

"Ugh." I put my face in my hands. "Why didn't I just tell him?"

Emily rubbed my back. "Keira, stop beating yourself up. Everyone makes mistakes. Part of being in a relationship is working through problems together."

"We're not in a relationship anymore. He broke up with me."

"You were both drunk. You had a fight. He didn't really break up with you. And there's no way he's sleeping with someone else. From everything you told me, up until that point it seemed like he was totally smitten with you."

"Why can't he just tell me everything I want to hear like you do?" I laughed and lifted up my head.

"Because he's a boy, not a man. You really should be dating men, Keira."

"Oh, he's definitely a man."

Emily laughed. "Okay, fine. But are you sure you even love him? Are you sure you don't just..." Emily looked away from me. "Are you sure you don't just want to be in love?"

I had thought about that a lot. But I didn't feel the pressure of getting married when I was with him. He had even told me he wasn't sure he'd ever be ready for marriage and I still wanted to date him. I did love him. Nothing else mattered. "When did you realize you loved Jim?"

Emily sighed. "Right away. But you know how I am. I easily fall head over heels."

"But it was different with Jim, right? You knew it was more than just a crush?"

"Yeah, it was different." Emily smiled to herself.

"Living with Rory made everything different for me. It kind of already felt like we were in a relationship somehow. I don't really know how to explain it. He's everything I ever wanted."

"I get it. When you know, you know."

"I lost him, didn't I? I chose my career over love. I never in a million years thought I'd be that person. I don't want to be that person, Emily! How do I fix it? I can't lose him this way."

"Okay, I'm pissed now too. This is ridiculous. No one makes my best friend grovel for hours for no reason."

"There is a reason..."

"No, there's not. I read the articles. They weren't even that specific." She picked up my phone and scrolled through my contact list. Then she picked up her cell, typed in some numbers, and pressed the call button.

"What are you doing?"

"Be quiet, I'm putting it on speaker."

"Hello?" Connor said.

"Son of a bitch," I mouthed silently at Emily. I had been texting him all day and he had never responded to me.

"Hey, Connor."

"Who is this?"

"This is Keira's friend, Emily. I just left her place and she's really upset. Why haven't you called her back?"

"Look, Emily, I've interfered in their relationship enough. She just needs to talk to Rory."

"Um...yeah. I agree. So where is he exactly?"

The line was silent for a second. I thought there'd be music blaring in the background, but it was really quiet. Maybe they weren't at a bar hooking up with random women.

"He's with me. Everything's fine. I'll have him home soon."

"What time exactly?"

"He'll be home in a few hours. Can you tell Keira that everything's fine?"

Emily smiled at me. "Will do. Thanks, Connor."

Connor hung up without saying goodbye.

"See," Emily said. "Everything's fine. They're probably just walking around town or something. And they're all together."

I sighed. "Maybe you're right."

"I'm definitely right. Connor just verified how right I am."

I laughed. It felt like a huge weight had just been lifted off my chest. Maybe everything was going to be okay. Maybe Rory would even forgive me. *Please let him forgive me.*

"Do you want to try to get some sleep?" Emily asked.

"Oh, geez, Emily, I'm so sorry. It's late. I know you have to wake up early for work."

"It's fine. But I am going to get going. I've been so tired recently."

"Yeah well there's a little human inside of you stealing all your energy."

Emily laughed. "Text me once everything's worked out."

"And if it doesn't work out?"

"Then I guess you'll just come over." She smiled at me. "But it is going to work out. He just needed some space."

"I hope so."

***

After an hour had passed a pit started to form in my stomach. Once two hours had passed I started pacing the floor. *He said a few hours, right?* A few meant two? Or was that a couple? Maybe a few meant three.

***

I looked down at my phone. I had texted Connor again after three hours. And now it had been four hours. It was 2 a.m. Rory wasn't coming back tonight. Either Connor had been lying about being with Rory, or Rory had refused to come home. He didn't want to see me.

I got up off the couch and walked over to Rory's room. I just wanted it to feel like he was here. *This is weird.* But I didn't care that it was weird. I might never get another chance to sleep in his bed. And I loved his bed. It smelled like him.

I opened up the door to his bedroom before I could change my mind. Even his room smelled like him. I lay down and curled up on his side of the bed. And I immediately started to cry. I didn't love his bed because it smelled like him. I loved it because he was always in it with me, snuggled up next to me, holding me, making me feel safe. I missed him. And now I was worried that I was going to have to miss him for the rest of my life.

Eventually the soothing smell of cinnamon engulfed me and I slowly drifted to sleep.

***

When I woke up, I half expected Rory to be in bed with me. But he wasn't there. *Where is he?* I looked down at my cell phone. There were still no new messages or missed phone calls. I couldn't wait around anymore. I needed to go find him. I climbed out of bed and walked out of Rory's bedroom.

I froze when I saw him. He was sitting on a stool at the kitchen counter, looking down at something on his lap.

"Rory?" My voice sounded weird in my throat.

He immediately looked up. "You slept in my bed." He smiled at me. There were dark circles around his eyes. He looked exhausted.

I didn't want to have to filter anything anymore. It was time to just be me. "I missed you."

"I missed you too."

I wasn't sure what to do. *Should I go to him?* For some reason I remained frozen by his bedroom door.

"I read the rest of the articles."

"Rory, I'm sorry. I shouldn't have written them. I..."

"I didn't realize how much I was hurting you."

"It doesn't matter. I don't care about any of that."

"I was an asshole," he said. "And honestly, I don't even know if we'd be together right now if you hadn't done all those things to get my attention. I think I might have needed that somehow." He scratched the back of his neck. He looked lost.

"It doesn't mean I should have done it."

"I'm glad you did, though. Like you said last night, you make me happy. Actually, I'm happiest when I'm with you." He picked up the sheet of paper that he had been looking at on his lap. "Is this true?"

I looked at the smudged paper. It was the first draft of my article for The Post. The one where I had poured my soul out. "Where'd you get that?"

"Connor gave it to me."

I thought about that night in the ice cream shop. Connor had picked up my trash. He must have kept that note once he had seen that the envelope was addressed to Rory. That's why he was so sure he could fix everything last night.

"Is it true?" Rory asked.

"It was true when I wrote it. But it's not true now. I'm not falling for you anymore. I know you don't believe me, but I do love you. I've completely fallen."

"Keira." He stood up and walked over to me, closing the gap between us. "I'm sorry about last night. I shouldn't have walked out on you."

"Where did you go?" It was weird to be standing so close to him without him touching me.

"I just needed to sober up before talking to you again. I swear that's it."

I didn't care where he was. If he hadn't slept with someone else, then it didn't matter. All that mattered was that he was here now. "I believe you." He still didn't try to touch me. That's how I'd know if we were okay. If he wanted me again. "Maybe we should just start over?"

He didn't say anything.

"Hi, I'm Keira," I awkwardly put my hand out for him to shake.

He looked down at my hand and then back up at me. "I don't want to start over." He stepped toward me, pressing my back against the wall.

I swallowed hard. "I don't want to start over either..."

He leaned down, silencing me with a kiss. His kiss was soft at first, but seemed to grow with intensity every second, until he was kissing me more passionately than he ever had. He grabbed my thighs, lifting my legs around him. I could feel his erection pressing against my thigh.

If this was the security he needed, I'd give him whatever he wanted. I wanted him to understand how much I cared about him. And it didn't matter that he had purposely hurt my feelings ever since he moved in. All that mattered was that he wanted to be with me now. And that he had come back.

"Promise you won't leave me like that again."

"I promise." His lips moved to my neck, placing hard kisses down to my clavicle.

"When we fight we have to work it out together. You can't just walk out on me."

"Or maybe I'll just punish you next time," he whispered in my ear. His words brought that familiar pull in my stomach.

"Do you want to punish me right now?" I thought about being blindfolded in his room. And then I thought about how he had aroused me with a spoon. I felt myself blushing.

There seemed to be a glint in his eyes when I asked. "Yes."

I wanted him to do whatever he needed to forgive me. And I was more than curious what he used the handcuffs for on his bedpost. "Then do it."

I saw his Adam's apple rise and fall. His hands slid to my ass as he pulled me off the wall and walked over to his bedroom door.

Suddenly all I could hear was my heart beating. I had thought I lost him. But here he was, looking at me the same way he had before our fight. Everything was back to normal. Except I was dripping wet with anticipation of what he was going to do to me. Rory kicked his door shut with his foot and tossed me down on his bed.

"Get undressed," he said as he stared down at me.

My hands were shaking as I slowly lifted off my tank top. The intensity he was staring at me with made me nervous. It was almost like he was seeing me undress for the first time.

Rory hooked his index finger in the middle of my bra and pulled me to my feet. "This next." He let go of my bra.

I quickly reached behind my back, unhooked my bra, and pulled the straps down my shoulders.

His eyes ran down my torso and landed on my yoga pants. He looked back up at me, arching his eyebrow.

I loved when he challenged me. I pushed my yoga pants and thong down my hips and thighs and kicked them off. God I wanted him.

His eyes wandered over my naked body, turning me on even more. He was looking at me like I was the sexiest thing he had ever laid his eyes on.

"Your turn," I said, looking at his shirt.

He smiled at me and shook his head. "That's not how this works, Keira."

"But..."

"Fine. I'll give you this one thing." He slowly pulled off his shirt, revealing his perfectly sculpted torso.

I looked at his chiseled abs and moved my legs together. I didn't want him to be able to see how aroused I was.

He smiled as he looked at my pressed together thighs. "But now you can't ask for anything else." There was a glint in his eyes.

And I realized I had made a mistake. I thought about when he had fucked me in the kitchen and he hadn't let me come for a long time. Is that what he was going to do to me? Even if I begged him to please me? I bit my lip.

"Sit in the middle of the bed."

I already wanted to beg him. And he hadn't even touched me. I turned around and climbed onto his bed. I watched him go over to his dresser and pull out a tie. My breathing hitched as he walked back to me.

The last thing I saw was his smile as he placed the tie in front of my eyes. His fingers didn't touch me at all, only the silky fabric. I so badly wanted him to touch me.

"Put your hands out in front of you."

I followed his instructions. A chill ran down my spine as I heard the clang of metal. A second later I felt the handcuffs being secured around my wrists. Again, he didn't touch me at all. *Fuck.*

"Lie down and lift your arms above your head."

I lifted my arms above my head as soon as I lay down. I felt the mattress sag slightly near my head and Rory tugged the middle of the handcuffs. When he got off the bed, I realized that I could barely move at all. He had somehow attached the handcuffs to his bed post. My heart started to beat faster. I had never been so exposed in my life. After a few seconds I started to feel nervous. *Why isn't he touching me?* "Rory?" My voice sounded so needy.

The bedroom door opened.

"Rory?!" I pulled on the handcuffs, but the metal dug into my wrists. "Rory?" I heard the fridge open and a cabinet shut. *What the hell is he doing?*

A second later I heard the door close again. Something clinked against his nightstand. *A glass maybe?*

The bed sagged between my thighs. I spread my legs, hoping that he'd touch me. I wanted his tongue, his mouth, his fingers. Anything.

I could feel the warmth radiating off his body as he leaned over me, yet the only part of him touching me were his thighs, insuring that mine stayed spread wide. A second later, something freezing cold touched my nipple. I gasped and tried to move, but I was locked in place. *Shit that's cold!* I squirmed some more.

As he encircled my nipple, I felt the wetness. *An ice cube.* He continued to tease my nipple with the ice cube as my body got used to the sensation.

A moan escaped from my lips as the ice cube dipped between my breasts. Rory moved the ice cube to my other nipple, encircling it, making both my nipples harden in response.

He moved the ice cube back between my breasts and released it from his mouth. I felt it slide down my torso, stopping in my bellybutton. My whole body shivered as the ice cube began to melt.

The warmth of his tongue between my breasts was a welcome sensation and I moaned again. His tongue traced the path of the ice cube and lapped up the excess water in my bellybutton. He kissed my stomach before taking the ice cube back into his mouth and traveling lower.

God yes. I lifted my hips, but that just made him move even slower.

"Please, Rory," I panted.

He put the ice cube against my clit and I gasped again. I tried to move my arms. It was too cold.

He pressed his nose against my clit, giving me a short reprieve, before plunging the ice cube deep inside of me with his tongue.

Oh God.

The metal from the handcuffs dug into my skin as my whole body shivered. It seemed even colder inside of me. His tongue moved the ice cube around inside of me, deeper and deeper. It was too...amazing.

I tilted my head back. He was going to make me come. But right before I did, the ice cube and his tongue were gone.

"No. Rory, please don't stop. I'm so close." I almost wanted to cry. I felt desperate for his tongue to be back inside of me. I pulled on my restraints again. "Please," I begged.

His cold lips pressed against mine and I immediately opened my mouth. Instead of his tongue, he dropped the ice cube into my mouth.

"I know, Keira." He ran the tip of his nose down the length of mine.

The ice cube was oddly sweet. I realized that it was my own juices I was tasting. Why did that arouse me even more? At this point I felt like anything would arouse me.

"Open your mouth."

I immediately parted my lips, thinking that he was going to remove the ice cube. But instead, he thrust his cock into my mouth.

"Fuck," he groaned.

I wanted to please him so that he'd please me. I swirled the ice cube around his shaft and tighten my lips. My whole mouth felt cold as he began to guide his cock slowly in and out of my mouth. The groan that escaped from his lips just made me even hornier. And it made me want his cock even more. I bobbed my head.

After only a few minutes the ice cube had melted, but he continued to fuck my face. When his tip pressed against the back of my throat, I had no problem taking him in. The ice cube must have numbed my throat. I didn't gag at all as he thrust his whole cock into my mouth.

He grabbed a fist full of my hair and slammed his cock into the back of my throat again.

I felt his cock pulse slightly. *Yes, he's going to come.* I wanted his warm liquid down my throat. But as soon as the thought entered my head, he pulled his erection out of my mouth.

A second after he pulled his cock out of my mouth, I felt a splash of warmth on my breast.

Oh my God.

Another blast of semen landed on my other breast. I hadn't realized how cold I was. Every splash of it felt amazing.

"Every inch of you is mine," he said in a low voice. He ran his finger between my breasts and then slid it into my mouth.

I licked the salty semen off his finger. I was so aroused that I'd do anything. A whimper escaped from my lips.

"You probably think it's your turn to come now, right?"

I felt like this was a trick question.

He placed something soft on my chest and slowly wiped away his sticky semen.

I couldn't take it anymore. "Yes," I said breathlessly.

He grabbed my hips, flipped me over, and slapped my ass hard. I cried out, but not because of him spanking me. The handcuffs were digging into my skin.

"Grab the headboard."

I blindly reached out until my fingers felt the wood. I gripped the headboard and hoisted myself up onto my knees.

He spanked my ass again.

I knew I was dripping wet. It almost felt like some of my juices were dripping down my thigh. But it might have been the water from the ice cube that had been inside of me.

"Did you know that you have dimples right above each of your ass cheeks?" he asked, touching my lower back on either side of my spine.

"Yes."

"I find it unbelievably sexy."

I felt an ice cube drop into each small dimple. My body shuddered and the ice cubes immediately fell off my back.

"Here's the game, Keira," he said and placed the ice cubes back into my dimples. "I'm going to finger you, as long as you keep the ice cubes on your back. If they fall,

I'm going to stop. And I'm going to spank you." His voice was so authoritative. I had never heard him like this.

"Okay."

"Spread your legs."

I slowly moved my thighs farther apart, trying hard to keep my back steady. I needed to feel his fingers inside of me. I needed to come.

He lightly touched my swollen clit.

I moaned and pressed my ass back. The ice cubes immediately fell from my back.

"Oh, Keira." He spanked my ass hard.

It just turned me on even more.

He rubbed the ice cubes where he had slapped me before placing them on my back again.

"Let's try this again." He ran his fingers up the inside of my thighs.

Stay still. He placed his palm against my aching pussy and I moaned loudly.

"I don't think you've ever been this wet." He thrust his finger inside of me.

"Yes!" I yelled.

But his finger immediately left me.

"No, no! Rory, please."

"You're bad at this game, Keira." He spanked me again, even harder.

I was determined not to move this time.

He leaned over me, pressing his erection against my ass. I heard the clink of the glass again and he placed two new ice cubes onto my back.

This time he didn't tease me, he just thrust his finger deep inside of me.

I held my hips steady and tried to dig my fingernail into his bedpost instead of moving.

"Focus on my fingers," he said as he slid another one inside of me. "Focus on me inside of you and don't move." He kissed my ass where he had been slapping me. "I want you to come, Keira. And I'll let you if you don't move."

I moaned and dug my fingernails deeper into his bedpost.

"Good girl." He hooked his fingers inside of me, hitting that spot that only he could find and I pushed backwards.

His fingers slipped out of me right before I was about to find my release.

"No! Rory, please! Please let me come!"

He spanked my opposite ass cheek. "You asked me to punish you."

"Rory," I begged.

He spanked me again and flipped me over, so that my back was once again pressed against his mattress. I pulled against my restraints. I couldn't wait any more. I wanted to touch myself. If I wasn't handcuffed to his bedpost I'd please myself right in front of him.

He spread my thighs with his strong hands and placed a long, slow stroke against my wetness. "I like when you beg me."

"Oh God!" I yelled as he placed one of the ice cubes inside of me. I tried to move my legs but he had me pinned down. He slipped the other ice cube into my aching pussy and lightly sucked on my clit.

And I completely shattered. My orgasm ripped through me as I screamed his name. I let my head drop back between my arms. I didn't care that the metal dug into my wrists. I felt amazing and exhausted and..."Oh!" I moaned as I felt his tongue thrust inside of me.

He pushed the ice cubes around with his tongue, sending them deeper than he could go. My body shivered as I felt myself climbing higher and higher again. His tongue swirled around, hitting all of my walls. I was going to come again. The contrast between the ice and his warm tongue was too much. He pressed his nose against my swollen clit and thrust his tongue even deeper.

"Rory!" I yelled as a second orgasm washed over me. It wasn't as intense as the first one, but it was just as relieving. I let my head drop back again as he continued to swirl his tongue inside of me, lapping up all my juices.

He lightly tugged on my nipple with his teeth. "I needed to feel your pussy clench around my tongue."

God his words were dirty. Just hearing them seemed to arouse me again. But I was done. I was completely exhausted. All I wanted was for him to un-cuff me and hold me until I fell asleep.

"And now I need to feel you clench around my cock."

"I can't. Rory, I can't take anymore."

"You'd be surprised by how many times you can orgasm in one day."

I wanted to experience everything he could give me. I let me legs drop back open. "Show me."

He leaned over me again and I felt his erection press against my stomach. I heard a drawer slam on his nightstand and the rip of foil.

"It doesn't seem like you're punishing me anymore."

"Is that so?" He flipped my body back over and pulled my waist up in the air.

I wanted him to spank me again. I liked the way it made me feel.

He answered my needs with a hard slap on my ass.

I moaned.

"I love how kinky you are." He pushed my thighs apart and slid a finger inside of me.

I pushed back on the headboard and he spanked me again and again, moving his finger even faster.

As soon as his finger abandoned its post, he grabbed my hips and thrust into me as hard as he could. His fingers dug into my hips as he started fucking me.

His fingers were great. And his tongue was amazing. But nothing felt better than his thick cock, spreading me wide. I tightened my grip on the headboard and tried to push back, meeting each thrust.

He was being rough with me, but it didn't hurt at all. I was used to this now, and I loved it. I loved being tied up and blindfolded and fucked hard. But I suddenly wanted more.

"I want to see you, Rory."

He slammed into me hard and then slowly pulled out of me. I felt so empty without him inside of me. He grabbed my waist and flipped me over again. I spread my legs, inviting him back in.

But then nothing happened. Instead of pulling away my blindfold or thrusting back inside of me, he lightly touched the inside of my thigh, sending chills down my spine.

"Are you clean, Keira?"

Why does that matter? I needed him again. Was this just another way for him to punish me? A slow, torturous bath or something? "I showered last night."

"No. I mean have you been checked for..."

"Oh God." I felt myself blushing. "Yes, I'm clean."

"Are you on birth control?"

Oh my God. "Yes."

He pulled the tie off my eyes and let it fall around my neck.

"There aren't many firsts in the bedroom that I haven't already experienced." He pulled his condom off and tossed it onto the floor. "Let me do this for the first time with you."

I looked down at his enormous cock. I had never had unprotected sex before either. That was...intimate. It was a whole other level of intimacy. And he wanted that with me. "Are you clean?"

"Yes, I'm clean." He smiled at me.

He wanted to cum inside of me. Right after he had cum all over my breasts. He had said that every inch of me was his. This was the last part of me that he hadn't claimed. I found that unbelievably sexy.

"If you don't want..."

"No. I want that too. I've never done that either."

He leaned forward and unhooked my handcuffs. My head dropped back onto his pillow. He kissed each of my wrists where the metal had dug into my skin, and then slowly left a trail of kisses down the inside of my arm.

He didn't seem to know how to say that he loved me. But this had to be the closest thing. He stared into my eyes as he slowly slid his length back inside of me.

It was different, but better. Definitely better. He felt bigger somehow. I could see in his face that he thought it was better too.

He kissed me gently at first, his tongue matching his slow thrusts. I felt his hand drift to the small of my back and he rolled over, pulling me with him so that I was on top, straddling him.

This was a first for both of us. I wanted to make it as good as possible for him. I put my hands on his shoulders to steady myself and slowly gyrated my hips.

He groaned and grabbed my breasts.

He looked so sexy. His torso glistened with sweat, somehow making his muscles even more defined. And he looked like he had never felt anything so good in his life. I was doing that to him. I was pleasing him. I slowly guided his cock in and out of me and leaned down to kiss him.

His fingers gravitated to my nipples and he began to slowly massage them. I moved my hips faster, trying to show him how good it felt.

He groaned into my mouth and moved one of his hands to the back of my head, deepening our kiss. His other hand slid to my waist and he started guiding my hips.

I didn't want to come. I didn't want this to end. But I could feel myself losing control. "Rory, I'm going to come again."

He rolled back on top of me, pinning me against his mattress. "And I'm going to cum inside of you." He placed a kiss on my neck and moved one of his hands to my thigh. His fingertips dug into my skin as he began to move his hips faster. Each thrust pulled me higher and higher.

I buried my hands in his hair. "Cum, Rory. I want you to cum inside of me." I pulled his lips back to mine.

He groaned in my mouth and I felt his dick pulse inside of me. Warmth seemed to spread up into my stomach.

He lightly bit my bottom lip as his warm liquid continued to shoot into me. I had never experienced anything so good in my life. I felt myself clench around him.

"Rory," I moaned. My orgasm washed over me as he continued to fill me.

As soon as he was done, he collapsed on top of me. His torso pressed against mine and I could feel his heart beating rapidly. "That was amazing." He kissed my cheek. And then my forehead. He kissed the tip of my nose and then placed a soft kiss on my lips. "Now I'm exhausted," he said and pulled out of me. He rolled onto his back and sighed.

I didn't like the empty feeling. "Me too." I put my head on his chest. "It's hard to sleep when you're not beside me." Last night I had a fitful night of sleep. Dreams of him banging other women wasn't great for peaceful slumber. A nap seemed like the perfect idea.

He ran his fingers through my hair. "I feel the same way."

I sighed and closed my eyes. I was completely spent. And I was just so happy to have him back. My eyelids felt heavy.

He continued to run his fingers through my hair for several minutes. "I love you too," he whispered.

I knew he thought I was asleep, or else he wouldn't have said it. So I didn't say anything. *He loves me too.* I closed my eyes and easily fell asleep.

CHAPTER 36

The sound of buzzing woke me up. I yawned and grabbed my phone off Rory's nightstand. But it wasn't my phone that had woken me. It was Rory's. Before setting it back down, I glanced at the screen to see what time it was.

There was a text message from Tiffany Five Stars, and I couldn't seem to pull my eyes away from the small amount of the message that showed on his screen.

"I'm really glad you called..."

I swallowed hard. He called Tiffany Five Stars last night? I set the phone back down on his nightstand. Why had he called her last night?

I sat up. My stomach twisted into knots. There was only one reason to call a girl that was rated on your phone as five sex stars. I looked down at Rory sleeping peacefully. *He cheated on me.* I wanted to punch his stupid, beautiful face.

No. No, he said he just needed to sober up last night. He promised me that was it.

His words from last night came back to me. He had said he was glad I hadn't deleted all those women's numbers from his phone. *Oh God, he definitely cheated on me.*

Connor must have lied to Emily on the phone. There was no way he had found Rory last night. That's why he didn't come home in a few hours like Connor said he would. Because he was sobering up with his dick inside Tiffany. *What the fuck?*

I got out of bed and stared down at his phone. He wouldn't lie to me. He wouldn't come back here and apologize even though I was the one that messed up. But maybe he wasn't apologizing for walking out during our argument. Maybe he was apologizing for sleeping with someone else last night when he was mad at me.

But he had that paper from Connor. So he had to have seen Connor last night. And Connor promised me that he wouldn't let Rory sleep with anyone else.

I put my hand on my forehead. I was going insane. *I'm a crazy person, fighting with myself.* Rory groaned in his sleep and turned onto his side. His arm reached out for me, but he didn't seem fazed that I was no longer beside him.

He's probably thinking about Tiffany.

I shook my head. He made love to me. Without a condom. He said that he loved me out loud, even if he thought I was asleep when he had said it. But did he only realize he loved me because he had slept with someone else? A person he thought was worthy of five sex stars? That wasn't a good reason to tell someone you loved them.

I looked down at his phone. I didn't care that I was invading his privacy or betraying his trust. If I didn't see the rest of that text, I might murder him in his sleep. And murder was definitely worse than spying. I picked his phone back up and slid my finger across the screen.

An icon popped up asking me for his password. I tried his birthday first, but that wasn't it. Maybe it was for the best. It was a bad idea anyway. *I shouldn't read his texts.*

I'm really glad you called...

Fuck it. I'll try one more thing. If my next try didn't work I'd stop trying. One more shot. I looked down at Rory. What would a single guy who slept with tons of women and never wanted to commit to anyone make his password?

Of course. He wouldn't be worried about anyone seeing his texts and phone calls. I typed in "password" and his phone unlocked. I took a deep breath and pressed on the text from Tiffany Five Stars.

"I'm really glad you called me last night. Your girlfriend is definitely going to freak. Stop by tonight too because I think Jamie might actually have what you're looking for. She's so much better than I am! You're going to love her."

There was a smiley face emoji at the end of the text. I felt like I was in shock. I read the text again. He did sleep with her. And Tiffany wasn't even enough for him. He needed to fuck Jamie too? Emily was right. He wasn't perfect. He was a cheating asshole. Why did I always fall for such jerks?

I wanted to text Tiffany back: "Damn right I was going to freak out when I found out that he slept with you, you slut!" But I didn't. I just stared at the message. Could that possibly mean something else? I bit my lip. Maybe if I read more of their conversation. I scrolled up to the start of it from yesterday. I didn't want to see their exchanges before that. Nothing mattered before we had started dating. And I definitely didn't want to know anything about what they did before we started dating. I already knew it was just tons of sex. Hopefully meaningless sex, but sex none the less.

Rory had texted her first: "Hey, Tiffany. Sorry it's been so long. Are you free tonight?"

It was a few hours after he had left our apartment. A few hours was enough to sober up. He knew what he was doing. He wanted to sleep with Tiffany. It wasn't even just a drunken mistake. Maybe I could have forgiven a drunken mistake. But it seemed like he missed her. I wasn't enough for him.

Tiffany: "I'm at work right now. But we can definitely meet up later, babe."

Babe? Gross.

Rory: "Can I just come there?"

Tiffany: "I can definitely make you come here. We're not busy and I'm closing up tonight. We'll have the whole place to ourselves."

There was another smiley face emoji. I wanted to throw up. Instead, I kept reading.

Rory had texted her a few hours after that. Just a little after midnight. "Thanks for working late tonight, Tiff. You know I appreciate the special treatment."

Winky face emoji? I threw the phone down onto the bed, just missing hitting Rory. *The special treatment? Ew!* I couldn't even look at him. He cheated on me and he joked around with her about it? He was disgusting. I felt tears stinging my eyes. I quickly got dressed and slipped out of his room.

I didn't know what to do. My answer always seemed to be to run over to Emily's house. I really wanted to run. How could I love and hate someone so much at the same time? I wanted to remember how he looked at me a few hours ago when he had finally come home. Like he had missed me. I didn't want that feeling to be gone so soon.

But this couldn't wait. I needed to confront him about this now. I was so sick of always running from my problems. And he wasn't just my boyfriend. He was my roommate. *Boyfriend.* That word didn't seem to mean anything. I felt so nauseous. Maybe the article I had written was right after all. Maybe we were just friends with benefits. He'd never get another benefit from me, though, that was for sure.

My chest started to hurt as I began to pace around the living room. *Fuck him.* Why would he do that with me this morning? Make love to me like that, right after he fucked Tiffany? He was such a pig.

I picked up one of the Nerf guns off the floor and aimed it at the dartboard on the wall. I cocked it and pulled the trigger, hitting one of the outside circles. I cocked it again and placed a shot a little closer to the center. I pretended it was Rory's face and continued to shoot round after round, hitting the last three foam darts right in the middle of the target. It was weird how good that felt. I grabbed the darts that were scattered around the floor and reloaded the gun. I cocked it again and shot another dart. Bullseye.

"You're pretty good at that."

His words were like ice in my veins. I turned around and kept my finger on the trigger.

"Whoa." He put his hands up in the air. "I surrender." He gave me one of his charming smiles. I looked down and saw the outline of his phone in his shorts pocket.

Without thinking, I pulled the trigger and shot him right in the groin.

"Fuck!" Rory put his hand over his dick. "What the hell, Keira?" His face was a grimace. "Shit that hurts."

"What were you doing last night?"

"I told you. I was just sobering up. I was hanging out with Connor and Jackson."

"You're lying."

"I'm not lying." He laughed and stepped toward me.

I raised the Nerf gun. "Don't."

"Keira." His smile was gone. "I promise that I was just with Connor and Jackson. You can even call them. They'll tell you. Whatever it is you think I did, I didn't do it."

"I bet they will lie for you. That's what friends do, right?" I shot him in the stomach.

"Ow. What do you think I was doing?"

Why isn't he just admitting it? Him pretending to be innocent made me even more upset. "Tiffany Five Stars texted you. She was so happy you called last night, you asshole."

His eyes got wide. "Wait, did you read my texts?"

"Who's password is 'password'?"

"Shit." He scratched the back of his neck. "What else did she say?"

Why did he care more about what she revealed than confessing the truth to me? "You don't want to just tell me what you were doing with her?"

"So she didn't say anything?"

"What is wrong with you? Yes, she did. I was just hoping you'd man up and tell me. That slut made it very clear that you two fucked last night."

"Whoa, what? I didn't sleep with Tiffany. Yeah, I've slept with her before. But I didn't last night, I swear." He lifted his hand off his penis.

I immediately shot him again.

"Jesus Christ, Keira! That fucking hurts!" He knelt down on the ground, holding himself in his hands again.

"She calls you babe? And jokes about making you come? You're disgusting."

"She just misunderstood why I was texting her."

"Bullshit, Rory. You were playing along. And then you thanked her for working late. And her special treatment. Of your *penis*."

He laughed. "Keira, you just don't understand."

"The only other thing that could mean is that she's a prostitute. Oh God, you have sex with prostitutes? And you didn't use a condom with me. I'm going to die of a terrible prostitute STD!"

"Keira..."

"And who the hell is Jamie?!"

"Jamie? What are you even talking about? I don't even know who Jamie is. Let me look at my phone, okay? I can clear this up."

I shot his hand with a foam dart.

"Stop shooting me! What is wrong with you?"

"You cheated on me! You said you would never cheat on me. I thought you might be last night when you didn't come home. And Connor lied to me on the phone."

"You talked to Connor last night? I specifically asked him not to take your calls. What the hell?"

"Why? Was it a gangbang or something?"

Rory laughed. "No. Of course not. I'm not into devil's threesomes."

I shot him in the chest again.

He lowered his eyebrows slightly.

"And Connor didn't take my calls," I said. "I was worried sick all night. He only picked up when Emily called."

"And what did he say to her?"

"Why are you so concerned about everything other people are saying? If you didn't sleep with Tiffany just tell me where you were. Or were you sleeping with someone else?"

"I didn't cheat on you last night."

"You're terrible at phrasing things. What does that mean? That you cheated on me before?"

"No. Damn it, Keira! I just worded it wrong. I've never cheated on you. And I never will cheat on you."

"Then where were you?"

"Keira..."

"Where were you, Rory?" My voice cracked when I said his name. I was quickly falling apart. "Why won't you tell me?"

He just stared at me.

Say something! "Get. Out."

"What?"

"Get out of my apartment, Rory! Get the fuck out!"

Rory laughed. "Keira, if you could just..."

"You need to leave! This isn't working out."

"You're kicking me out? Seriously?"

"Tell me where you were. Just tell me what you were doing. Just tell me!"

He stared at me for a few seconds. "I'm sorry. I can't, Keira."

"Fine. Then you're officially evicted. Get out!" I threw the Nerf gun at him.

He stood up and caught the gun in his hands. "Evicting me, huh?" He raised his eyebrow at me.

"Stop. Stop looking so sexy! I'm not changing my mind. I can't even look at you right now. We're done, Rory. Get the hell out of my apartment."

"You're being ridiculous. We just agreed earlier today that we'd talk about our problems from now on. I'm not leaving."

"Cheating on me isn't something that we need to discuss. It's a deal breaker, Rory. And I've tried to talk to you. You won't tell me what you were doing. I don't have anything else to say. Clearly too much has happened between us. So I'm definitely not your girlfriend anymore. And you can't be my roommate now either. We're done!" I was so mad. And I hated how calm he was. He was the worst boyfriend ever. And definitely the worst roommate ever. And the sexiest. *Damn it!*

Rory's phone started buzzing in his pocket as he stared at me. "Fuck." He pulled out his cell and answered. He locked eyes with me. "Not great," he said into his phone. He put his hand over the receiver and held the phone out to me. "It's Connor. He'll tell you that he was with me last night."

"I don't care about him or Jackson being with you. I just want you to tell me where you were. And what you were doing with a girl that you think deserves five stars because of how good she is at sucking your cock! Is Connor going to explain all that to me if you give me the phone right now?"

"No."

"Then I don't want to talk to him. And I'm definitely done talking to you." I couldn't stand being in this room anymore with him. I couldn't look at him. My tears had already started to fall down my cheeks. I crossed my arms in front of my chest and walked toward my room.

"Keira." He grabbed my arm.

I shook him off of me. "Don't touch me, Rory. Don't you dare touch me." For the first time since he had come out of his bedroom, he actually looked concerned.

"I just need you to trust me."

"I can't trust you."

He didn't say anything. He watched me as I retreated into my bedroom. As soon as I closed my door, I collapsed onto the floor and started crying. He was a coward. He didn't love me. And I didn't love him. He was right. How could anyone love someone like him?

I started to cry even harder. Because that was a lie. I loved him more than I realized I could love someone else. But I couldn't forgive him for this. Even if he was telling the truth, it didn't matter. Whatever he had done with Tiffany Five Stars was probably just as bad as cheating. And he was keeping something from me. He had asked me to trust him. I would never be able to trust him. How could I possibly love someone that I didn't trust?

I heard something crash outside my door. It sounded like Rory had thrown the Nerf gun against the wall. I heard the front door open and close. And my gut told me that he was going out again. To cheat again. But this time it wouldn't really be cheating. I had just broken up with him. And evicted him. I put my face in my hands.

Is that why he kept saying he hadn't cheated? He had technically broken up with me before he stormed out last night. Maybe that didn't count. But it still hurt. I couldn't forgive him. I had just told him I loved him and he walked out on me and hooked up with a prostitute. I'd never forgive him for that. I thought he was sweet and kind and charming. But he was just like every guy I had ever met. He was a complete asshole. If I had given him a chance to talk, I'm sure it would have ending with him saying, "It's not you, it's me."

A part of me thought I was fixing him. Maybe it was because Connor and Jackson had said that to me. I thought he didn't want to be a player anymore. It seemed like he wanted to settle down. But the other night he had told me that people don't change. I was trying to change him. He didn't want to be changed. He couldn't change. I would never be enough for someone like him.

I leaned my back against my bedroom door and hugged my knees into my chest. In the end it didn't really matter. I thought being with him would make me happy. But I wouldn't have been happy down the road. I wanted to get married. I wanted children. I wanted all those things that he said he wasn't ready for and may never want. It was better that we ended it before it got any more serious. Every logical part of my brain was telling me that he wasn't good for me. So why did I miss him right now? Why did it physically hurt me to know that he was hurting? I put my chin on top of my knee. I thought he was the broken one, but maybe it was me.

I needed to call Emily. I stood up and opened my bedroom door. I walked into the living room and grabbed my phone off the coffee table. The Nerf gun I had been shooting Rory with was cracked in half, laying underneath the dartboard. There were shards of plastic scattered around it. I could add anger issues to all the reasons why I shouldn't be with him. I pressed on Emily's name and held the phone to my ear as I went back into my room.

After ringing several times, the call went to voicemail. Maybe she was still at work.

"Hey, Em. It's me. Rory came home." I sat down on the edge of my bed. "I ended it. Actually I kicked him out." I put my hand on my forehead. "I really need to talk to you. He cheated on me. So why does it feel like breaking up with him was a mistake? Please call me." I hung up and looked down at the screen. It was past 6:30. She should have been off by now. Why hadn't she answered my call?

My phone buzzed while I looked down at it. It was a text from Rory. I swiped my finger across the screen.

"I left okay? I know you need some space. And I can see how you may have misunderstood that text. But we need to talk about this. Let me take you out to dinner tonight."

Did that mean he canceled his plans with Jamie and Tiffany? That didn't make me feel any better. I couldn't be bought with a fancy dinner. But maybe I needed to hear him out. If he was willing to tell me what he was doing last night, maybe we could work this out. *If.* It really didn't seem like he was though. And the only reason I could think of was because he had in fact cheated on me. My phone buzzed again.

"I'm friends with the chef of this really nice restaurant a few blocks away from our place. He was able to get us on the list for tonight. I'll pick you up at 8."

That cocky bastard. I opened up my computer and pulled up Craigslist. I quickly typed out an ad about the empty room in the apartment. At the end I added, "men need not apply," in all caps. Perfect. I pressed the submit button. The sooner I found someone to move into Rory's room, the sooner I could move on.

I sighed and slammed my laptop closed. I didn't want to forget about him. I never wanted to forget the way he looked at me or the way he made me feel. But it all came down to trust. I could never trust him. Rory was a player. And he'd always be a player. I picked up my phone and quickly typed out a response to him.

"I'm interviewing potential new roommates tomorrow. Please let me know when you want to come pick up your stuff so I can make plans to not be around." I pressed send.

I needed a fresh start. In a lot of ways Rory was amazing. I couldn't deny that. But he wasn't my future. It was like he said. I wanted to be happy in the future. That was the ultimate goal. I didn't want to be constantly worried that I wasn't good enough for him or that he was out hooking up with someone else. And the worst part was, he knew how it felt to be on the other side of this. His ex had cheated on him. Why would he do this to me?

My phone started buzzing. It was Rory. I just stared down at the screen. I didn't have anything to say to him.

When it finally stopped buzzing I slowly exhaled. A minute later my phone beeped. He had left a voicemail.

"Keira." There was a pause. "Screw the restaurant then. Let's just go somewhere. Let's take a vacation. Just you and me. Wherever you want. I'll take you wherever you want to go. Let's go to Italy. You'll love it there." He sighed. "Please call me back."

What? I lay down on my bed. *What is he doing?* I didn't want to go to Italy with him. He'd probably see one beautiful girl with long black hair and tan skin and run off with her. *Stupid Italy.*

I tried to call Emily again, but it went straight to her voicemail this time. I stared at the ceiling. My life had seemed so full this morning. And now I had never felt more alone. I hadn't just lost Rory. Connor and Jackson had basically been living here too. They had become two of my closest friends. Connor had somehow become one of my closest confidants.

I picked up my phone and found Julie's number. If I couldn't fix my own relationship, maybe I could fix things for Connor. It was the least I could do after he had tried so hard to help me.

The phone rang

"Hi, Keira." Her voice sounded slightly cold.

Deservedly. "Hey, Julie!" I said with as much cheer as I could muster. "Connor told me how much fun he had with you the other night."

Julie laughed. "Yeah, I don't think so, Keira. He hasn't even texted me."

"He told me that he really likes you."

"Was that after he ran after you and left me alone in your apartment?"

"Um...yes."

"I don't really know what you're trying to do, Keira. Clearly he likes you. Why'd you even set us up in the first place?"

I laughed. "Likes me? Julie. Psh. I'm dating Connor's best friend. Connor and I have just become really good friends in the process."

"Really?"

"Yeah. He's such a sweetheart. He knew that I was upset and came running after me. He's just a really good friend."

"Oh."

"Look, Julie, he's super embarrassed, that's the only reason he hasn't texted you. He's so caring. If you give him another chance, you won't regret it. You'd be lucky to have him in your life."

"Are you sure there's nothing between you two?"

It didn't seem like I was ever going to see Connor again. So it didn't matter at all that we had hooked up that one time. Fixing things with Julie would be my goodbye present to him. "There's absolutely nothing going on between us. I really think you two would make an amazing couple."

Julie sighed. "So you think I should just text him? I really did have a good time."

"I think you should definitely text him."

"You know, I actually haven't been able to stop thinking about him. I just assumed that he didn't have a good time."

"Trust me, he did."

"Geez, Keira. Okay. I guess I'll text him."

I could hear the smile in her voice.

"Thank you so much for clearing that up."

"Of course. It was just such a crazy misunderstanding."

Julie laughed. "Maybe the four of us could go on a double date sometime?"

"Yeah, that would be fun." I didn't want to talk about this with Julie. I just wanted her to give Connor another shot. Apparently I was a good matchmaker. I could just never find anyone for myself.

"Okay, I'll text him now. Thanks, Keira!"

"Bye, Julie." When I hung up I looked down at my screen. Emily still seemed to be screening my calls. *Goodbye, Connor. Goodbye, Jackson. Goodbye, Rory.* I had never felt so alone.

CHAPTER 37

Only one person had responded to my ad on Craigslist. Her name was Rebecca Johnson. She didn't have a Facebook or any social media presence as far as I could tell. She was a complete ghost online. But her name seemed normal enough. And she was female. If a man showed up named Rebecca I'd just close the door in his face. *Never again.*

I put my laptop down on the coffee table and picked up my pint of Ben & Jerry's ice cream. The only thing better than forbidden chocolate was Chunky Monkey. Ben and Jerry were the only men that seemed to understand me.

The apartment was a complete mess. Rory's stuff was still everywhere. There were beer cans on the poker table and water rings on the coffee table. Nerf darts were scattered on the carpet and the broken Nerf gun was still on the floor.

But if Rebecca couldn't accept that, then I didn't want her as a roommate anyway. I needed someone that wouldn't judge me if I ate a pint of Ben & Jerry's ice cream every day until I felt better. I wasn't sure I'd ever feel better. It still felt like I was making a mistake. And I couldn't bounce around my ideas because Emily still wasn't answering my calls. I had even called Jim. But he didn't answer either. I was starting to worry that something terrible had happened to them. Or the baby. I put my carton of ice cream back down on the coffee table. Then I really would be all alone.

A knock on the door brought me out of my pity party. It was probably Rebecca. She was exactly on time. That was a good sign already. Even though the apartment was a mess, I had changed into a nice pair of jeans and tank top. A potential roommate might forgive a little bit of a slob, but not if I was gross. Besides, I always felt better when I took time making myself look good. This was one of those instances that even a nice outfit couldn't seem to fix, though. I took a deep breath. I suddenly wanted to cry again. Hopefully I could hold it together while talking to a stranger.

I opened the door. *Rory*. I immediately tried to slam it in his face, but he put his hand out to stop it.

"Can I come in?" He was holding a bouquet of beautiful flowers in his other hand. He held them out to me.

I had demonized him in my head so much after I had kicked him out that I had almost forgotten how handsome he was. "I'm busy, Rory. I'm interviewing new roommates."

"So lots of people answered your ad?"

"Just one. But she sounds great. She should be here any minute. So, I can't really talk right now."

"Just one? I guess it's just me then."

"What? No. Her name's Rebecca."

"Yup." He pushed past me and walked into our apartment.

Come on! "Please don't tell me that you're Rebecca?"

"Yeah. That would be me."

"So you have a girly middle name too?"

He laughed. "No, I made it up so you'd let me in."

"I don't want you here." I was surprised by how much I was keeping it together. Just a half hour ago I was sobbing and stuffing my face with ice cream.

"Keira, I didn't cheat on you."

"Then what were you doing?"

"This isn't how I wanted this to happen. I made reservations at a really nice restaurant last night. And I was willing to buy tickets to anywhere you wanted to go. But if you want to do this right here, then fine, we'll just do this right here."

"Talking in a restaurant or in Italy won't make a difference, Rory. I don't think I can forgive you."

"Actually it would have made a difference. But you love making everything difficult. You have this way of crawling under my skin. And even when I'm mad at you, I can't seem to stop thinking about you."

"I can't stop thinking about you either." I let the words slip out before I realized what I was saying. It was the truth, though. And I couldn't seem to think straight when he was staring at me like he was. He had a way of making me feel like I was the only thing that mattered in his whole life.

He put the flowers down on the kitchen counter. "I was scared, okay?"

"Scared? Scared of what?"

"You." He scratched the back of his neck. "Of the way I feel about you, I mean. That's why I went on that date on Friday night. I was scared of taking the next step with you. But that was ridiculous. I mean, we were already living together. Making you my girlfriend didn't even seem like that big of a step. It just seemed right."

"And that's why you went on a date with Tiffany two nights ago too? Because you're still scared of how you feel about me?" I wanted to understand where he was coming from. I wanted him to make me understand why he had done it. It almost seemed like it was somehow my fault. Like I drove him into the arms of another woman.

"No. This is coming out wrong." He scratched the back of his neck again. "I didn't go on a date with Tiffany. Keira, I would never cheat on you. I'm never going to cheat on you. I'm sorry that I hurt you before. I'm not going to hurt you anymore."

He still wasn't telling me what I needed to know. "Rory..."

He put his hand on my elbow. "You're really cute when you're upset. Please, just let me get this off of my chest."

I missed his hands on me. "Okay."

"When we were fighting the other night, everything just suddenly clicked. When you asked me if you make me happy. That's all that matters right? I've never been happier. You're it for me, Keira." He put his other hand on my cheek. "And I thought that I'd be scared of making the next step with you too. But I'm not. The only thing I'm scared of is losing you. And when we make this official, that's it. You're the one. And I want to make that step. I'm in love with you. I'm so in love with you, Keira."

Oh my God. I put my hand over my mouth.

"I don't want another roommate ever again. I want to fall asleep every night with you by my side. And I only want to wake up next to you."

"Rory..."

"And I know I'd be happiest with you by my side for the rest of my life. Keira, I want you to be my roommate forever." He got down on one knee and pulled a box out of his pocket.

I wiped away the tears that had started to fall from my eyes. "But Tiffany?"

"She works at a jewelry store. Her friend Jamie, who I only met yesterday, found the ring I was looking for." He opened up the box.

It was beautiful. It was elegant and sophisticated, and not over the top or garish. It was exactly what I would have picked out.

"Connor and Jackson were with me the whole time. I told them they couldn't talk to you because I knew they'd blab. Neither one of them is any good at keeping secrets. And I called Emily to find out your ring size. I swore her to secrecy too."

"Why didn't you just tell me? I shot you in the...Rory, I'm so sorry." I put my hands on both sides of his face. "I'm so, so sorry."

He laughed. "I didn't have the ring yet. And I wanted to propose at a nice restaurant. Or somewhere exotic. Or just anywhere you've ever wanted to go. But maybe this was the best place. My life changed forever when I first knocked on your door. That is, if you say yes." He smiled up at me. That charming smile that made me fall so hard for him in the first place.

I knelt down in front of him, holding his face in my hands. "Rory, I thought you..."

"I know." He kissed my palm. "But I didn't."

"Rory, we barely know each other."

"I know you, Keira." He kissed my other palm. "I know every inch of you." He kissed my forehead. "And I love every inch of you." He kissed me softly on the lips.

I put my arms behind his neck. "I love you so much."

"Then marry me." He pulled the ring out of the box. "I should have known you'd make this hard too. I know I'm a mess. I know that I need..."

"You're not a mess. Rory, you're perfect. I think everything about you is perfect. And you're definitely perfect for me."

"You're killing me. Say yes, Keira."

"Yes. Of course, yes!"

He leaned down and kissed me. It was soft, yet passionate at the same time. He grabbed my hand and slowly slid the ring onto my finger.

"Rory, it's beautiful."

He stood up and lifted me in his arms, twirling me around in a circle. I couldn't help but giggle. I didn't think I had ever been so happy. As he lowered me down, my torso slid against his. He kept his arms wrapped tightly around me as I looked up at him.

"I thought you never wanted to get married?"

"I don't think I had any idea what I wanted until I met you." He kissed me again.

There was a loud knock on the door. "Can we come in now?!" Jackson yelled.

I smiled up at Rory. "The door is unlocked, guys!"

Jackson ran into the room, followed by Connor, Emily, and Jim. I laughed as Jackson put his arms around us. "I knew you two would work it out," he said.

He was quickly followed by the rest of our friends, as they all embraced us in a big circle. I had felt so alone earlier. And now I had never felt so full. I don't think I had ever been happier in my whole life. Each big moment with Rory had made me feel like that. I couldn't help but think that each day going forward he would make me happier and happier. And he was absolutely right. At the end of the day, happiness was the only thing that mattered.

EPILOGUE

"It's perfect," I said. It probably looked like I was staring up at the freshly painted sign, but my eyes were glued firmly to my new husband's butt. God did Rory look good in swim trunks. Although he insisted that he had to wear a shirt during our new ice cream shop's business hours, I was pretty sure in a few more weeks he'd abandon the policy. After all…we were at the beach. No shirt, no shoes…who the hell cared? I sure didn't. I preferred him without a shirt. And as far as I was concerned, the swim trunks weren't necessary either.

Rory looked down at me from the ladder he was standing on. "Hey, eyes up here, Keira," he said and waved his hammer in front of the sign.

I laughed. "I *was* talking about the sign."

"Of course you were." He stepped off the ladder and joined me on the boardwalk. "It really is perfect, though," he said.

"Sure is." The sign was great, but I was still talking about his ass. "I still can't believe we're actually doing this." Sweet Cravings was scrawled across the top of our new storefront. *Our new storefront.* It felt like I was still dreaming. One minute we'd been touring all the beaches on the east coast during our honeymoon, and the next minute we were buying this shop on the Rehoboth boardwalk.

I never wanted our honeymoon to end, but eventually we'd have to go back to Philly. Our next venture was a catering company in the town where we'd met. But for at least this summer we were staying put. We had to get our new shop off the ground and make sure things were running smoothly before we left it in the hands of a manager. And I was going to enjoy every second of our summer here. I leaned into Rory's side.

He wrapped his arm around me. "Now I have to bring it up one more time before we scare all the patrons away…are you positive these flavor names are the way you want to go?"

I stared at all the flavor names that were posted outside the storefront. "What's wrong with the flavor names?"

"Um…nothing," he said.

I laughed. "If we're going to stand out, we need to do something different than the other five ice cream places on the boardwalk. This is going to be our thing."

"Right. You don't think our 100 unique flavors are enough?"

I shook my head. "Nope. We need the outlandish names too." Outlandish was probably an understatement. Lots of them were sexual. Most of them inappropriate in one way or another. But all of them were hilarious and made sense. The awesome names were what made our shop stand out. "You got to have the final say on all the flavors because you're the one with the discerning chef's palette. And I got to do the naming because I'm the author in the family."

"Well, if you think Sex in the Sand is a great name for banana ice cream with graham cracker crumbs, what do I know?"

"Exactly."

Rory laughed and placed a kiss on the side of my forehead. "I've been meaning to ask. Remember that time Connor and I found you on the floor of that ice cream shop looking for your earrings?"

Kill me now. I had kind of hoped that once we got married we'd never talk about all the awkward things I did to get his attention before we became an us. I didn't know where this conversation was going but I had a feeling I didn't want to know. "Hmm…no that doesn't sound familiar."

"Right. Because you were lying."

I squirmed out of his grip. "I was not."

"Keira."

"Rory."

He lowered his eyebrows. "And the day after when you were deep throating that banana, asking me if you gave good head because you were practicing for another man…"

"I don't recall any of that." I was pretty sure my face was bright red. It was still hard to believe I'd done either thing. Well, mostly just the banana one. I ate ice cream all the time.

Rory reached forward and tucked a loose strand of hair behind my ear. "Did you really have a date either of those nights?"

I laughed. "You think I'd make up a date? Psh." I shoved his shoulder.

"No." He smiled. "I just remember you were eating this huge bowl of chocolate ice cream…"

"Mmm. Forbidden chocolate."

"Forbidden chocolate. That's a pretty normal name."

I rolled my eyes at him. *Too tame.*

"Anyway," he said. "I remember wishing you'd been thinking about me instead of some other guy while you'd been at that ice cream shop. I wanted it to be me on your mind. Always."

I pressed my lips together. God, he was so sweet. And I owed him the truth. "Well, I did have a date the night I was in the ice cream shop. It was just with…myself. I was definitely thinking of you."

He pulled me back into his arms. "Yeah?"

"I was always thinking about you. I still am." I laced my fingers behind his neck. "And the banana thing? You know I was just trying to make you jealous. Can we please never talk about it again?"

His forehead dropped to mine. "You don't have to be embarrassed. I was being a dick. It made total sense to suck a banana in front of me."

I groaned and pushed on his chest, but he held me firmly in place.

"I love you, Keira."

He had a way of making me melt. "I love you too." I thought after he quit La Patisserie that he'd no longer smell like cinnamon all the time. But the scent never left his skin.

"One more question," he said.

I looked up into his hazel eyes. "Ask away."

"Sweet Cravings. Why when all the ice cream flavors have such raunchy names is our shop named Sweet Cravings?"

"Because it's ironic. But more so…because it makes me think of you. Because you, sir, are sweeter than any flavor of ice cream." It was a cheesy thing to say. But I still meant it.

He smiled in that way that still made my knees weak.

"Hey, are you guys open?" someone asked from beside us.

"Yes!" I realized I sounded too excited, so I cleared my throat. "I mean…yeah."

Rory laughed. "It's our first day, but we're officially open. What can we get you?" We both went inside our store and stood behind the counter all professional-like.

I knew you were supposed to smile at your patrons, but I didn't have to force one on my face as I watched our first customer. He was a young lifeguard, just off the beach. And unlike my wonderful husband, he realized that shirts weren't necessary.

"See…" I whispered to Rory. "You don't need a shirt."

"He's a lifeguard," Rory whispered back.

"I don't see your point."

Suddenly the lifeguard started laughing. "Wow." He was staring at the ice cream flavors listed on the outside of our storefront. "You guys are going to kill it here."

I was pretty sure I couldn't smile any harder. "You like the names?"

"They're hilarious."

"And here my husband didn't believe in them." I hit my hip against his.

Rory held me to his side. "I just wanted to make sure we weren't going to scare people away."

The lifeguard shook his head. "It's great. I'll have a Dirty Sanchez, as long as you promise it's actually ice cream," he said.

"I swear it's just chocolate," Rory said as he went to get him a scoop.

"What's your name?" I asked. "You're our first customer and I want to ingrain this in my memory forever."

The lifeguard laughed as he handed me some cash. "J.J. I'm sure I'll be stopping by again soon. I'll be working here all summer."

"Well, it was nice meeting you, J.J. I hope you enjoy your Dirty Sanchez!"

He laughed. "Thanks."

I squealed as he walked away. "We did it! We're a success!"

Rory smiled down at me. "One customer doesn't pay the bills. But...we officially opened our first place together."

"And did you see what he was wearing? He was shirtless!"

He laughed. "I noticed."

"So...you should take yours off."

He lifted up our Now Hiring sign. "Maybe after we hang this up."

I sighed and put my elbows on the counter. "He was very handsome you know. He's going to make all the girls drool this summer."

"As long as he's not making you drool."

I shook my head. "We both know I'm much more attracted to sexy chefs."

J.J. disappeared down the boardwalk, but not before I noticed how quickly he ate his ice cream. Our first customer was a great success. And even though I wasn't checking him out, I could tell he was definitely going to break some hearts this summer. I was so glad to be out of the dating scene. I'd married the love of my life and I couldn't be happier.

Rory hung our Now Hiring sign up outside and I got even more excited. It was really happening. Our dreams were coming true. And I knew this was going to be a summer to remember.

ABOUT THE AUTHOR

Ivy Smoak is the USA Today and Wall Street Journal best-selling author of *The Hunted Series*. Her books have sold over 4 million copies worldwide.

When she's not writing, you can find Ivy binge watching too many TV shows, taking long walks, playing outside, and generally refusing to act like an adult. She lives with her husband in Delaware.

TikTok: @IvySmoak
Facebook: IvySmoakAuthor
Instagram: @IvySmoakAuthor
Goodreads: IvySmoak

Made in the USA
Monee, IL
09 June 2024

59630592R00194

Made in the USA
Monee, IL
09 June 2024

59630592R00194